ABOUT THIS BOOK

I started thinking about writing this series of books back in 2016 as I was remembering my grandfather on the 100th anniversary of the Battle of The Somme in World War One. He was there on the first day of the battle when 19,420 British soldiers were killed.

I retain memories from my early childhood of my grandparents' village house – small, Victorian, red brick, end of terrace – with its rarely used front parlour, zinc bath hanging on the back of the stairs, the outside privy, the long garden laid out to vegetables, the old water mill down the lane.

My grandfather was invalided home in 1917 with trench feet (a polite euphemism for gangrene). In my presence, he never spoke of the war again.

S.T.

Published in Great Britain in 2024
By Diamond Historical

ISBN 978-1-915649-28-7

Copyright © 2024 Stephen Timmins

The right of Stephen Timmins to be identified as the author of this work has been asserted in accordance with the Copyright, Designs and Patents Act 1998.

All rights reserved.

No part of this publication may be reproduced, stored in a retrieval system, or transmitted in any form or by any means without the prior permission in writing of the publisher, nor be circulated in any form of binding or cover other than that in which it is published.

All characters appearing in this work are fictitious. Any resemblance to real persons, living or dead, is purely coincidental.

Diamond Historical is an imprint of Diamond Books Ltd.

DIAMOND BOOKS

Book cover design:
jacksonbone.co.uk

Also by Stephen Timmins

The Stanwood House Chronicles
Volume 2 – Kit's War
Volume 3 – Aila's Peace

And Published by Diamond Crime

The Fortieth Step Thrillers
Volume 1 – Legacy
Volume 2 – Revenge
Volume 3 – Promise

DIAMOND BOOKS

For information about authors and
other books published by Diamond Books visit:
www.diamondbooks.co.uk

To Elaine
who loves family histories

STANWOOD HOUSE
VOLUME ONE

Aila's War

STEPHEN TIMMINS

CHAPTER ONE

FRIDAY 18TH MAY 1908

The World Turned Upside Down Pub, Raunds,

Northamptonshire

Aila Smythe ran back into the stables behind the pub as the horse shrieked, its hooves cutting the air over the frightened men. They ran too – ducking for cover into the rear door of the pub, the lane, anywhere away from those sharp edged, metal weapons.

The horse whinnied once more, screaming out its rage at a world of whips and spurs and reins and stupid, ignorant, cruel riders. The stable yard was almost empty now. Aila peered out over the half door, her mouth dropping open in surprise. A single boy remained, still, unafraid, clicking his teeth then talking soft, kind words to the terrifying, terrified animal. The boy walked forward, hand outstretched. The horse dropped onto its front hooves, panting, watchful, ready to fight once more, ready to run, ready for trouble. But more than anything, ready for the calm, gentle voice of the boy with the outstretched hand, talking to it in soft words only it understood. Heads began to appear, the landlord first, then the ostler. The pub landlord turned to the ostler, Fred Hammond.

"Your boy, Fred. Him and horses. They go together. They trust him."

They watched as the boy stroked the horse's muzzle, still talking to it. The landlord walked forward and patted him on the shoulder. "Will, my boy, you've got a feel for 'em, ain't you. Thanks, lad. Thanks indeed."

The boy looked at him and nodded, not really listening, still feeling for the horse's mind. "You should tell whoever owns this horse to stop beating him. Poor thing's terrified."

The landlord glanced towards the bar. "Careful now, Will, it belongs to the Honourable Dudley Smythe. You need to watch what you say round that one bearing in mind the company he keeps."

The boy shrugged and turned back to the horse once more. Aila emerged from the stable leading her pony. She walked across the stable yard and stroked the horse's muzzle too, watching the boy out of the corner of her eye. "That was very brave of you. What's your name?"

The boy looked uncomfortable. "Will Hammond, Miss, and it wasn't nothing. Horses don't want to hurt you. Just this one's been badly treated and that isn't right. He needed to feel loved again."

The girl turned and looked him straight in the face. "My name is Aila Smythe." She stroked the horse's mane. "His name's Prancer. He belongs to my half–brother."

The boy stepped back, expecting trouble, but the girl shook her head.

"I'm not going to tell tales on you. My half–brother is horrible. He's cruel to everything and everyone. You did a good thing here, today. Thank you."

She held out her hand and, wondering, Will shook it.

A loud, overbearing voice sounded from inside the pub. "Aila? Where is that stupid girl? Aila?"

The girl turned to Will and spoke quickly. "That's my brother. You'd better go. He's been drinking and my father's estate owns the pub so no one dares stop him. Please go. He really is horrid."

Footsteps sounded in from within the pub and she pushed Will towards the stable door. He stumbled inside and waited in the half dark watching as the young man reeled out of the pub's back door laughing over his shoulder at the two men who followed him into the yard. Will's eyes narrowed. What would the son of Lord Augustus Smythe of Stanwood be doing in the company of the least pleasant of the Stanwood estate's tenant farmers, Alf Naylor, and his cousin the equally unpleasant huntsman, Oc Chown? The two men waved the young aristocrat goodbye and then walked back into the pub laughing and slapping each other on the shoulders.

CHAPTER TWO

MONDAY 21ST MAY 1908
Stanwood House

It was still a muddy brown. She stirred her paintbrush in the water jar, wiped it, selected more paint and tried again. No. Bother! She looked up at Miss Johnson, her governess, who was completing an annoyingly perfect watercolour of a vase of flowering stocks. She shrugged, pulled her plaited hair round in front of her eyes and peered at it. The governess stirred.

"What on earth, Aila Smythe, are you doing?"

Aila chewed her lip in concentration.

"Well, Miss, I'm trying to paint a picture of my pony and I'm sure his coat is the same colour as my hair, but I just can't get it right."

Aila was sure that her governess was hiding a smile. She pushed her plait back. In her vainer moments she was proud of her brown hair and her brown eyes and the arched nose her grandmother told her was so pretty. Her governess' smile did not rise to the surface though. She spoke instead. "Enough painting for today I think, Miss Smythe. Now, kindly do me the honour of conjugating the verb amo?"

Oh no! Why Latin? She could understand (just) why her father insisted she learn to read, write and do arithmetic, but Latin! She put her paint brushes back in the jug of water, stifled a yawn and stared out of the window to where she should be, out riding Danny, her mischievous old pony.

She searched her memory. The first bit was manageable.

"Present indicative, Miss: amo, amas, amat, amamus, amatis, amant." She paused. "Present Conjunctive: amem, ames, amet, amemus, ametis, ament."

She paused once more, attempting to find a way out of the awful boredom.

"Future, Miss: Amabo, amabis, amabit..."

Aaah! There was a way out. She raised her hand. "Miss Johnson, may I ask a question, please?"

Her governess regarded her with suspicion, raising an eyebrow in a manner that Aila had almost given up trying to emulate.

"Well Miss, if amo means 'I love', how can you talk about the future? How can you say I will love? I mean surely the Romans didn't wake up one morning and decide they were going to love someone next week, Miss. It just doesn't make sense. You know what I mean, Miss, 'I will love Marcus Aurelius on Tuesday 14th of next month.'"

She batted her eyelids and looked up at her young governess wide eyed. Edith Johnson's face was still rigid.

"Aila Smythe, you know perfectly well that amo is a regular Latin verb that we teach as an example in order to give you a sense of the structure of the language. Now, let me try a short Latin sentence on you: 'non equitandum'. If you can translate that command into English, you may leave now."

A huge smile appeared on Aila's face. "I will then, Miss Johnson, because my Danny's a pony not a horse so that means I can ride him because you just said you will not ride a horse in Latin, not you will not ride a pony. So there."

They both laughed at the same time and Aila put on her best pleading face.

"Are you going to ride out with me, Edith? It's a beautiful day for it. You can test me on my Latin nouns as we ride. I promise. Please, please."

She slipped her free arm through that of her smiling governess and they walked together towards the stairs with Aila bubbling over with chatter the whole way.

"I wish Papa were not in London at the House of Lords so often. I'd like him to see how well you're teaching me, Edith. I think that, for once, he might even be proud of me to see how much I've learned."

She tilted her head to one side and paused. "I do still wonder if I remind him of my mother, Edith. I mean I know she passed over so many years ago, but I think it upsets him still and that's maybe why he doesn't want to see me. Poor Papa."

They walked on down the stairs past the family portraits hanging on the walls. Aila glanced at them, half noticing the sudden silence and nervous glance in her direction from her governess.

"Why is there no portrait of my mother, Edith?"

CHAPTER THREE

SATURDAY 14TH NOVEMBER 1913
Stanwood, Northamptonshire

Aila loved Juno. Her father, Lord Augustus Smythe, had bought her the colt as a fifteenth birthday present and she had taken every possible opportunity to ride him over the course of the year, even on the Hunt – the dreaded Hunt. She was aware that her half-brother, Dudley, loved all the things about hunting that she loathed. She loved the day in the saddle, the wild gallops, the hedges jumped, even the endless milling around chatting, while the huntsman set the hounds on a new scent.

Dudley fretted at these delays, barking senseless orders at the whippers-in, yelling at the huntsman, ordering the hunt followers out of his way. To be in at the kill, to witness the violence, see the blood, laugh at the suffering of the poor exhausted animal – all these he loved. All these she loathed.

And today was no different. She had, as ever, enjoyed the first few hours of the Meet when the fox was far away; when the overexcited horses skittered and danced on the cobbled street; when the hounds milled round under the control of the huntsman; when the bright scarlet of the Master of Foxhounds' coat was not streaked and spattered by mud.

But by mid-afternoon she was tired; Juno was tiring, the useless (thank goodness) huntsman had lost two foxes in the morning and clouds were building over the distant hills. Juno's ears went up and flicked forward. The riders beside her began to trot then canter. Tthe view halloo had sounded. Juno joined the fun, tiredness forgotten. Aila leaned forward on the side saddle and called out encouragement into his ear, all the while hoping the poor animal would escape.

* * *

Will Hammond yawned and shivered as the westering sun dipped towards the hills and the new weather front crept across the valley. He pulled his cap further down onto his forehead and tightened his tarpaulin coat round his neck with one hand, the other never leaving the harnesses. He wished now he'd stopped for food earlier. But he'd not wanted to break the rhythm. Harry was as strong a young horse as you could ever want and old Dickon was always so willing.

He allowed himself another glance along the perfect furrow then felt the sudden change in the horses' gait. Something had spooked them. He heard it then himself. The View Halloo – distant, but clear. He pulled the horses up and waited. Dickon saw the fox first as it skirted the field staying close to the hedgerow and shook his massive head in its direction. And then the hounds were there, breaking through the hedge, still baying their excitement. But the dog fox had been hunted before. It turned, jinked, changed direction again and darted across the freshly ploughed soil, the hounds closing all the time. Will realised what was about to happen and groaned in despair.

The first riders were through the gate and crossing the perfect furrows before he even had time to drop the harness and grab the horses' heads. He should have known better – the Hunt was not famed for its care of farmland. He hung on to the shire horses, calming their minds, ignoring the yells and insults, even the back handed slash across his face from the huntsman's crop. It was over in moments, half a day's work ruined, the shire horses almost too spooked to control and blood running down his cheekbone.

* * *

Aila pulled Juno up at the gate of the freshly ploughed field not wanting to ruin the ploughman's hard labour. Other riders had simply crossed the field and were crashing through the distant hedge as she turned Juno away, glancing up to see the sun creeping down towards the horizon behind a bank of cloud and feeling the first drops of rain.

She trotted her colt back down the lane and turned into the track through Prior's Wood to take the short cut back to Stanwood House. It was much darker in the wood than Aila had expected, but she had walked and ridden this way home for most of her young life. At least the leafless trees formed some kind of protection against the biting wind and sleet. She leaned forward and patted Juno's neck.

"We'll be home soon, Juno, dear. Home and dry."

She smiled as his ears flicked back. He was so intelligent and aware of everything around him. He turned his head and whinnied and she glanced round in turn. A group of riders from the Hunt was closing on her at the trot. She tightened her grip on Juno's reins and slowed to a halt. The riders — she could see there were three now — weren't slowing. In the faint light of a small clearing, she could see scarves wrapped over their faces against the sleet. Their horses were unrecognisable too, covered as they were with mud spatter. Juno skittered, spooked by the strange sight.

And they were on her, the first rider raising his crop and slashing it across her head, knocking her sideways off the saddle, the second rider whipping at her frightened horse. Juno reared, shrieking. She raised her arm to protect herself from the next blow, slipped from the saddle and fell to the ground. An agonising stab of pain hit her left hip as she landed, her boot still caught in the stirrup as Juno bucked and whinnied and dragged her down the path. Her head hit a tree root and she knew no more.

CHAPTER FOUR

SATURDAY 14TH NOVEMBER 1913

Alf Naylor, tenant farmer on the Smythe estate and the community's leading misanthrope, was talking animatedly to his mud–covered cousin, the Huntsman, Oc Chown. They turned at the sound of the heavy hooves in the stable yard. Will Hammond half heard the Huntsman's voice.

"He said now she's... to get rid..."

Will missed the end of the sentence as Dickon snorted and pulled him and Harry towards their stables. Safe on the back of his hunter, Oc Chown raised his crop once more. "I oughta teach you a lesson you won't never forget, Will Hammond."

The huntsman stood in his stirrups, raising the crop above his head. Will looked up at him. "I wouldn't do that Mr Chown, if I was you. Aren't many people who get a free hit on Will Hammond. Think on that before you try it again."

The huntsman hesitated. It was true that there was something about young Will that gave even big hard men pause. It may have been the steady gaze; it may have been that everyone in the village knew that his father had taught Will to box from his earliest years; it may have been the long, lean, muscular body and sinewy arms. He turned to his cousin and blustered. "Mr Dudley will be wanting words with you, Alf Naylor, employing troublemakers like this."

Will walked the shire horses into their loose boxes, removed their harnesses and started to rub them down with smooth steady strokes – Dickon first, then Harry. As he was checking the hooves for stones, he heard the tenant farmer's harsh voice close behind him.

"So did you finish the field?"

Will didn't look up. He spoke over his shoulder.

"Best not to raise your voice, Mr Naylor. Harry was spooked by the hunt and you don't want him getting excited and kicking holes out of your stables now, do you?"

The farmer growled. Will sighed. "The hunt trampled across half the field. Your man, Chown, he's a liability and you know it, and it was lucky it was me he hit and not Dickon or Harry. Now that would have been trouble. I'll finish it off tomorrow morning, Mr Naylor, and catch up before Sunday. You can trust me for that."

"I won't be trusting you with nothing no more, Will Hammond. Your services are no longer required at Glebe Farm. Once you've got these two settled you can get out and not come back. Mr Dudley don't like troublemakers."

Will finished combing out Harry's tail and walked round to comb the mane. He glanced across at the farmer. "I'll be coming in to collect my wages then before I go, Mr Naylor."

The farmer spluttered with rage. Harry's ears twitched backwards and forwards nervously and Will clicked his tongue, stroking the broad head. He turned towards the farmer and watched him.

"I'll be coming in for my wages, Mr Naylor. Don't think otherwise and remember that I know how to count. You can pay me for half a day today if it makes you feel better."

He heard the stable slam, grunted with amusement, and turned to the horses. "Well, big fellas, looks like our working days together are over. Can't pretend I'm not going to miss you two. You're the best pals a chap like me could have had. Have a care now."

He patted the horses' withers and walked out, not looking back. The rain was still horizontal and he ran to the farm's back porch, shaking out his tarpaulin coat before knocking on the door. He paused, hearing raised voices inside.

"What do you mean, Alf Naylor, you got rid of the troublemaker? Young Will Hammond, a troublemaker? Are you mad? He's the best ploughman in the county by a mile. And half the fields not done and it's late October. What have you done?"

Will counted five and knocked the door. He heard the rustle of skirts and pulled his cap off. "Evening, Mrs Naylor. I'm sorry to be a bother, but I've come for my wages."

The elderly woman patted his arm. "Come on in, Will. I'll make sure you get 'em."

Will shook his head. "I'll wait here if it's all the same to you, Mrs Naylor. I don't want to be the cause of any trouble in your house. I'm owed one pound nineteen and seven pence. Mr Naylor knows that and I said I'd take only a half wage for today to make him feel better."

Tears shone in the farmer's wife's eyes. "I'm sorry, Will. I know this ain't right."

The inner door opened and a hand threw money out into the porch, the coins scattering and rolling. It was to be expected. Mrs Naylor ran back inside shouting and crying, coming back after a half minute of sob filled silence with an oil lamp. Together they searched the ground coming up with everything bar a single penny.

***

It was three miles back home. Will pulled the string of the tarpaulin coat tight round his neck once more and trudged on, singing Harry Lauder's *Roamin in the Gloamin*, as loud as he could. It was his favourite song of the moment and one that he felt quite suited the time of day if not the weather. When he forgot the words, he whistled. When it rained too hard to whistle, he hummed, and it was during an extended hum that he heard it first. He paused and stopped. No, perhaps not. He started again but... yes. There it was again, a faint whinny. It was a horse and a horse in pain. He tilted his head to try and take a bearing. Yes. There.

He backtracked into the trees, calling out as he did so. The whinnying was clearer, close by now. He started to talk, soothing, gentle words. The horse fell silent and in the silence the rain paused, the moon floated high above shreds of cloud and by its light Will could see clearly. The horse was caught by its reins in the branches of a coppiced tree and across its head was a terrible gash, the flesh pulled back to the bone on either side. Will whistled through his teeth and then spoke his soothing litany once more, seeing the terror begin to fade from the animal's eyes. It took him ten minutes to release the horse, ten minutes in which he wished twenty times over for a bow saw to attack the heavy branches. But he did it, bit–by–bit, branch–by–branch, until eventually the young colt was free. He stroked its flank feeling it trembling and quivering with residual fear.

"Well young fella me lad, I know where you belong. You've been out with those silly hunters who just lost me my job. Let's get you back home then."

He paused, jaw dropping in amazement. There was a riding boot, upside down, hanging from the stirrup. By its size the boot belonged to a woman. He peered at the horse's back – of course, it was a side saddle. He breathed out.

"Well young chap, what happened to your rider then, eh?"

He glanced up at the moon – another squall was on its way, but the light was just enough for the while. He crouched and saw a small pool of dark liquid framed by small spots. Blood. Someone was hurt. He didn't need to hold the reins. At this moment the horse wouldn't have left him for ten bucketfuls of mash. He followed the spray of blood for twelve, thirteen, fourteen paces. The squall was about on him. Then he caught a glimpse of fabric on a bush – a strip of torn riding habit. A veil was next and then a hand, fingers upturned on the forest floor. He knelt beside her, feeling for a pulse. It was there – weak, slow, intermittent – but there. He studied the body – there was no way the left leg should be sticking out at that angle. He slipped off his tarpaulin coat, straightened the leg, wincing as a heart-rending groan came from the woman's throat. He wrapped the coat tight round the slight figure and lifted her on to the side saddle, running the stirrup leather as low as he could and attempting to rest her body against the pommel. He touched the velvet of the horse's muzzle.

"Come on young fella, let's get her home and then we'll see to that face of yours."

He walked beside the horse, holding the unconscious body as steady as he could against its easy gait. It took him almost half an hour and the squall had, by now, not so much passed as transformed itself into a torrential downpour. His first thought had been to ring the doorbell at the front of the house, but the habit of a lifetime reasserted itself and he skirted the main building and headed for the stables, calling out for help as he entered the yard. No answer. Strange. He found an empty stall, lifted the girl's body off the horse, trying desperately to keep the leg straight, laid her on a bale of hay in the darkness of the stable, talking to her gently when she groaned.

"There, there. It's all right, Miss. You'll be home in no time at all now."

He turned away and tended to the horse, promising himself he'd come back and stitch that wound before he left.

The girl was unconscious again – if she'd ever come round in the first place. Will found a plank resting against the wall outside the stall and lashed it to her leg with all the loose tack he could find. Then, wrapping her once more in his tarpaulin coat, he lifted her bodily and headed through the driving rain to the servants' quarters, calling out as he pushed through the door. No one, not a soul. What was going on here? Butler's pantry? Empty. Scullery and kitchen? Empty. He pushed on through the corridors until he reached it. The boundary, the dividing line, the green baize-backed door at which people of his class turned back unless on strict instruction. He hesitated, squared his wide shoulders, and backed through the swing door into the rear of the brightly lit hallway.

The unexpected electric lighting blinded him for a second and he failed to see the elderly woman standing by the door, peering out into the rain lashed night. He called out once more and turned towards the main drawing room, looking for a place where he could lay his burden down. The old woman turned, saw what appeared to resemble a giant holding a dead body. She cried out once and staggered to a chair, half fainting.

Will laid the body of the young woman on a chaise longue. Her eyelids flickered open once more and this time there was recognition in them. He smiled at her.

"You're home now, Miss. They'll get a doctor to you now. I'd better see to the old 'un. Reckon the sight of me caused her to collapse in a heap. And I can see her point mind."

Will was delighted to see the faintest of smiles crossed the exhausted face as he straightened and turned to help the old woman to her feet. Before he had moved more than half a pace there was a crash of footsteps and three men raced through the open front door. The first man, Will recognised. It was his Lordship still in muddy hunting clothes; the second was the butler, soaked to the skin in his house clothes. The third Will didn't have time to see before he was grabbed and hurled across the polished floor to crash against the fire surround. His Lordship saw none of this so fixed was he on the figure on the chaise longue.

"Aila? Aila? My dear child you're safe back."

He dropped to his knees in front of her and stared at the tarpaulin coat and the roughly lashed leg.

"Oh, Good Lord, you're hurt. Livens, send for the doctor immediately. Use the telephone, man. Dudley?"

Lord Augustus Smythe turned towards where Will had picked himself up was walking deliberately towards the man who had thrown him there. His Lordship glared.

"Who the devil are you? How did you get here? Dudley, throw him out."

Dudley swallowed and backed towards his father. "I've got a dozen servants who can be in here at a moment's notice, so don't you try anything."

He jumped towards the bell rope as Will kept walking forward and past him.

"Excuse me, my Lord, I just want to collect my coat then I'll be on my way. The lady's got very bad breaks to her thigh and hip bones so I wouldn't move her 'til the doctor gets here. She's lost blood too. I couldn't tell how much. It was too dark to see where I found her in Prior's Wood. I'd wrap her in something warm quick though. She's cold as ice."

He touched his forelock to the stunned aristocrat and turned towards the servants' quarters as three footmen ran in. Will looked back at Dudley Smythe, looked at the footmen, shook his head in pity and walked past them and out once more into the stables. He lit a hurricane lamp, found iodine and a needle and thread and crossed to the young horse with the gashed face, talking in his quiet, reassuring voice.

"This is going to hurt I'm afraid, young fella, but you know I'm going to be doing my best to sort you out."

The horse flinched as he poured the Iodine onto the torn flesh, then quietened as Will, still talking gently, sowed and stitched, closing the cut across its cheek, drawing it tight and finishing with the finest small stitching he could manage in the ill lit stable. It took him a full half hour of careful work before he could stand back and admire the results.

"Well, you're never going to win a beauty competition now, but it looks a sight better than before. Yep, you'll do, my dear."

He rubbed the exhausted animal down, brushed out the knots in its tail and mane, managed to convince it to lie down in the soft straw and then sat beside it singing until the big, gentle, liquid eyes closed. Will crept across to the stable door and peered out. The rain was lashing across the yard, water already filling the gutters and drains. He sighed, walked back across to the sleeping horse, pulled his snap tin out of his coat pocket and began to eat the thick hunk of bread and cheese his mother had prepared for his midday meal. He reached up for the hurricane lamp, blew out the flame, and burrowed into the straw. His eyelids drooped and, as he began to doze, he thought of the faint smile on the young woman's face when he had laid her down. So that was Lord Augustus' daughter, Miss Aila. Poor soul was going to have a world of pain to live through now.

* * *

Warm breath on his cheek brought him to the surface. He tried to ease the crick in his neck while the young horse watched him. Will laughed and examined his stitching in the half–light of dawn. Not too bad. Not too bad at all. The colt pushed its head against him and he smiled, stroking its muzzle, then turning to the hayfork hanging by the stable door. By the time the stable boy arrived at six thirty, Will had mucked out and found more feed and water for the injured animal. The boy watched him nervously over the stable's half door.

"It's all right, young un. I'm Will Hammond, the ploughman. I found this horse last night with a young lady badly injured so I brought 'em both back home."

The youngster squeaked with excitement. "That was his Lordship's daughter, Miss Aila, wasn't it? Doctor's been with her all night. Word is it was a really bad break of her leg. Will you get a reward?"

Will laughed. "Not I, young un. I got threatened for my trouble. Definitely not my best day."

He turned back to the horse and examined the stitching in the morning light. "Young un, this poor chap got badly cut about last night. Make sure he gets a bit of exercise, but no one's to ride him until the scar's healed. See?"

He indicated the face. The stable boy whistled as he saw the wound. "His name's Juno, Mister, and he's Miss Aila's favourite, but they'll get rid of 'im, straight off they will. No one'll want to ride an ugly horse, they'll say. He'll be for the knackers' yard, for certain."

Will reached out a long arm and lifted the stable boy off the ground, holding the amazed lad quite still in mid-air. "Now you listen to me, youngster, a scar on the face means nothing. It's what's inside that counts and this is a good horse, gentle, kind and willing. If a man had a scar like that, would you send him to a knackers' yard? Well, would you?"

The boy shook his head. Will eyed him for a moment longer, then dropped him to the ground and turned once more to the horse. He rested his head against its cheek and stroked it, speaking over his shoulder.

"Anyone says anything about this horse going to the knackers' yard, you come and find me and I'll have words."

The boy nodded again. Will picked up his tarpaulin coat and strode out of the stable yard. A middle-aged man in an old Ulster coat, watched him leave, detached himself from the shadows by the stable doors and walked across to the young horse, nodding at the boy.

"Morning, Jimmy. How's Juno?"

He indicated the injured animal.

"Dunno, Mr Chant, sir. That man, Will Hammond, he stitched him up. You come special to see Juno?"

The vet shook his head. "I just came over to check all the horses after the hunt. Too many injuries these days now The Honourable Dudley Smythe's in charge."

Jimmy looked over his shoulder. All the staff, whether in the stables or the house itself, knew how unwise it was these days to express any sentiment against the young master of the house. The vet leaned forward, examined the needlework on the horse's face and nodded appreciatively. This was very good work. He spoke to the boy once more. "So, tell me about this Will Hammond, then."

The boy shrugged. "He's a ploughman, Mr Chant, sir, won lots of prizes for his work is all I know."

The vet nodded, still examining the horse's scar. How did this Will Hammond know to pull the flesh together in this way? If he'd done it any other way the scarring would be terrible. He thought for a while.

"Jimmy, you're not to tell a soul about this scar. And make especially sure that Mr Dudley doesn't get to hear anything about it. Understood? Not until Miss Aila is well enough to come and see the poor thing for herself."

The boy nodded, worried now. "Yes, Mr Chant, sir."

"You just do exactly what that Will Hammond told you. Understood?

"Yes, Mr Chant, sir."

CHAPTER FIVE

WEDNESDAY 7TH JANUARY 1914

To say that Aila Smythe was not happy would have been a considerable understatement of the case. She had been confined to her bed for over nine weeks now and she was bored. Boredom was something she was more than used to at Stanwood House, but up until now she had been able to relieve it by riding out on her young colt, Juno. And that of course was one of the inordinate number of things she was no longer permitted or able to do.

The point is, she told herself, that someone had rescued her. She was sure she remembered a face smiling down at her and talking to her soothingly. She had demanded to see the vet – maybe he could explain why Juno had thrown her; but in the meantime... she eased her leg in its cast and scratched down inside it with the knitting needle, sighing with pleasure as the itching stopped.

Who was it? Who? She glanced at her maid who was standing by the window, half watching a roe deer in the park below and half watching out for her mistress.

"Maisie? Maisie, I..."

Her voice trailed off in a sigh. Maisie smiled and crossed the room holding Aila's perfume bottle. Aila hardly dared tell Maisie that while a squirt of Guerlain's Après 'Ondée may have been one of the luxuries she liked best in the world, it had no healing properties. Maisie did not agree. She sprayed the spring flower scented mist over her mistress, sniffed the stopper on the bottle with hedonistic pleasure and placed it back on the dressing table. Aila shook her head with a faint smile. "Maisie, please accept my apologies for my behaviour. It's just that I'm..."

She paused and stared out at the rain lashed window. The sixteen-year-old maid trotted back across to the bed. "It's just that you're very, very bored, Miss Aila. I do understand."

She patted her patient's hand and smiled at her. Aila looked up at her and laughed. She had become so fond of her young maid. "Maisie, I don't know how you put up with me, I really don't."

Maisie made her bob and headed for the door, balancing the breakfast tray on one hand. With the door open she turned, eyes sparkling. "Well look at it from my point of view, Miss Aila, it's either looking after you or caring for your Grandmamma. And on balance..."

She slipped through the door as Aila reached behind her for a pillow to throw. The door half opened again and Aila hurled the pillow with all her recovering strength, laughing out loud as she did so, delighted to have got one over on her pert little maid. But, ah! The figure entering her bedroom was not a teenage girl, but a burly, red–faced man in his fifties. As he closed the door behind him and made his bow, Aila could hear the rattle of breakfast plates and Maisie's helpless, half–suppressed giggling in the corridor outside. She took her hands away from her mouth and offered a weak smile.

"Good morning, Mr Chant. It's good of you to come. Did Maisie offer you a cup of tea to keep out the cold?"

The vet stooped to pick up the pillow and passed it back to her with a broad smile. "No, Miss Aila, I can't say she did. She seemed to be in a dreadful hurry to show me in for some reason or other."

Aila covered her face with her hands and tried her best not to laugh. "I'm very sorry, Mr Chant. I shall, of course, discipline her."

His smile broadened further. "No need for that, Miss Aila. Nice to see a young lass in high spirits. She's always been a good girl has Maisie Brown. Now, I understand you wanted to see me?"

She nodded. "I just wanted to ask how Juno was. Everyone's too busy to tell me anything about him and it was such a bad fall I just wanted to make sure he was recovering well."

The vet considered. "He's recovered well, Miss. He misses you, I know, but apart from that dreadful scar on his face he's in good health. He needs exercise, of course, but I gave orders..."

So that was it. Juno had been badly hurt and no one had wanted to tell her. She had to be careful now. The slightest false tone and the vet would clam up like the rest of them. "Is the scar healing though, Mr Chant?" She dissembled. "I heard it had made him very ill."

The vet smiled and shook his head. "Not at all, Miss Aila. Young Will Hammond, him who found you in the wood, sewed it up as neat as I've ever seen stitching. I, er, I've been that busy with the practice, I've not had time to go and tell him so myself, but at any rate his Lordship will have thanked him for saving your life."

So that was his name. She blinked at a sudden memory of a strong-jawed young man smiling down at her in the drawing room. And it was a name from her past too. She was sure she remembered the name from when she was a child. But where? When?

"Yes, I'm sure he has, and when I'm allowed out, I'll go and visit him myself. I think my father said he lived in Wellingborough, but my memory of the first few days after my fall is more than a trifle hazy."

Mr Chant tried to smile reassuringly. "No, no, Miss Aila. So far as I'm aware the Hammond family lives in Stanwood village, in one of those little terraced houses down West End."

Aila nodded and yawned, suddenly tired. The vet jumped to his feet and pressed the bell push for the maid as Aila held out her hand. "Thank you so much for coming to see me, Mr Chant. I'm sorry I get tired so quickly. I'm afraid I'm just a nuisance to one and all. And thank you so much for caring for Juno."

The door opened and Maisie peeped into the room. The vet laughed at the expression on her face. "You are a lucky girl, Maisie Brown. Your mistress is too tired to lift a pillow now, let alone throw one."

Maisie half smiled, peered at Aila and ran to the bed. "Miss Aila? Can I get you something, Miss Aila? Should I call for the doctor?"

The vet nodded with approval at her concern and left the room as Maisie lifted Aila up on her pillows, plumping them and fussing with the counterpane. Aila took her hand and squeezed it. "Dear Maisie."

CHAPTER SIX

TUESDAY 24TH FEBRUARY 1914
West End, Stanwood

Aila rubbed her hip, noticing again how much the pain had diminished over the last six weeks. She tapped on the window separating her and her maid from the chauffeur. Henderson slowed the Rolls Royce and tilted his head as she spoke into the speaking tube.

"Henderson, go down West End please and stop when I tell you."

The chauffeur raised a gauntleted hand in acknowledgement and as the mid-afternoon sun slipped towards the hazy horizon, the long, sleek automobile crept down the lane towards the end terrace house where a man was digging over an empty vegetable bed.

Aila leaned forward and peered through the side window. Was this the one who had saved her life? She could see little of him beyond brown hair flopping down over a broad forehead and tanned muscular forearms visible below where he had rolled the sleeves of his collarless shirt up. She saw him look up towards the car, his blue eyes narrowing as he recognised the vehicle. What a fine-looking young man, was her first thought. How tall, how wide shouldered. How unlike the bottleneck shouldered, buck–toothed youths her grandmamma insisted on introducing to her at the various public functions she had been forced to attend in the county.

She tapped on the glass between her and the chauffeur. The latter engaged the brake, and stepped down. Aila used her sticks to lever herself to her feet, but for the moment that was as far as it went. Maisie leaned forward to assist, clearly anxious as to whether she could help her mistress step down out of the car.

Aila moved one foot forward, caught a look of astonishment on Maisie's face as she was lifted to one side and then was, herself, picked clean off the floor of the car by a pair of powerful arms and deposited gently on to the road. She rested on her sticks, laughed and turned to the maid. "You see, Maisie. It seems that Will Hammond comes to the rescue every time he sees me."

She raised her motoring veil to look him straight in the eye.

"Miss Aila." He touched his knuckle to his forehead. "Well, I have to say you look a sight better now than when I last saw you."

She held out her hand. "Mr Hammond, I'm sorry that I'm the last member of the family to thank you, but I'm afraid I've been rather ill. In fact..." She indicated Maisie who was watching the two of them uncertainly. "... If it weren't for Maisie Brown here, I don't think I would have lived at all and then all your bravery would have been for nothing."

She wondered at the mockery in his smile as he shook his head.

"There was nothing brave about it, Miss Aila. I just found your poor horse in the storm, saw your empty boot in the stirrup, and managed to follow the trail of blood back to where you hit the ground."

She searched his face. "And could you tell why Juno had thrown me, Mr Hammond?"

She watched him as he looked over the Rolls into the distance, considering her question. He shook his head once more. "No, Miss. I can't say I thought about that. Funny thing was, though, he'd managed to get his reins completely wrapped up in the branches of that tree. Not usual for a horse to do that. Not usual at all."

What clear eyes he had and what a steady gaze. She shivered as the chill struck through her coat and turned back towards the car door, surprising herself by how pleased she was to be lifted in those strong arms once again. She leaned forward to speak to the ploughman once more, trying to act as her father always did with tenants.

"And how is the ploughing, Will Hammond?"

She noted the bitter twist to his mouth. "I wouldn't know, Miss. The day I found you in the woods was the last day's ploughing I did and, by the looks of it, it'll be the last for years to come."

She glanced towards the end terrace house, hearing a woman's cry. He turned and she could see the sadness in his eyes.

"Excuse me, Miss, but I've got to go. That's our mum, and it sounds as though our dad's taken a turn for the worse. It would have been good if one of your father's tenants had let me work for them so our dad wouldn't have had to starve this winter, as at this rate I don't doubt it'll be his last."

He moved away then turned back as the chauffeur cranked the car. "Miss Aila, I'm sorry, I should have thanked you for coming. It was very kind of you. And by the way, you're the first Smythe to show their face at our house." He glanced at Maisie. "But you'd have known that wouldn't you, Maisie Brown?"

He touched his forehead, swung himself up on to the wall and ran for the house, not pausing to look back. Aila rearranged her veil and thought about the encounter, noting how Maisie had tried her best to shrink into the corner of the seat.

But if there was one thing that her accident and convalescence had added to her strange and lonely upbringing it was patience. She thought over the conversation, then turned to her maid.

"Maisie, you'd better come to my room this evening after supper and tell me what has been going on. And you are not to tell anyone about the conversation with Will Hammond. Is that clear?"

Maisie gave a little sob. "Yes, Miss Aila."

* * *

Maisie broke all her previous records that evening. She dropped a plate; she spilled the soup; she cracked a wine glass; she was rapped over the knuckles by the housekeeper. Aila watched her out of the corner of her eye and realised her dearly loved maid was shaking, her bottom lip trembling as she lifted the tray off the side table and walked towards the door.

"Maisie?"

The maid looked up at her, tears filling her eyes. Aila held out her arms. "Maisie, dear Maisie. I didn't mean to torment you like this. I'm being so cruel. You come straight over here and be hugged."

Maisie's face crumpled and she ran to her mistress's armchair, throwing herself on her knees, and sobbing into her mistress' lap. Aila stroked her hair. "Maisie, you are the best, the truest, the kindest, the dearest friend I have ever had. Now just tell me everything, and all will be right again."

The sobbing quietened to sniff and gulp. "It was all instructions from Mr Dudley, Miss Aila. He said no one was to mention Will Hammond's name and that he'd made sure that he'd never work again for any of the farms on the Smythe estate as it was his fault you'd had your fall."

Aila wrinkled her forehead. "But how can it have been Will Hammond's fault, Maisie? I thought he was the one who found me and brought me back here."

Maisie shook her head. "It wasn't his fault. It was the huntsman, Miss Aila, that man Chown – they call him Oc in the village. The word was he missed two foxes in the morning and they got onto one late in the afternoon and it went through a field where Will Hammond was ploughing. He didn't have warning of it coming through I was told, and it was all he could do to hang on to the horses and then Oc Chown hit Will Hammond across the face with his crop because they lost the fox. And Alf Naylor, the farmer, he dismissed him that very night and from what Mrs Naylor told my Aunt Eliza, he tried not to pay him his wages. And then he put the word round that Will Hammond was a Bolshevist or something. And then Mr Dudley forbade any of the other farmers on the estate taking him on. And then

Mr Dudley called me in and said that I was not to mention a word of this to you and that you were probably going to die. And even if you didn't, you would never inherit anything anyway. And then he laughed at me something cruel when I started crying at the thought that you might die. And..."

... And Maisie ran out of things to say. Her eyelids drooped as Aila kept up the gentle stroking of her hair. She gazed unseeingly at the glowing coals in the hearth, worrying at something that seemed to be just out of reach in the back of her brain. She looked down at the sleeping maid and smiled. But what had Maisie meant about her not inheriting anything? Was this something about her mother again? The mother she had never known. The mother no one ever talked about.

CHAPTER SEVEN

West End, Stanwood Village

Will got up late. Two nights of sitting by his father as he hacked and coughed had left him more than tired. If he'd had something to eat, the fatigue would have been manageable, but the gnawing pain in his gut had reached a stage where it could never be filled by cold water from the pump.

It was still pitch black outside so if he hurried, he could get to the woods and back with some logs for the fire before his mother came downstairs.

He pulled on his boots, tied his old tarpaulin jacket round his waist and went to open the back door. Bloody thing was jammed again. He pushed harder. No, it wasn't jammed. Some idiot had put something very heavy against it. He straightened, panting, crossed the floor to the kitchen window, pushed up the sash, squeezed through, paused with one leg on the ground and the other halfway through the window.

It couldn't be! He stepped forward, moved the bags, stopped, laughed, sank to his knees on the cold, grey paving stones and wept. Gulping, angry at himself for having shown weakness, he wiped the back of his hand across his face and shuffled towards the bags on his knees. A ten-pound bag of sugar, ditto flour, a dozen eggs, sacks of potatoes, carrots, swedes and turnips, a tub of beef dripping, a pound of butter, four loaves of bread and half a side of mutton. And last of all, against the scullery wall, two hundredweight sacks of coal.

And there were other, smaller offerings behind the food; a bottle of rum, twists of cloves and nutmeg, and at the very back, almost unnoticeable on the stone slabs, a small leather nameplate cut from a horse's noseband. Just one word: 'Juno'. He breathed out.

"Miss Aila. Well, I'll be. Miss Aila, you saint."

It took a while to load the coal into the bare coal shed and stack the food in the scullery. He laid the fire in the grate, lit it, put the kettle on to boil, made his father a hot toddy from the rum, nutmeg, cloves, sugar, butter and boiling water and carried it upstairs.

CHAPTER EIGHT

FRIDAY 6TH MARCH 1914
Stanwood House

Aila drove out in her father's Rolls Royce every day of the first week of March, breathing in the fresh, damp breezes of early Spring, watching the buds on the west side of the valleys fluff out into new-born leaves, and the blackbirds, jackdaws, crows, thrushes, finches and tits complete their frantic round of nest building. On the Thursday she directed the chauffeur to drive her over to see the vet in Finedon, not sure why she had done so even as Maisie helped her climb down from the running board. Mr Chant greeted her with a laugh of pleasure.

"Well, good morning to you, Miss Aila. No pillows to throw at me this time I trust?"

Maisie blushed pink as Aila held up her hands, palms forward. "We come in peace, Mr Chant. Forgive me for bothering you, but I just wanted to ask you about the stitching on Juno's head. Did Will Hammond really do all that by himself?"

The vet motioned the young women to sit on the low wall beside his stables, smiling as Maisie fussed again with a blanket for her mistress.

"Yes, he did, Miss Aila. I er... I don't know how to say this, Miss, but I wanted to go and see him. I did. You know, to congratulate him. I, er, I was told not to, Miss Aila."

Aila nodded her head. "That would be my half–brother, I presume, Mr Chant?"

He nodded, shamefacedly, then managed to smile once more. "I should tell you, though, Miss, how Will Hammond had a go at young Jimmy, the stable boy. The lad was on about how your family would send Juno off to the knackers' yard 'cos of him losing his good looks. That Will Hammond, he just looked at him out of the corner of his eye and picked him up by his shirtfront. The look on Jimmy's face... He thought he was in for a thrashing for sure."

The vet shook his head at the memory. Aila watched him. "What did Will Hammond do, Mr Chant?"

"Why, he just spoke to him, Miss Aila. I'll never forget it. He said, *'a scar on the face means nothing. It's what's inside that counts and this is a good horse, gentle, kind and willing. If a man had a scar like that, would you send him to a knackers' yard? Well, would you?'* And young Jimmy – he didn't know what to say. His eyes were big as saucers, but I reckon it went in as he cared right proper for Juno all winter."

Aila was quiet and thoughtful all the way back to Stanwood House that morning. She reached for the speaking tube. "Henderson, take the motor into the stable yard."

She glanced at Maisie who was watching her with an expression of acute worry on her face. "You can look as miserable as you like, Maisie, but I intend to ride again as soon as I am able, and Juno and I know each other so well I know he'd never hurt me."

It still took her another fortnight before she dared climb up onto the colt. For the first time though, she felt not the restriction, but the benefit of the side saddle, as it supported her mended hip so well.

She walked Juno round the yard and smiled to see Maisie's determined expression as Jimmy helped her up onto the back of Danny, the old pony. A further week, and she could trot without pain and Maisie could walk round the yard without falling off – although she still complained bitterly about her stiff thigh muscles and sore backside.

* * *

It was on Tuesday April 22nd, that Miss Aila Smythe rode out once more. It was a sparkling spring morning after a rain filled night. Wind-blown, dust free, filled with the cacophony of bird song and the lowing of cattle happy to be out in their pasture after the long boredom of winter in the byres.

Aila, followed by Maisie on the old pony, walked Juno down to the village, up past the church, towards the West End of the village where Will Hammond was digging over the bottom of his vegetable garden and singing as he did so, his brown hair tumbling down over his forehead, his shirt sleeves rolled, his waistcoat unbuttoned. She drew on the reins and listened.

"In Scarlet town where I was born
There was a fair maid dwelling
And every youth cried well away

For her name was Barbara Allen."

She smiled and joined in with her sweet soprano voice, singing a descant to his tenor.

*"Twas in the merry month of May
The green buds were a swelling..."*

Will stopped singing and smiled at her as she nudged Juno closer to the garden wall.

"You have a fine voice, Will Hammond, but such a sad song to be singing on so perfect a spring day."

He touched his forehead with his forefinger and walked forward. "You have the right of it, Miss Aila. I hadn't thought about the fact that they're both dead by the end of the song. I was just thinking about the green buds a swelling in the merry month of May."

They both laughed, happy to be in each other's company once more. Juno shook his head at Will as he stepped forward. Will smiled at the colt, stroking the velvet of its muzzle.

"Hello, young fella. I see you remember me. How are you faring?"

He lifted the sheepskin noseband, examined his stitching and stepped back, stroking the horse's muzzle again and smiling. "Well, that's not so bad as it could have been, Miss. I've seen worse stitching from a vet." He glanced across at Maisie on the pony, paused and squinted.

"Maisie Brown, I don't know who prepared your pony for you, but his girth's too loose. Hop down and I'll tighten it for you, else you'll be going home upside down with your feet in the air."

Aila laughed at the thought and even Maisie condescended to the faintest of smiles. Will stooped beneath the pony and spoke over his shoulder to Aila. "And I want to thank you, Miss, for the food and coal. Our dad's a sight better." He gave a snort of amusement. "Trouble is he's getting a real taste for those hot rum toddies."

He concentrated on tightening the pony's girth while Danny concentrated on trying to breathe out so the girth would still be loose. Will straightened and walked round to look the pony in the eye.

"Now you listen here, old chap, you're just being plain naughty." He tapped the surprised pony on the nose. "Stop messing me about. You breathe in and behave yourself."

The pony had the grace to look embarrassed. Will tightened the girth and held out his cupped hands so Maisie could step up into the stirrups. She eyed him, but he just smiled, shaking his head.

"He won't mess you about now, Maisie Brown. He knows when he's been found out." He rested his cheek against the pony's head. "Don't you, old chap? Now you be good to her as she's a friend of mine and I expect you to take proper care of her. So, no more of your tricks, right?"

The pony tossed its head and snickered. Will stooped, cupped his hands once more, and Maisie put one booted foot in them, allowing herself to be swung up into the saddle. Danny stood rock still and then moved forward at a tongue click from Will as he strolled back over to Juno and smiled up at Aila. "Don't worry, Miss. I've got a fair idea why Mr Chant hasn't come to see me himself."

Aila sighed. "I'm sorry, Will. This is all my fault."

He shook his head. "Not your fault your horse threw you, Miss. I've been thinking, mind, and I reckon it was someone's fault." He stopped stroking Juno's head and looked up at the young woman, his jaw hardening, then relaxed once more. "I got a job, though, Miss Aila. Start Monday."

She smiled in delight. "Oh, I'm so pleased, Will. Who's taken you on?"

He smiled back at her. "The army, Miss. They've a paddock full of horses over at the Wellingborough army camp so I went over there and showed the Farrier Sergeant Major how I was used to handling horses. Trubshaw his name is - great big chap too. I wouldn't want to upset him. Anyways, he offered me a job on the spot."

She looked at him, worried. "Well don't go and join up, Will. You must have been hearing all the rumours of war with the Kaiser."

Will shook his head. "It'll only be a short war I'm thinking, Miss Aila, if it ever happens. And if I'm with the horses, that should keep me well out of harm's way."

She was looking down at him, still concerned about the danger, when the comment he had made about her fall sank in. "What do you mean 'it was someone's fault', Will?"

He looked at her blankly for a second and then nodded. "I think maybe I let my tongue run away with me, Miss. I can't prove anything either way."

She bent forward and studied him. He half smiled.

"Miss Aila, if I can find out what happened to you in that wood, I will. But like I said, I let my tongue run away with me. I'm sorry, Miss."

She nodded, respecting his honesty. The church clock struck one in the distance and behind them Maisie cleared her throat making Aila laugh once more. "She's a tyrant, Will, an utter tyrant. If I am more than one minute late for my tonic, she starts humphing and grumphing. I get no peace, no peace at all."

Will laughed at the discomfited maid who narrowed her eyes at her mistress' back. He turned back to Aila. "I hope you'll come back again soon, Miss Aila. It's good to see you looking so well."

She smiled at him. "I will, Mr Hammond. It would be my pleasure."

He laughed and bowed before jumping up on to the garden wall to wave goodbye. Aila found herself humming Barbara Allen and smiling as she did so. Behind her, Maisie rolled her eyes and shook her head.

Will turned over a few more clods of earth, whistling to himself. He paused, his hands resting on the garden fork. He straightened, glanced at the sun to get an idea of the time, jumped down from the garden wall and strode up the lane in the direction of Prior's Wood. It was time he got to scratch that itch at the back of his mind that had been there from the very moment he had first found Juno tangled up in those branches.

It took him nearly a half hour of searching until he came across the mess of coppiced branches in which Juno had become so entangled. This year's leaf growth had rendered the area pretty much unrecognisable, but he was sure this was it. He began to feel across the sprouting nettles on the ground, the palms of his hands leather–hard after years of physical labour. His fingers touched something. He felt again.

Yes, there it was, something like a branch or a twig, but too smooth. It took him another three minutes of careful prodding and probing before he could see it. He whistled through pursed lips and squatted on his haunches to think about this. The smooth twig was a riding crop. Couldn't have been Miss Aila's though, as she'd fallen some way off.

CHAPTER NINE

FRIDAY 17TH APRIL 1914
West End, Stanwood

Aila had begun to run out of excuses for riding out every day especially as she didn't want to be rude to Maisie and go alone, but today Maisie and the other maids had to help the housekeeper with the annual stock–taking of the linen.

She turned her horse and walked down West End, only half admitting to herself that she was hoping to see that handsome young ploughman again. And there he was striding up the lane carrying a bunch of flowers in one hand and smiling up at her. She laughed down at him.

"You're not carrying posies about on the off chance of bumping into me are you, Will Hammond?"

He laughed back up at her and touched his forehead with his knuckle. "Well, if you promise not to tell my mum, they're yours for the taking, Miss Aila." He held the flowers up and bowed.

She laughed again. "Let me guess. For a family grave?"

He nodded, still smiling, and took Juno's bridle, turning him in the lane and walking beside the horse's head. "It is indeed, Miss. Want to see which one?"

Within five minutes Juno was tethered at the churchyard gate and Aila was seated on an ancient gravestone watching Will arrange the flowers in an old vase in front of his grandmother's gravestone. He glanced up and smiled. "You ought to be careful who you're sitting on, mind. Some of the inhabitants might take offence."

She looked down. "Well, whoever's under here..." She tapped the lichen coated gravestone with her knuckle. "...lost their name many years ago. I do hope it wasn't a Hammond."

Will smiled once more. "Well certain sure it's not a Smythe."

He pointed towards the family vault. They both sat, silent, watching the westering sun. Will stirred uneasily and Aila glanced at him from under her eyelids. "Come on, Will. Out with it."

He raised his eyebrows. "How did...? Oh, I know. It's one of those things my mum calls 'woman's intuition'."

She gave a mock sigh. "It's nothing to do with intuition, Mr Hammond. It's just that when you see a brow, which is normally smooth and untroubled by either thought or concentration, wrinkled and pinched, you know something must be amiss. Now, what have you found out?"

He snorted with amusement then hunched forward, breaking off a blade of grass and chewing at it. Aila made no attempt to hurry him, quite content just to sit and study his profile, and it was only after almost a full half-minute of indecision that he started on the story of his afternoon in Prior's Wood. She said nothing until the end. "So you have the riding crop at your home?"

He nodded.

"That's not safe, Will. They could get the police to search your house and then you'd be accused of theft or worse."

He nodded again and Aila laid her hand on his arm. "And, Will, Dudley has taken on a new gamekeeper and he and his deputy look to be the most horrid thugs. You need to be careful. They'll be looking for an excuse to beat you."

Will shrugged. "Will you take the crop, Miss Aila?"

"Of course."

"And would you know if it was Mr Dudley's?"

"I believe so."

He looked at her out of the corner of his eye. "You'll need to be careful too, Miss Aila."

He helped her to her feet, breathing in the elusive, spring flower perfume that he now associated with her, and they walked together down the path to where Juno was waiting. The colt tossed its head, stamped the ground and snickered at his two favourite humans, bending his head to sniff at Will's outstretched open palm. Aila stroked Juno's mane and half smiled.

"You know you impressed Mr Chant no end, Will."

Will raised a cynical eyebrow. "You mean with my sewing?"

Aila placed her boot in his cupped hands and was lifted into the saddle. "Did you not know he was there on that morning – the morning after you rescued me?"

Will stared at her, puzzled.

"He heard what you said to Jimmy, the stable boy, about Juno. You remember?"

Will shook his head, puzzled. Aila smiled. "Well think about it, Will Hammond. It was important. Think about it." The smile died on her face as she thought. "I'll collect the riding crop now if you don't mind, Will, just to be safe."

CHAPTER TEN

SUNDAY 19TH APRIL 1914
STANWOOD HOUSE

Seated on the bath chair on the south terrace of Stanwood House, Aila was feeling the healing warmth of the spring sun penetrate the bones of her damaged hip and ease the thin, biting ache. She yawned, wondering if an extended stay in the warmth of a Mediterranean resort would rid of her of the continual nagging pain.

She turned at the sound of hurried footsteps. Maisie was scurrying down the path towards her, anxiety evident in every step. Aila smiled up at her. "It can't be that bad, Maisie, dear."

"It can, Miss Aila. It can." She knelt by the chair and whispered into her mistress' ear. "It's Will Hammond, Miss Aila. Mr Dudley, his gamekeeper and his assistant, they've beaten him. I've heard he's hurt real bad, Miss Aila."

Within seconds Aila was on her feet, limping back to the house to confront her father. He was seated at the huge desk in his study turning the pages of Friday's Times newspaper and sipping a cup of tea. He glanced up and smiled in her direction.

"Good morning, Aila, dear. Are you joining me at church today or had you forgotten it was Sunday?"

She shook her head and seated herself across the desk. "Papa, I need to talk to you. It's serious."

Lord Smythe sighed, pulled off his pince–nez, and studied the agitated girl. "Must you, Aila? Before church?"

"Yes, Papa."

It took her five breathless minutes to explain, at the end of which she realised her father was studying her stern-faced, twiddling his pince–nez between his fingers.

"Let me make sure I have not misunderstood you. You have been seen publicly consorting with an agitator who was dismissed by Dudley. Yes? You are claiming that Dudley was responsible not just for disciplining this agitator, but for causing your fall from Juno?"

A discreet tap at the door was followed almost immediately by Livens' entrance bearing gloves, top hat, morning coat, prayer book and bible. Her father stood. "We shall discuss this in the presence of Dudley after lunch. At three o'clock."

She sat still, listening to the bustle in the entrance hall, and then turned to stare at her reflection in the mirror. "Idiot."

* * *

At one minute to three Aila limped down the main staircase and made her way to the library. As she turned the door handle the raised voices stopped. She glanced from her father to her brother and could scarcely hide her smile. Dudley had two black eyes and his very obviously broken nose was taped. He glared at her. She curtsied to her father and sat down. "Papa, I would like to apologise for ruining your morning for you. It was quite unforgivable of me."

She placed her hands in her lap and waited for the diatribe. To her surprise it didn't come. Instead, her father sipped his brandy and studied them both before speaking. "Dudley's version of the happenings of Saturday afternoon differs from yours in several key elements, Aila. Do you wish to change your story?"

"No, Papa, not at all. I appreciate that this is a private matter within the family, but if you wished to have verification of the events you can ask any of the villagers who pulled Dudley and his two cronies off Will Hammond and witnessed Dudley stamping on his head. I understand that they are still very angry."

Dudley Smythe sneered. "Of course you would take the word of that rabble over mine, wouldn't you, half–sister?"

Lord Augustus ignored him. "And the story about your fall from Juno? Do you wish to repeat your accusation of that as well?"

This time Aila allowed her smile to show as she nodded. She made sure that it was gentle and respectful and aimed solely at her father although she was well aware of what its impact would be on Dudley. He exploded. "What the devil are you trying to say, you stupid, underbred bitch?"

Lord Smythe straightened and slapped the palm of his hand on the table beside him. "Dudley, you will never address your sister like that again. How dare you?"

Aila raised her eyebrows. What was he talking about? Underbred? She was a Smythe wasn't she, his half–sister? Well, let him talk his way out of this.

"I have a very faint memory of another rider beside me grabbing my reins when I was thrown and an even fainter one of Juno being led away, but again, if it is evidence you need, then perhaps this will help."

She walked across to the two-hundred-year-old painting of Stanwood House in its previous guise as a Jacobean mansion, pulled it forward and reached behind. She turned towards her father holding the riding crop that Will had recovered from the wood.

"This, Papa, is Dudley's riding crop, and it was found at the site where Juno was tangled up in the coppiced tree. If you look at this end..." She handed the crop to her father. "You will see that there are blood stains on it, probably from poor Juno's head."

Dudley exploded again. "What kind of preposterous nonsense is this? How dare you, you little...?"

He strode across the room, his fist raised, ready to strike his sister. She straightened her back and raised her chin, showing not the slightest hint of fear. "If it's preposterous, Dudley, then why aren't you just denying that it's your crop? If it's preposterous then why aren't you accusing me of placing it there myself? I'm not a stable boy you can beat to death for not having your horse ready in time, or a ploughman you can ensure never works again and then have beaten half to death by your thugs. I may be just a girl but you do not frighten me one bit."

She turned back to her father who was turning the riding crop over in his hands. He looked up at her and she could see in his eyes the warmth and respect that she valued so much. He turned towards his son. "Answer your sister."

Dudley took a deep breath. "Of course I didn't drop that crop there, father. She's just had one of her ghastly little village friends place it there to implicate me."

Lord Smythe continued to watch him. "And young Ben, the stable boy? I had heard from Livens that there was some unpleasantness."

Dudley blustered, flushing a dark, unhealthy red. "The boy was incompetent, lazy and cheeky. You have to teach people of that class a lesson once in a while or they lose all respect for you, like that Hammond agitator."

Aila blinked at him in amazement. "Will Hammond, an agitator? You used that word earlier too, father. He's a ploughman. He's never been associated with any of that kind of behaviour." She turned to her father. "And may I say now that the reason I went to see Will Hammond was to thank him for rescuing me and for saving my life. And I discovered that no one else from Stanwood House had been there. And I also discovered that his father was starving to death because Dudley had stopped any of the tenants from employing Will Hammond as a ploughman." She paused and calmed herself. "I apologise again, Papa. I did not mean to be disrespectful."

Her father nodded and raised his hand as Dudley started to bluster again. "You will be quiet."

He sat still for one moment and then stood. "These are my decisions. Do not think for one moment that they are subject to discussion. I have been far too lax with both of you. Dudley, you will join the county regiment as every Smythe has done for the last five generations. This will be done immediately. You will no longer go to our London house. You will no longer have any say in the management of any aspect of this estate."

Dudley's face bled from red to white. Lord Smythe turned to Aila, his face softening. "Aila, I am afraid you must see no more of this Will Hammond. Now, with regard to your future: if it hadn't been for your fall, I would have been discussing with your grandmother how we might arrange for you to meet a potential husband, although this is not without difficulties. I shall discuss this with her now. You will see her tomorrow."

Aila stared at him, mouth opening to ask what the difficulties would be, then closing it again as he began to pace the room. He turned and faced them. "I intend to retain an open mind on the issue of Aila's fall, but I have to say that the evidence of the riding crop works strongly against you, Dudley. I will not talk to either of you on these matters again. Is that understood?"

Aila stood and curtsied. "Yes, Papa."

He smiled briefly at her and turned to Dudley whose face was mottling up once more. Aila glanced at him and judged her moment to a nicety. "Dudley, please do not offend Papa any further. We can get past these events and become a family again."

As she had hoped, Dudley exploded. He really did have no control over his temper. "A family! With the likes of you? How dare you?" He rounded on his father. "I'll be damned if I join up now with a war against Germany likely. And I'll be damned if I don't go to London."

He scowled at his father. The latter seated himself once more, swilled his brandy round in the glass, warming it with the palms of his hands, sniffing the bouquet. He directed a brief, uninterested glance towards his son. "In which case, Dudley, you will be damned. Allowances can be stopped. Wills can be changed. Expectations of inheritances can be lost at the stroke of a pen. If you do not join the regiment tomorrow morning and decide to go instead to London, I will cut you off without so much as a penny. Now leave my sight. I shall write a letter to the regiment's commanding officer which will be waiting for you on the table in the hallway tomorrow morning."

Aila limped back up the stairs to her rooms, turning over her father's words in her mind. She stepped into her room and closed the door, careful to lock it. She pointed at the wall between her drawing room and Dudley's bedroom and spoke loudly and clearly. "Maisie, I have to talk to my grandmother tomorrow. Please tell Jimmy that I shall not be riding Juno."

CHAPTER ELEVEN

MONDAY 20TH APRIL 1914

Aila paused outside her grandmother's drawing room, gathered her thoughts, knocked and entered. The straight backed, elderly lady seated on a chair as straight backed as herself, raised her lorgnette and studied her in silence. Aila curtsied and waited for her cue. The maid finished arranging the tea tray and the silence continued until she was dismissed and a single, imperious finger indicated that Aila should pour. She crossed the room, pulled a chair alongside the occasional table and started the afternoon ritual.

"Your limp would seem to have lessened, Aila."

Aila smiled, attracted as always by the gentle Highland lilt in her grandmother's speech. "Yes, thank you, Grandmamma. There are days now when the pain is quite bearable."

She passed the cup and offered the cake stand. Her grandmother placed two lumps of sugar into her tea and accepted an iced bun. Aila sipped her own sugar–free tea and waited.

"Are you eating enough, child?"

"Yes, thank you, Grandmamma."

She took another sip of her tea and made sure that her face showed no expression at all. She counted up to five and then looked up into her grandmother's eyes, saw the twinkle, and burst into laughter. The old lady laughed back at her, lifted her stick and rapped her on the knuckles.

"You, Aila Smythe, are a wicked minx. Now tell me all, and don't think for a second that you are going to get round me by making me laugh."

Aila stood, crossed to her grandmother's chair and kissed her cheek. The old lady batted her away. "Don't think you can get round me like that either, minx. Tell me all. Now!"

Aila crossed her hands in her lap, arranged her thoughts and went through the events again including, this time, Maisie's account of her meeting with Dudley. At the end she paused, half opened her mouth and then closed it.

The wise old eyes studied her. "Is there something else you wish to say, Aila?"

Aila thought for a further few seconds and then shook her head. "No, Grandmamma."

The elderly woman watched her grandchild as she rubbed her hip. "A pair of crocks we are, child, are we not?"

Aila looked up and spoke almost fiercely. "No, Grandmamma. No, we are not. You are very fit and hale and I'm still recovering from a fall that we all know was caused by Dudley. Grandmamma, that means he tried to kill me. That is attempted murder, Grandmamma. Murder! Of his own sister! Now, will you please tell me what it is that I need to understand?"

Her grandmother's eyes narrowed. Aila straightened her back, holding her hand up. "No, Grandmamma. I am not a child anymore. I think I've known forever that there is something wrong here. I just know it."

The dowager Countess of Chichester sighed and leaned forward, patting Aila's hand. "I will tell you, my dear. I will, but not until you tell me what it was you just started to say and then stopped."

Aila looked into her grandmother's eyes and tears filled her own. "I... I..." She paused and took a deep breath. "The doctor told me and I swore him to secrecy, but I will never be able to have a baby. The injury to my pelvis was too great and my womb was damaged. I think..." She bowed her head. "I think that was what Dudley wanted to achieve, if not my death. He wanted there to be no issue from his half-sister. Grandmamma, I would never want to give him the satisfaction of knowing this."

Her grandmother reached across and pulled Aila down to rest her head on her lap. Aila cried quietly as the old, veined hand stroked her hair.

"I am so sorry, my dear wee bairn. So very, very sorry."

Aila pulled herself upright, wiped her eyes and took a deep shuddering breath. "Right, Grandmamma! What is this secret that everybody else apart from me knows?"

Her grandmother pulled her back into her arms. "Aila, dear, you are a credit to our family. You are brave and loving and courteous and kind. Your father loves you and is proud of you."

Aila nearly smiled. "But, Grandmamma! But. There's a 'but' coming up isn't there?"

She heard the soft sigh. "Yes, my dear. Yes, there is. I can think of no other way to say this." She paused again. "Your father's relationship with your mother was... irregular. Dudley's mother died, as you know, in childbirth. Your father was devastated by the loss. Thirteen years later your mother arrived at Stanwood House as the governess to Dudley. She came from the county of Rutland not so very far away. Your father was very attracted to her. They began a, um, a liaison. And you are the result of that liaison."

Aila blinked twice. "They were not married?"

Her grandmother lowered her eyes.

"But my mother? I've always been told she is dead. You mean she is not?"

The dowager Lady Smythe sighed deeply. "We do not know for sure either way, child. Your father received information from the maid who cared for you when your mother disappeared. He believes she may still be alive." She raised a hand before Aila could speak. "We do not know where she is. Your father spent many years trying to find her."

Aila sat back and closed her mouth, the revelations spinning in her mind. Her mother was not dead. She had a mother. Tears filled her eyes. Questions spilled from her lips. "But where did he look? How old would she be now? What does she look like? Why did she run away? Oh, Grandmamma, my poor, poor mother."

Lady Chichester shook her head helplessly. Aila stared at her through the tears half blinding her. She had to think. She had to do something. She jumped to her feet and ran from the room.

Lady Chichester sighed once more and called out. "She has gone, Augustus."

The door to her study opened and her son entered and seated himself in the armchair. "Well, mother? How did she react?"

She shrugged. "As you would expect from the dear child, Augustus. As you would expect. Her first thought was not of herself but of the mother she has never known. She will not let that knowledge go, my son. But the thing that she did not want to mention, Augustus, is also serious, maybe even more serious."

She recounted the conversation concerning her internal injuries. Lord Augustus sighed. "My poor darling Aila."

His mother studied him.

"Now, Augustus, tell me what you plan to do. I am sure a Minister of the Crown such as you would have planned for the time when your daughter found out the true nature of her birth."

He shot her a glance from under his eyebrows. "I was hoping for some of your good advice, mother."

"Hah! You have spent the last seventeen years ignoring my good advice and largely ignoring your daughter. Yet you spent five fruitless years trying to find her mother. You spent thousands of pounds on this quest. And now, all these years later your daughter has learned the truth about her parentage and the truth also that your son is a man who would murder his own half-sister in order to keep her from having a penny of his inheritance."

She shook her head. "I suggest that you delay matters as long as you can. The news about her condition needs to be considered and if I know anything about your daughter, she would never be party to any kind of marriage arrangement that she believes to be fraudulent. What you can do to stop her wasting her life away in a futile search for her mother, I simply do not know."

CHAPTER TWELVE

TUESDAY 4TH AUGUST 1914
Stanwood House

The talk of war, the newspaper headlines of war, the music hall songs of war, the politicians' rhetoric of war – all far beyond rational discourse, beyond hysteria. War was now a certainty. For the last week Lord Augustus had ordered a copy of every national daily newspaper. Henderson had collected them from the mainline station in Northampton each morning. Mr Livens had ironed each copy and his Lordship had then spent the remainder of the mornings reading the headlines and editorials and using the telephone to speak to the Permanent Secretary at his ministry in Whitehall.

Finally, on the 4th August, Henderson had been summoned in the early afternoon. Mr Livens supervised the footmen and valet loading the Rolls and the master of the house departed for Wellingborough to catch an evening train to London. Aila was left with an almost indefinable sense of guilt for her lack of understanding of so cataclysmic an event. As the Rolls carrying her father passed through the gates at the far end of the drive she turned to the butler.

"Mr Livens, I asked Maisie to tell Henderson that I want to take the motor into Northampton. Could you please ensure he will be ready tomorrow?"

The next afternoon she sat on the jump seat in the back of the Rolls, watching Henderson's every move through the window. It made very little sense to her at first and Maisie's scarcely hidden amusement did nothing to help. Henderson parked the Rolls at the station and was sent to collect the bolt of silk she had ordered from Paris. The second his back had disappeared through the station door Aila hauled herself into the front seat and started practising her moves. It was not easy.

She climbed back into the rear seat of the Rolls before Henderson could catch her and stared at the newspaper boy yelling the news from the far side of the street. The crowd around him was too thick for her to be able to see the headlines on the newsstand, but watching the excitement in the faces and the springs in the steps of the men buying the newspapers, the awful realisation sank in. She placed a coin in the palm of Maisie's hand and waited for her return. Together they stared at the thick, black headline. ENGLAND AND GERMANY AT WAR. In smaller type in the left-hand column beneath: 'Result of British Ultimatum – German refusal.'

* * *

Will started again on the back of the same sheet of paper, wrote half a dozen words, licked the pencil stub, sighed, started once more and eventually ended up with something approaching a draft. He pushed the pencil behind his ear and unscrewed the pen top.

Northamptonshire Regiment Army Camp,

STANWOOD HOUSE

Wellingborough,
Thursday 7th August 1914

Dear Miss Aila,
This is just to let you know that I felt I had to volunteer and join the army to fight against the Kaiser. We have just completed our basic training and we are off tomorrow to join the rest of the regiment at Blackdown, near a town called Aldershot, where most of the army seems to be based. I think we then set sail for somewhere called Le Havre in France on 13th. I am not allowed to say too much as it is all supposed to be a big secret. Which is a bit silly as everyone knows we're going and we have to be going to France because it is the next country to us, if you see what I mean.

I am sorry I am not up to much as a letter writer, Miss Aila, and I am very sorry not to have seen you. I miss our talks in the churchyard. You may have heard about what happened there with your brother and I very much regret being the cause of so many problems for you.

You will not see me again for a while I'm guessing, but when I get back, I would be deeply honoured if you would meet me once again, although you might well be married by then.

Please give my regards to Maisie and tell her to take good care of you.
Yours respectfully,
Will Hammond

He stared numbly at his neat copperplate, sighed, folded the paper, inserted it into the envelope, addressed it, sealed it, and turned to a second letter.

Dear Mum and Dad,
I don't think I am going to get any time to come home before we leave here, but the word is we are off to France soon, so I am sending you this letter to let you know I am fine and I promise to keep out of any danger.

He smiled.

I will make sure my pay gets sent to you and I look forward to the time when I can come home again.
Your loving son,
Will.

He went in search of his Platoon Corporal. "Corp, can I go out to the post office at the Midday meal break? I'll be back within the hour."

The Corporal nodded. He'd come to like this tough, self–contained youngster and, like the rest of the Company, he respected him for his honesty and his fearlessness. "I'll come across to the Guard House with you to tip 'em the wink. You'd better be back in time for your turn in the ring, though."

Will smiled. He'd been entered in the regimental boxing competition. The contest was an inter–company event with weight matching being little more than a vague approximation.

Once back from the post office, he stripped to his waist, wrapped the linen strips round his knuckles, watched with mild interest as his excited seconds pulled the leather boxing mitts on to his hands and straightened to attention as Lieutenant Scott hurried across.

"Hammond, have you boxed before?"

"I have, sir, yes."

The Lieutenant shook his head. "Look, man, they're putting you up against an ex-professional. You must give him thirty pounds in weight too."

He pointed to the far corner of the ring where a giant of a Military Police Sergeant, stripped to his vest, was staring in his direction. "I've said I'll fight sir and I have no intention of backing out of it now. It'd let the Company down."

* * *

Not just the Company, but the entire regiment did little but talk about the fight for days, no, weeks, after. The giant lasted two and a half rounds, worn down by Will's speed, skill and dexterity and as the third minute of the third round had ticked away, Will altered tactics, took the attack to his opponent, finally throwing an uppercut to the point of his jaw and then stepping away to watch. The sergeant toppled forward, hitting the canvas with a massive thud, dust rising in a small cloud. There was a second of silence as Will walked back to his corner and then the roar from three sides of the ring hit his ears. He let the referee raise his arm over his head in the victory gesture and then held out his hands for the gloves to be removed. The men of Will's own company, Lieutenant Scott among them, were leaping up and down, chanting his name. He smiled slightly and jumped down to the ground wishing above all that he could just be allowed to be alone with the horses in their paddock.

* * *

Aila had spent a fruitless half hour coming up with increasingly impossible scenarios for separating Henderson from his beloved motorcar while Maisie laughed at her. Eventually it was lunchtime and Maisie was dispatched to the kitchen for sustenance. Two minutes later, minus food but bearing news, Maisie rushed back in. "Miss Aila, Miss Aila, Henderson has a stomach ache and the Rolls Royce is sitting in the stable yard with no one watching it."

Minutes later Aila was seated in the driving seat while Maisie kept a look-out by the entrance to the stable yard. She started the vehicle almost immediately and after several false starts and some terrifying grinding screeches, she steered the long bonnet out into the yard. For a further fifteen minutes she manoeuvred its enormous length round and round the yard and finally reversed it back into the stable from which she'd taken it. She climbed down and did a little skip across the cobbled stones towards her maid. Maisie grabbed her.

"Miss Aila, do take care. These old cobbles are slippery."

"I don't care, Maisie. I am now a qualified chauffeur." She paused. "Maybe that should be chauffeuse."

CHAPTER THIRTEEN

FRIDAY 7TH AUGUST 1914
Stanwood House

The ringing of the bell at the side door announced the arrival of the postman. Maisie trotted down the passage and opened the door to find young Allan Luff, the junior postman, grinning at her.

"Morning, Maisie. Didn't know Mr Livens trusted you with the post these days."

She tossed her head and looked superior.

"Not many today, anyways. His Lordship's letters must be going to the London house. There is one for your Miss Aila though. She got a fancy man, has she?"

Maisie glared. This was going too far. "You mind your business, Allan Luff. I shouldn't have to tell you that Miss Aila is a proper lady."

She grabbed the handful of letters, slammed the door, paused, riffled through them, found the envelope addressed to her mistress and dropped it into the pocket of her apron. The distant chime of the grandfather clock in the hall reminded her it was time to carry up the mid-morning drinks for both Aila and her grandmother and five minutes later she was holding out the envelope in front of her puzzled mistress. She slit the envelope with her paper knife, pulled out the page, read, gasped and raced to the stable block. Maisie picked up the letter.

* * *

The army tents had been dismantled and packed and now the regiment was queuing to draw chitties for luxuries like pipe tobacco or ciggies; queuing to collect rail warrants, queuing for the barber; queuing to sip endless cups of stewed tea. By ten they were lined up by platoon and company and counted off as they started the one-hour march from the camp to Wellingborough station from where they would entrain for the trip to London and from London to Aldershot and then to Southampton docks and so, finally, to France.

* * *

Aila hurried across to where the Rolls Royce was housed and prepared the engine, weeping with frustration when it refused to fire. After three attempts the motor caught, she engaged the gear, and crept out of the yard and onto the drive. Confidence growing, she accelerated up to a terrifying twenty-four miles per hour, braked hard beyond the gates to swing the long bonnet in the direction of Wellingborough and prayed that no sheep or cattle were being moved from field to field on the way. Wellingborough was packed with soldiers. The Rolls crawled through the crowded streets until she gave up, abandoned it a hundred yards from the station and ran, scarcely noticing the pain in her hip in her anxiety.

* * *

The entraining had started. Will picked up his kit bag and rifle and waited his turn. The jostling, joshing, laughing mass of khaki moved towards the train doors, pausing as an overenthusiastic private managed to drop his rifle between the train and the platform.

He shook his head and turned back, wondering if Miss Aila had ever received his letter – and if she had, then what would she have thought about it. Probably just that he was a pushy young country bumpkin labourer who didn't know his place. He climbed up onto the step of the third-class carriage, hoisting his kitbag in front of him.

And then above the laughter and shouting, above the hissing of the engine, above the roared orders of the NCOs, he would have sworn he heard his name being screamed out. He paused, half turning, until the laughing corporal pushed him into the carriage.

* * *

Aila rushed into the station entrance ignoring the harassed stationmaster's shouted order for her to buy a platform ticket – and stopped dead. She had never seen such a crowd. Never! The most people she had ever seen in one place had at the county show and that had been bad enough – but the noise here! The smell! She crept forward, squeezing and pushing her way into the dense throng as the mournful hoot of the steam engine filled the platform.

She stepped up on to a bench, fanning her face with her pocket-handkerchief, peering across the mass of humanity as the smoke cleared. And there he was, half a head taller than the rest of the men surrounding him, his face sombre, withdrawn. She screamed his name. It seemed to her as if he heard her, for he turned his back on the train and gazed round at the crowd. She saw him shake his head and step up into the carriage and screamed once more. He half turned again and was pushed into the carriage by a laughing soldier.

The guard's whistle sounded through the racket. The engine answered with a desolate hoot. With a modicum of wheel slip the engine started and it rumbled its slow way out of the station, with the men still cheering, singing and waving out the windows. Aila stood on the bench, clutching her handkerchief, sobbing, desolate.

AT WAR
1916 – 1918

CHAPTER FOURTEEN

MONDAY 18TH JANUARY 1916
Walmer and Kingsdown Golf Course, Kent

"He'll never get it on to the green in one."

His fellow golfer studied the terrain and smiled slyly.

"Care to wager, old chap?"

A half crown was held out and inspected and both men turned back to third member of the outing.

"Hurry up Gillies, we haven't got all night, you know. Embarking tomorrow morning for France, in case it had slipped your mind!"

The tall, athletic, thirty-two-year-old looked up from where he was addressing his ball, studied the other two for a moment, and laughed.

"All right, all right, what's the wager, then?"

Two fingers holding a third bent over beside them were held up. The man they had addressed as Gillies laughed. "Well, if it's only half a crown I'll use my mashie niblick – make it a bit more unpredictable, you know."

"But it's more than a hundred yards, man."

The two men groaned as Harold Gillies took a last look at the green, bent his head, and swung. The ball soared, straight and true, bounced on the edge of the green and rolled towards the pin. Half a crown changed hands as the still smiling Dr Harold Gillies walked back across the springy

South Downs turf, swinging his golf bag on to his shoulder. The winner of the wager laughed and slapped him on the shoulder.

"Bloody Kiwis. So competitive! All I can say is if your surgery is half as good as your golf, Gillies, your wounded soldier boys are in for a treat. Now, do you think there's any chance of getting up a cricket team once we're in France? Medics against the rest?"

They discussed the possibility as they headed towards the eighteenth hole. They continued to discuss the possibility over dinner and were still discussing, although with considerably less enthusiasm, as the Dover Ferry was mooring in Boulogne the next morning.

"I say, Gillies, there's the chap over there you wanted to meet."

Gillies stared across the dock. "Why? Does he play cricket?"

"Don't talk rot old fellow, he's half French and half American. Course not. Name of Valadier – Auguste Charles Valadier. Works out of the 83rd General Hospital just north of Boulogne at Wimereux – dentist johnnie. Set up a special medical unit for treating jaw wounds. Jolly interesting technique he's got too, but as he's not a surgeon he has to be supervised by one of us medical doctors. Let me introduce you."

CHAPTER FIFTEEN

TUESDAY 19TH JANUARY 1916
Stanwood House

Aila slit the envelope and reached in for the letter. A second, smaller page fell out. She hunched closer to the coal fire and tilted both missives towards the winter light slanting through the window. In pencil, at the top she saw that her cousin Amelia Burkett–Smythe had written a quick note.

Aila dear,

This was sent to the doctor for whom I am working in Rouen, Captain Harold Gillies. It was from a friend of his at a Casualty Clearing Station just back from the Front Line. I'm afraid it shows you what a dreadful state of affairs it is there. By the by, having said that I am in Rouen it looks very much as though I shall soon be back at a hospital in Aldershot. You really should try your hand at nursing, Aila, instead of wasting your life away in the wilds of Northants...

Aila smiled, shook her head and read the enclosed note.

'On the morning of the 2nd, I was wakened up at six o'clock and went to the hospital. The commanding officer had previously told the D.M.S., much to my annoyance, that we had accommodation for 800 cases, and when I arrived nearly every square foot of both buildings was filled with lying cases and more were pouring in... As long as I live, I *shall never forget the next three days— climbing over stretchers, trying to sort the cases out, removing the dead and dying, getting some operated on and sending others to the train, but always finding more cases in unlikely spots. Never have I felt so utterly helpless and ashamed at being able to do so little...'*

She wiped her eyes and picked up her pen to reply to her cousin.

CHAPTER SIXTEEN

SATURDAY MARCH 26TH 1916
Burton Latimer, Northamptonshire

Aila sat beside her grandmother in front of a south facing brick wall trying to draw warmth from the early spring sun at the garden party. She watched the procession of young men in their brand-new officers' uniforms parade past the seated debutants and their chaperones. She leaned across to whisper in her grandmother's ear.

"Grandmamma, why am I here?"

The dowager Lady Smythe glowered at her. Aila glowered back. "You do not seriously mean to tell me that Papa and you are still contemplating marrying me off? How could you? And anyway, look at them."

She waved an arm in the direction of a passing group of junior officers – one waved back. Aila abandoned glowering and giggled. "Grandmamma, they are so very young. I'd have to buy a pram to carry one of them in."

Her grandmother struggled to retain the severity of her demeanour for a few seconds, failed and burst out with a distinctly unladylike snort of laughter. "You, Aila Smythe, are still a disgrace and a minx. Come along, we have been invited so we must circulate, as I believe the modern term has it. And we must speak to that young man whether you like it or not."

She pointed with her chin at a tall, bespectacled lieutenant who was seated in the shade reading a book. His long legs were stretched out beneath his kilt in front of him. His Gordon Highlanders Glengarry lay on the table beside him. He glanced up, caught her eye and looked back down immediately.

Aila leaned across the table to whisper once more. "Well at least he can read without moving his lips."

That elicited a rap on the knuckles and another half-suppressed laugh.

"Who is he, Grandmamma?"

"His name is Sir Alastair McDonald. His father's the laird and I know the family well. My branch of the family is a sept of theirs."

Aila widened her eyes in mock dismay. "But he's wearing a skirt, grandmamma, and he's foreign. I may be no more than the barren, natural child of an English Lord, but surely you don't expect me to stoop so low as to marry a skirt wearing foreigner."

Her grandmother narrowed her eyes and tapped her on her the back of her hand with her forefinger. "Remember that a McBride was good enough for your grandfather so a McDonald would do just fine for you. And since you think it is funny to make mock of the tartan of the greatest clan in the greatest nation on earth, you will now walk across with me to meet him. Try not to limp."

Aila pushed her chair back to stand up and saw her grandmother's eyes soften.

"Aila, my dear child, you do look bonnie today. You really do."

Together they walked across to talk to Second Lieutenant, Sir Alastair McDonald.

She liked him, she realised, after ten minutes. He was earnest without being dull and had a brain which, unlike so many of his braying fellow junior officers, he had clearly put to good use. He enthused some more about the book he was reading. "You'll have read any George Eliot, Miss Smythe?"

Aila shook her head in embarrassment. "I'm sorry Sir Alastair, but I'm not a great reader. I know I should be, and I know my father has all her books on his library shelves. See, at least I do know George Eliot is a woman. Now if you had asked me to conjugate a Latin verb, I'm sure I would have done far better." She struggled to remember one of the book titles from her father's library shelves. "One of her books is called Silas, er, Silas..."

McDonald smiled at her. He had a kind smile, she thought. "Marner, Miss Smythe, Silas Marner. But this one," He held up the book. "Middlemarch, is her masterpiece: a truly engrossing and morally powerful book. I'm afraid to say I'm reading it for the third time. I find the character of Dorothea quite fascinating." He blushed. "I'm so sorry, Miss Smythe. I'm babbling. My mother says I either babble or haver."

Aila laughed out loud at this as her grandmother straightened to her feet. "Come Aila, we must be going and we have yet to thank our hosts. Great Nephew, I trust you will remember me to your father and mother."

The young Lieutenant leapt to his feet and bowed in her direction, looking uncertainly towards Aila. "It would be my pleasure Great Aunt. And, er, I..."

He stumbled over the words and looked helpless. Aila took pity on him and laid her hand on his arm. "It gives my grandmother great pleasure to hear a Scots voice, Sir Alastair, so I do hope you will be able to find the time to call on us before you embark for France."

She took her grandmother's arm and they walked away towards the main house. Her grandmother patted the back of Aila's hand. "Well, granddaughter? Well?"

Aila looked down at the gravel path beneath her feet and tried not to laugh. "Weeell, my wee Highland granny. Weeeell. He's nae bonnie o' course and he is outwith my normal circle, but he's, he's..." She reverted to her normal accent. "He's nice, Grandmamma. Now listen while I speak very slowly and clearly. I am not marrying him. In any event you do know that this whole marriage market is deeply, deeply primitive, don't you?"

She glanced sideways at the old woman beside her who snorted in irritation.

"You've been talking to your cousin Amelia, haven't you? I don't know where she gets her ideas from – and her my granddaughter and the daughter of an Earl!"

Aila walked on beside her grandmother slowly, glad to be able to limp again now that they were out of sight of the young Lieutenant. "She gets them, Grandmamma, from a sense of justice; from a sense that for too many years too many women have been crushed by men as stupid, vicious and evil as Dudley. Just because your generation and my father's generation went through this game does not mean mine has to.

"And there's no point in getting angry with me, Grandmamma. You know that even if I am forced to marry,

I will be exposed as a fraud. Whoever it is that I marry I'll not be able to have children and that's what this..." She waved an encompassing arm at the strolling pairs of chaperoned young women. "... dynasty, breeding, inheritance matter is all about, isn't it? It's as if I'm supposed to be a thoroughbred dam. All I want to do is to find my mother. I want to find my mother."

She bowed her head. wondering yet again about her deep sense of double loss, of why the pain of knowing her mother might be alive felt as every bit as painful to her as the knowledge that she would never be able to have a baby, her own child.

Her grandmother took another few steps, glancing across at the weeping girl. Aila took two deep, trembling breaths and wiped her eyes, half expecting a telling off and another lecture on the responsibility of being a Smythe. Instead, her grandmother guided her to one side, off the gravel path.

"My dear, dear, Aila. I do understand. As your father has said many a time, you are far too bright, which is not an attribute likely to guarantee you position and success as a woman in our society. And I cannot in all honesty answer your question. I know I was lucky with my husband, but I also know many who weren't, poor girls."

Aila shook her head. "But if I cannot have children what is the point?" She held up her hands, palms upwards, fingers curled. She breathed out. "I do not want to fight with you, Grandmamma. I love you too much." She straightened her back and tried to smile. "I do not want to fight with you, Scots granny o' mine?"

Lady McBride sighed, nodded to herself and then at Aila. "And I not with you, my wee bairn." She paused. "And by the way, granddaughter, that was the worst attempt at a Scots accent I have ever heard. And I am not now, nor ever will be your 'wee Highland granny'."

They both laughed, relieved to have averted a row. Aila hugged her grandmother's arm and, judging the time to be as auspicious as it could be, raised her next point.

"Grandmamma?"

A suspicious eye was cast upon her.

"Grandmamma, with all these people giving so much for what the newspapers call 'the war effort' – you know, Papa in the War Office and even Dudley hiding somewhere behind the Front Lines in the army. Well, I think I should make an effort too."

She glanced down at her grandmother, noting the pursed lips and half raised eyebrow.

"I want to train to be a nurse, Grandmamma. I have been speaking to cousin Amelia. Not about breeding though, I can assure you! She has already trained and she has asked me to join her twice now, but I cannot go until I have done some training."

Her grandmother patted the back of her hand. "Just so long, minx, as we do not fight again, I shall recommend this course of action to your father."

Aila smiled. "I quite like being a minx you know, Grandmamma."

She stooped to kiss the old cheek and they walked on together, her grandmother temporarily relieved, Aila's wounded soul still unhealed.

CHAPTER SEVENTEEN

WEDNESDAY 29?? MARCH 1916
Rouen Railway Station, France

"First class isn't packed, Doc. Look, there's a half empty carriage."

Harold Gillies looked down from his considerable height at the young Cockney medical orderly carrying his bag for him.

"You know, I'm pretty sure you're supposed to call me Captain Gillies, or Sir possibly, but not Doc."

The orderly shrugged and pushed the bag up through the door.

"You'll be in Paris by lunchtime, Doc."

He proffered a sketchy salute and turned to wander back through the packed platform of Rouen station. Gillies laughed and returned to the book that the American dental surgeon, Bob Roberts, had loaned him. He had struggled with the French medical text but the pictures of jaw and mouth surgery fascinated him. If it was possible to use surgery to rebuild rather than just cut out and destroy. He studied the pictures once more and pulled out the sketchpad that accompanied him everywhere and began to draw the musculature of the jaw, working out where best to pull together and restore. A fellow officer leaned across to see what he was sketching, blenched, and went back to his perusal of a week-old copy of The Times newspaper.

Three days later, Harold Gillies realised his entire life had been turned upside down. He boarded a train back to his hospital in Rouen still thinking about the surgery he had just witnessed, grabbed a piece of writing paper and started a letter.

Sir William Arbuthnot Lane
Head of Army Surgery
Royal Army Medical Corps

Dear Sir William,

You will, I trust, recall our last meeting at the Cambridge Military Hospital in Aldershot. I am writing to you now concerning the possibility of setting up what I am calling a 'facial reconstructive, plastic surgery' unit in order to cater for some of the worst of the facial wounds caused by snipers and shrapnel amongst our troops.

I have been witnessing the work of Dr Hippolyte Morestin in Paris and already the French medical...

The train jolted back into Rouen station.

CHAPTER EIGHTEEN

WEDNESDAY 31ST MARCH 1916
British Army Reserve Trenches, Belgium

He pictured his home village, humming the tune of Barbara Allen under his breath, remembering the erect bearing of Miss Aila on Juno's back.

"Colour S'arnt Hammond?"

He returned to present day Belgium, folded the tattered letter from Aila once again, pulled himself to his feet and stood to attention.

"Sir?"

Major Scott smiled at him. "How goes it, Will? That was a pretty awful few weeks, eh?" Will smiled back. Strangely enough, this officer had become his only friend, ever since his bout in the boxing ring back at the training camp in Northampton a lifetime ago. He pointed over his shoulder.

"Only a handful of us left now, sir. Any idea when the new conscripts are due?" The Major shrugged, lit a cigarette and offered the packet to Will who shook his head.

"Best not to, sir. We ran out of fags a week ago and I wouldn't want them to see me smoking when they don't have any." The Major grimaced. "Sorry, Will. Sorry. Should've thought." He passed the packet across. "Share 'em out, would you?"

Will smiled and watched the Major squint at a small cloud of dust growing larger by the second. "Put the men on alert, Will. That's a Staff car. Could be information." Will saluted, fought off the fatigue and strode away radiating confidence and energy.

He reached his group of slumped, exhausted men, grinned, and held out the packet of cigarettes. "Compliments of the Major, boys. Should be enough for one each." The men cheered faintly and lit up. A corporal squinted up at him. "How come you look so bright and perky all the time, Sarge? You on a special diet you ain't telling us about?"

Will stared down at them straight faced. "I am wrapped in the warmth of my love for the high command of our army. My respect for them provides me with all the nourishment I require to function at the highest level."

A chorus of raspberries greeted this comment. He smiled. At least they could still laugh. After what they had been through in what they were now calling the Battle of the Somme, he was amazed they could raise a smile. A drawling upper-class voice cut across his reverie and he straightened to attention.

"You there."

Will glanced round. An immaculately turned-out Staff Lieutenant was staring at him out of gooseberry eyes and smacking his swagger stick against his highly polished boot.

"Sir?"

"You're a disgrace to the British Army. Your uniform's filthy." He walked round the silent Will. "Your puttees aren't properly bound. Your boots! Good Grief man, they're not even regulation issue. Where did you get them?"

Will glanced down at his feet. "Off a German, sir. He no longer had any use for them."

The gooseberry eyes goggled. "What? That is tantamount to treason! Can you not see that there's a General over there in the Staff Car? What do you think he'd make of such behaviour? The very least I can do is have you put on a charge today before I leave."

He jumped as Major Scott tapped him on the shoulder. Will saw that his major was quivering with rage, but when he spoke his voice was soft, almost gentle.

"Lieutenant, allow me to introduce you to Colour Sergeant Will Hammond, DCM, MM, also Mentioned in Dispatches four times. Colour Sergeant Hammond has led the remnants of his Company back here to the Reserve Trenches after three weeks of continual fighting during which more than four hundred of his battalion fell in action. Without Colour Sergeant Hammond I doubt that even this many would have returned alive. He may look slightly rough round the edges, Lieutenant, but that is because neither he nor his men have had the chance to wash, shave, sleep or even eat in the last thirty-six hours."

The Staff Lieutenant flushed. "It's still no excuse for standing there looking like a tramp."

The Major stared. "I think you forgot something at the end of that sentence, Lieutenant." He glared at the junior officer not caring if he turned out to be the General's son or the Prince of Wales. "I'm waiting."

The Lieutenant tried to swallow the word, furious at his humiliation. "Sir."

Out of the corner of his eye, Will saw the General in the back of the staff car straighten up to listen. The Major's anger was beginning to evaporate. He rocked on the balls of his feet and blew his cheeks out.

"It is every excuse, you blithering idiot. Colour Sergeant Hammond is a fighting man. Perhaps I should recommend to the General that you spend a few months at the Front attached to his company as part of your basic training. It may help to give you a little understanding about what this war is all about."

The General strolled in their direction. Will brought his men to attention as the General tapped the brim of his cap in their direction with the tip of his swagger stick. "As you were, men." He studied Will for five long seconds. "I seem to recall pinning a gong on your chest a while ago. Am I right?"

Will opted for brevity. "Yes sir."

The General nodded. "I seem to recall further that your tunic was rather cleaner than it is now." He looked down at Will's feet. "Well made, German boots, aren't they? A tad better than our apology for footwear." He turned to the enlisted men. "Chaps, I know you had it rough up there and I'm sorry. I'm even more sorry to tell you that you'll be required back at the Front all too soon. There aren't enough top rate fighting men like you to go round, but I can at least offer you a two week break back at Divisional HQ training up new conscripts. Put the fear of God into them, chaps." He half turned, then paused. "Well done, Major. And thank you, men. Thank you for what you do. It puts old men like me to shame." The Company stared.

Will thought quickly. "Three cheers for the General. Hip Hip..." The General turned away, but Will could see the shake of his head and the tears in his eyes. The Company collapsed back against their packs and Major Scott sighed as Will glanced at him sardonically.

"You'll never make Colonel if you keep on upsetting Staff officers, sir."

They both smiled – this had become a standing joke between them.

CHAPTER NINETEEN

SATURDAY 19TH JUNE 1916
Stanwood House

Aila had long ago realised she knew little of men. Her half–brother, Dudley, was one of the very few she knew at close quarters, and she presumed, hoped rather, that he was not a typical example. He had only returned home once in his Lieutenant's uniform, showing off in front of the servants and then informing their father that he was transferring into the Royal Artillery as heavy armaments were the future of warfare. To Aila it was obvious that his main wish was to be stationed safely behind the Front Line with the batteries of guns.

On the other hand, Second Lieutenant Sir Alastair McDonald was quiet, studious and quite untroubled by Dudley's brand of male vanity. He had stayed at Stanwood House four times now. Not that there was anything inherently suspicious about this. Was there? After all, he was stationed nearby; he was a second cousin; he was a Scot, he was a gentleman; her grandmother liked him. Aila frowned. Was she being manipulated? She yawned and sat bolt upright. This was why he was coming here this weekend. She *was* being manipulated! Alastair must have spent all this time plucking up the courage to ask for her hand. And, of course, Lord Augustus' continued absence in

London had stopped him, as her father's permission had to be sought first. How dare they? This was not only unfair on her but also on poor Alastair.

The door opened. No knock so it could only be her grandmother. Aila managed not to scowl as she bustled in and Maisie jumped to her feet to fetch a chair. Before her grandmother could utter a word, Aila launched into her diatribe.

"So, I take it you've come to tell me that Alastair is going to ask for my hand in marriage when he comes next weekend?"

Her grandmother sat down.

"So, I am right. Well, no Grandmamma. No, no, no! How many times do I have to repeat that? I mean does Alastair even know about my condition? Or about my being illegitimate?"

The elderly woman straightened her back as Maisie tried to disappear into the shadows. "I have spoken to his mother in general terms about your health."

"In general terms, hah! And not about my illegitimacy, of course. Let me guess, Grandmamma, you or Papa have come up with a plan for that. Please do share the information with me."

Her voice was heavy with bitter irony. Her grandmother glanced across the room.

"And before you say another word, Grandmamma, Maisie stays in this room. She knows all my secrets. She has never once betrayed me and whatever happens to me, wherever I am forced to go, I hope dear Maisie will go with me."

Maisie stared down at her sewing.

"I am waiting, Grandmamma."

"I… Your father… We…." She breathed deeply and started again. "I recommended to your father that he should consider disinheriting your brother in favour of your cousin Amelia's branch of the family."

She waited for the onslaught. Aila stared at her, shocked. "Then who would inherit Stanwood House, Grandmamma?"

"Your cousin, Roland, of course. He is the eldest male. Should he die then it would go to his younger brother, Huon."

Aila shook her head as the horror of this hit her. She raised her hand before her grandmother could speak again. "Grandmamma, I do not want, nor do I intend to argue with you about this. If you cannot see the basic injustice of this course of action, then I… then I…. Well, you should. You, of all people. It's disgraceful. And what happens to me? Where do I live? Do you expect me simply to be shunted off from my home and from my family to some castle in Scotland with a man whom you know I do not love and for whom I could not bear children?"

She jumped to her feet to rage at her grandmother. "What have I done to deserve being treated with such contempt? What have I ever done? Is it my fault that no one knows where my mother is? Is it my fault that I am a bastard?" She spat the word out. "Is it my fault that my own half-brother tried to kill me and then left me barren?"

She ran to the door and slammed it behind her. Maisie leapt to her feet to follow then stopped, her arm still outstretched towards the handle. She turned back to where Lady Smythe sat, watching her tears drip on to the backs of her folded hands. Eventually the old woman wiped her eyes, blew her nose, stood, picked up her stick and walked to the door, where she paused.

"She is not wrong, you know, Maisie Brown. My granddaughter is not wrong. Let her know that I will speak to her father. And, Maisie? Please help her. She listens to you, and I know you love her as much as I do."

Her voice broke. Maisie opened the door, touching – almost stroking – the thin arm that held the stick.

"I'll do everything I can, M'Lady, everything I can."

* * *

An uneasy truce remained in place until the next weekend and the visit of the McDonalds. Aila had ridden Juno every day, leaving the stables early in the morning and returning as the sun dipped towards the woods behind the park. Maisie had said little, watching as Aila found some kind of peace in her rides around the lanes, fields, meadows, woods and coppices she loved so dearly. By the day of Alastair's and his mother's arrival she knew her mistress had regained much of her equanimity.

* * *

Aila moped through the boredom of the Sunday morning ritual – the trip to church, the heavy luncheon, culminating in a cream slathered syllabub. She asked to be excused, ignoring Alastair's pleading look, seated herself on the west terrace and waited... and waited. At three forty-five, just as she had managed to doze off in the mid–summer warmth, a cough from Maisie alerted her and she opened her eyes to see that Alastair's mother had arrived at her side. Maisie was waved away from the chair and the onslaught began.

"Aila, I admit to being confused and however odd this may sound I would be grateful if you would inform me of what your intentions are towards my son."

Aila made the mistake of catching Maisie's eye at this juncture and nearly dissolved into a giggling fit. She covered it with a cough and smiled. "Lady McDonald, I have no idea what you have been told about me, about my status and about my infirmities."

She paused and waited. The older woman raised her forearms, palms upwards, shoulders raised, in a whole-body shrug. "I understand that you have had certain health problems, but what that has to do with Alastair I cannot yet tell."

"Ah." Aila leaned forward, rested her right elbow on the arm of the chair and her jaw on the palm of her hand. "Did they tell you that I was forbidden to say anything about it, Lady McDonald?"

"Tsch, Aila, don't be so formal. They told me it was up to you what you told me about your health. Your father seems to have considerable respect for you, my dear."

Ah, so yet again the subject of her illegitimacy had not been mooted. Her father must be hoping against hope that she wouldn't mention it, although he had had the decency not to force her hand. Aila thought for a moment. "I think I had better tell you the story of my half–brother."

It took her over five minutes and by the end her throat was dry. She signalled Maisie to bring tea. Lady McDonald stared at the ground and Aila could tell she was considering her options. Before she could speak, Aila completed her argument. "So not only am I completely unsuitable as a wife for dear Alastair, I am also not in the least inclined to marry anyone. Lady McDonald, I like your son a great deal. He is intelligent, modest and gentle and quite unlike other men of my acquaintance. But I do not want to marry. In fact, I intend to become a nurse."

The Scotswoman sipped the last of her tea, came to her feet and allowed a smile to cross her face. "Aila, dear, I am not sure what to make of all this, especially as I would be very proud to have you as a daughter. I shall send my son out to speak to you now."

Aila threw her arms up into the air and raised her eyes heavenwards as Alastair's mother hurried away. She turned to Maisie, shaking her head in despair.

"Maisie, dear, you'd better make yourself scarce. Not that I would dream of having an argument with the poor boy but I may become slightly intemperate."

Maisie picked up the tea tray as Alastair emerged through the French windows. Aila waved at him and smiled as she saw the worry on his face. "Dear Alastair, let's get this over with as quickly as possible, shall we? I have tried to explain to every member of my family and to your dear Mama whom I find, by the by, quite adorable, that I do not intend to marry. This is not an insult to you, Alastair, as I happen think you are quite the nicest man it has ever been my pleasure to meet. Now, has your mother told you about my medical condition?"

They spoke for a further five minutes, heads close together, he nervous, she reassuring. Then she slipped her arm through his and they walked together into her father's study, smiling at the crowded room, both now enjoying the confusion their unexplained happiness was causing, both refusing to raise a glass in a toast to anything. Eventually Aila saw her father beckoning her across. To her surprise he smiled at her affectionately. "My dear daughter. You are a true Smythe. You really are."

Aila tilted her head, eyes narrowed, then went up on tiptoe to kiss his cheek. "If by that, Papa, you mean I can be nearly as Machiavellian as you then, yes, I do try to live up to the family tradition. Now, what is it that you really want from me?"

Her father glowered at her until she batted her eyelids at him. "Oh come, Papa, you know that you never call someone across a room to give them a compliment. You forget I have been watching you for nearly twenty years. You want something. What is it?"

She saw his eyes twinkle and he gave a quite uncharacteristic grunt of amusement. "Your grandmother says you are a minx and that if you ever get around to marrying you will probably make the poor young man's life a misery."

He nodded in the direction of Alastair. Aila shook her head. "I may laugh at him, Papa, but I do it with genuine affection. He is a fine young man and I respect him."

She tilted her head to one side again. "Papa, thank you for allowing me the choice to tell Alastair and his mother about my mother. I said nothing." She detected the slightest hint of relief in his face. "But I wish to talk to you about this Papa. And I will talk to you, whether you like it or not. With regard to Alastair and my inheritance you must know from grandmamma that I have no desire to marry."

She raised her hand as he started to talk over her. "Papa?" He paused and she continued. "I do not understand what you or the family gains by this, but in any event, I shall finish my nurse training whatever you or grandmamma may have to say about it and after that I shall consider Alastair and he shall consider me. I have made it clear to him that I have nothing to offer him. Unfortunately, for me, this seems to make no difference to the way he feels about me. His is a calf love, Papa. I hope that in the next year or so he will mature sufficiently to see the error of his ways."

Her jaw came up and she stared her father down. He glanced round the room. "Very well, Aila. Very well. Now you asked me why I had summoned you. I have, er, arranged for Alastair to be transferred out of the Gordon Highlanders and into the Royal Horse Artillery."

Aila looked across the room to where Alastair was listening intently to her grandmother lecturing him on some issue. She turned back to her father. "Does he know this, Papa?"

Her father shook his head. "No, the order will come through to him next week. Dudley has requested the transfer so he can be near to his, er possible, future brother-in-law."

Aila narrowed her eyes. "Papa, Dudley no more likes Alastair than he does anyone else. It's you doing this for me, isn't it? You want to make sure that Alastair is kept well back behind the Front Line with the artillery, don't you?"

Her father raised an eyebrow and remained silent.

CHAPTER TWENTY

JANUARY 3ᴿᴰ 1917
Whitehall, London

War Office   Captain Harold Gillies MD
Whitehall   Rouen Army Medical Hospital
London SW   January 3rd 1917

Dear Gillies,
Following on from our recent correspondence and your conversations with Head of Army Surgery over the last six months I take great pleasure in requiring and directing you to transfer from your current posting with the Medical Unit in Rouen to Cambridge Military Hospital, Aldershot, on or before 11th of January 1916 for special duty in connection with Plastic Surgery. The details of your new posting are attached herewith.

Sincerely,
Lieutenant General Alfred Keogh, M.D., M.Ch., R.U.I.
Director of Army Medical Services,

Harold Gillies read the letter three times, stood up, sat down, walked round his desk, and rubbed his hands together in glee. This was it. He was to be Britain's first plastic surgeon with full responsibility for getting the Aldershot unit up and running. He yelled for an orderly.

CHAPTER TWENTY-ONE

THURSDAY 19TH APRIL 1917
Aldershot General Hospital

Lieutenant Henry Tonks dusted pastel off his fingers, replaced the colour in the neatly laid out box on the small table beside his chair and studied the wounded solider once more. Harold Gillies, newly promoted to Major, reached across, pulled the sheet of pastel paper off Tonks' easel. He walked to the window and stared at the perfectly executed pastel image of the shattered face without speaking. As the nurse came in to wheel the soldier back to the ward, Gillies tugged something out of his pocket. "I had these printed for doctors to tie on head wound patients' uniforms at the Front. What do you think?"

Tonks studied the labels and pulled at the string attached to one of them.

'Jaw / Head Injury. Urgent. To be referred to Captain Harold Gillies (MD), Plastic Surgery Unit, Aldershot Hospital. Immediate'.

He smiled in his stern fashion. "How on earth did you get the War Office to stump up for these?"

Gillies laughed. "Didn't. Paid for them myself. Cost me a tenner no less. Anyway, probably worth it. They've agreed to send the labels out to all Field Stations at the Front. I'm not printing off any more now I've been promoted either!"

He handed the drawing back to the artist.
"We'll see."

CHAPTER TWENTY-TWO

FRIDAY 20TH APRIL 1917
Army Training Camp, Belgium

The rain eased, then stopped. Colour Sergeant Will Hammond pulled off his cape and helmet as the clip clop of hooves and the jingle of harness made him glance up. A troop of horse artillery was deploying in the neighbouring field.

A nearby gunner stepped down off a wagon and fell forwards as one of the horses moved in its traces. He staggered to his feet and lashed out at the cowering animal. Will was over the fence in a second. Three quick steps and he swung the gunner up with one arm and bounced him on to the grass. The gunner scrambled to his feet, took one look at the tall, tough NCO with a chest full of ribbons, un-bunched his fists and turned away to find support.

Will turned to the horse, stroking its muzzle, patting its flank and talking to it gently. It stopped trembling as Will pulled a full nosebag from the wagon and hooked behind the horse's ears. He reached into the wagon and unobtrusively adjusted a rope as a bellow sounded across the field. It was a bellow that Will was sure he recognised. He murmured quietly to the horse, then turned and straightened to attention. An Artillery Captain was riding an eighteen-hand hunter across the field shouting as he came.

"You there. What the devil do you think you're doing assaulting one of my men?"

Will's breath hissed out from between his teeth: Dudley Smythe, as he lived and breathed. And he was still yelling. Will stood rigidly to attention and replied in the formal tone of an NCO when addressing an officer.

"Sir, that Gunner was attacking this horse. If he'd done it any harm and the horse had bolted, your Howitzer could have rolled off the wagon, sir. As it's not fixed properly, sir!"

Another officer arrived, also on a horse while the Gunner stuttered that it had been properly fastened. The second officer studied Will, then swung himself off his horse, peered myopically into the wagon and spoke in a soft Highland accent.

"The Colour Sergeant's right, Smythe. The fastening is loose."

Dudley puffed himself up once more. "That does not provide an excuse for assaulting one of my men."

He paused and stared at Will more closely. "Don't I know you from somewhere?"

Will continued to stare straight ahead. "Shouldn't think so, sir. I've been at the Front for the last three years."

The second officer hid a smile as Dudley turned his horse, yelling over his shoulder.

"Get his name, McDonald. I'll have him put on a charge."

So, Dudley's friend was a Scot – two officers who could stay behind the lines and sleep comfortably in comfortable beds at night. Captain Alastair McDonald cleared his throat. "You did know Captain Smythe, didn't you, Colour Sergeant?"

Will flicked a glance at the tall Scot. "Yes sir. Before the war, sir."

McDonald nodded. "And judging by the look on your face you were not an admirer of his."

Will didn't move. A half smile crossed Captain McDonald's face as he pointed towards Will's beribboned chest. "Seen more than your fair share of action then."

"Sir."

The Scot touched his cap with his crop. "Good luck to you then, Colour Sergeant, and thank you."

He indicated the horse. A bellow came from the other side of the field.

"Come along, McDonald! I doubt my half-sister would ever contemplate marriage if she knew you consorted with riffraff like him."

Will came to attention and saluted. He stared at the officer's retreating back. So, Aila wasn't married yet and that was the man who was trying to win her. He sighed. Seemed like a decent enough chap too.

He looked for the Gunner who had hit the horse and saw him cowering behind two of the biggest men in his platoon. Without a second's hesitation he strode towards them. The two men stepped aside. There was no way they were going to become the object of this one's wrath. Will studied the quivering soldier. "My name is Colour Sergeant Will Hammond, First Northants. You want me, all you have to do is come to the Front Line and get me."

He nodded at the two other gunners and strode back to the fence, vaulting it effortlessly.

CHAPTER TWENTY-THREE

MONDAY 23RD APRIL 1917
Aldershot General Hospital

"His name is Rifleman E. Moss. Um, I think.'"

Sister Amelia Burkett–Smythe squinted at the doctor's scrawl on the label attached to the soldier's tunic, then glanced up as two medical orderlies entered the ward carrying in yet another soldier on a stretcher. She groaned as she saw the label hanging from his tunic and turned to the trainee nurse beside her. "You'd better fetch Major Gillies, Ruby, though Lord knows how we'll cope, he's the fifth one in two days."

The young nurse scurried off and within a minute the Major strode in, grinning enthusiastically. "Morning, Sister. More patients, I see. Excellent. Excellent." He beamed down at the latest arrival reassuringly. "Don't worry, old chap. We'll have you sorted out in no time."

He strode back out of the room as another patient arrived. The Sister grabbed an orderly and issued exact instructions as to where to put the new arrivals. By ten in the evening the seventh and last of the facial injury patients had been placed in a bed and she went to find the Major. He was painstakingly filling in musculature on a prosthetic model on his desk and studying one of Lieutenant Tonks' pastel drawings. He glanced up. "Evening, Amelia.

Everything hunky dory, as our American cousins apparently say?"

She pursed her lips and sat down uninvited. "Harold, we won't be able to cope. We only have thirty beds allotted to us here and we've had seven new patients in the last two days and there are more scheduled for tomorrow."

He tore his eyes away from his model and grinned at her. "Fear not, Sister. Uncle Harold has been working his magic once more!"

Amelia groaned. "Not again, please."

"Now, now, Sister. It's new premises. The top brass finally agreed!"

He scrabbled at the pile of papers on his desk and pulled out a War Office letter and scanned it. "Yes, here it is, er...

'... not possible to enlarge the Cambridge Hospital, nor, indeed, are the surroundings suitable, in any case, for patients of the type in question. Quiet, good air and ample space, we understand, are amongst the essential conditions for securing success...'

Anyhow, long and short of it, chap called Kenderdine, a trustee of the Roehampton amputee place has recommended we buy Frognall House down in Sidcup. The Joint War Committee has put up funding, so's that marvellous Sir Heath Harrison fellow. And, bless her heart, her Majesty has also coughed up. There, what do you think of that, eh, eh?"

Sister Amelia shook her head and did her best to sound pompous. "I don't think our gracious Queen has ever 'coughed up' anything in her life, Harold. You Colonials most definitely lack due respect for the mother country's institutions."

His mouth twitched as he laid on a New Zealand accent. "Just 'cos you got presented at Court don't mean you can put one over on me, Sister." He studied his model again and nodded in satisfaction. "Right, time for the night rounds."

He unlocked the cupboard behind his desk, pulled out two bottles of champagne, and picked up as many small, surgical bottles as his fingers could hold.

The Sister groaned again. "One day, Harold, someone's going to peach on you. Especially as you walk round all day ordering the men to swear off drink and tobacco for ever."

Gillies raised a finger. "Good point, Sister, good point. Now where did I put the ciggies?"

As she walked towards the door laughing, he called her back. "Amelia, one thing. We really, really could do with some more nurses in the Amelia Smythe mould."

Amelia smiled. So, I'm mouldy now, am I?"

"Quite definitely. But if some of your posh relatives have hearts and could bring themselves to help out, it would be jolly, jolly useful."

Amelia paused, tilted her head and nodded. "I think you'd like my cousin, Aila. I've already written to her about it and I'll write again before I go to bed. If you ever give me any leave, I might be able to see her in person. I've got an invitation to a ball in some castle in Perthshire in August." She shook her head and shivered. "And you may think it's mid–summer here, but in a castle in Scotland it'll be freezing. The things I do for you, Harold. Good night."

CHAPTER TWENTY-FOUR

FRIDAY AUGUST 24TH 1917
Perthshire, Scotland

Maisie shook her head. It was all very well for Miss Aila, she could drop into a Scottish accent at the drop of a hat, but she couldn't – well, wouldn't rather. I mean it was late summer and it was still freezing in this castle. And she had scarcely seen her mistress for three days.

She sighed again, completed her fine sewing and held the black satin dress up, admiring the silver roses at the waist. She twirled before the mirror to make the jet and silver sequins on the bodice and hem glitter and dance in the light. The door opened.

"Maisie Brown, you're not going to try my gown on, are you? You'd never get it over your front bits."

Maisie tried to look affronted as Aila came up behind her and hugged her. "I've been missing you, my Maisie."

They looked at each other's reflections in the old mirror and Maisie tried her hardest not to show how miserable she felt. Aila rested her chin on her maid's shoulder and whispered into her ear. "I have some news for you, Maisie, dear. Alastair has been ordered to join his regiment in three days so I am planning to get us all back to Stanwood House the day after tomorrow. How does that sound to you?"

She laughed at the delighted smile on her maid's face and threw herself in one of the armchairs. "It comes to something when I am more worried about my maid's welfare than I am about the man to whom everybody is trying to marry me."

She raised her hands as Maisie raised her head and her eyebrows. "No, no, no. Not going to marry. Not going to. Cross my heart and hope to die."

They both laughed.

"Do I need to try the dress on again, Maisie, or is it as perfect now as only you could make it?"

There was a knock on the door and it whipped open before Maisie had a chance to put the dress down and hurry across the room. Both women stared in amazement and Aila leapt from her chair to throw her arms round the new arrival. "Cousin Amelia! I thought you couldn't get away from the hospital. How wonderful. Now we shall have two people at the ball who speak English — well three if you count our Grandmamma."

Her cousin laughed. "Well, I have to say, my dear little Aila, that you have been sending me so many missives about your past and future that I thought I would use this event as an excuse to grill you. And if you won't cough up the information I shall move to my secondary attack and bribe Maisie Brown here — or threaten her — whichever is easier."

Maisie hid behind her sewing, listening to the ribbing and smiling at the jokes. A distant gong sounded, and the cousins hurried from the room waving at Maisie. She smiled after them, put down her needle and thimble and considered her state. She'd thought of nothing but serving

Miss Aila since… when? Since her 'front bits', as Miss Aila had just called them, began to grow.

She walked to the small window and stared at the dark forest at the edge of the park stretching up to the mountain range.

Since when her sister had first noticed her father giving her funny looks… and then when he had made yet another drunken grab for her one night and her big sister had fought him off. Since that next morning when her sister had walked with her up the long, long drive to the dauntingly big house, holding her small bag of possessions and had introduced her to Mr Livens, the butler. Since the time the very next day – she tilted her head and smiled at the memory – when a pretty girl of about her own age, with a mass of beautiful brown hair, had run down the main staircase past where she was polishing the banister and trying not to cry. The pretty girl had paused to crouch in front of her and ask her for her name.

"Don't cry, Maisie Brown. I'm sure you'll be happy here." She had stood and was about to run back down the stairs when she paused once more. "Are you good at sewing, Maisie Brown?"

She had nodded.

"Good. Good. I'll send for you this afternoon. By the by, I'm Aila Smythe, Lord Smythe's daughter, but you're supposed to call me, Miss Aila."

She had made her bob and said, "Yes, Miss Aila," which made them both laugh.

"Oh look, you've got dimples. How I wish I had dimples. I shall see you later, Maisie Brown."

And she had, and it had turned out her own maid was leaving to get married, and within a fortnight she had become Miss Aila's maid. And it was like having an older sister again and it had made her feel so utterly secure that she had never wanted anything more since that day. And now Miss Aila spoke of leaving Stanwood, of nursing, but not yet of marriage, thank the good Lord.

CHAPTER TWENTY-FIVE

WEDNESDAY 26TH SEPTEMBER 1917
First Northants Positions, British Front Line, Belgium

"Colour Sarn't Hammond, the Major would be grateful for a word."

Will nodded at the runner, stood up into a crouch and looked round the troop once more. "Just stay quiet and still lads. Reckon this will be over soon."

The German barrage was near continuous now as he followed the runner, making sure he stayed on the duckboards and out of the filthy quagmire. He pushed through the heavy rubber gas curtains and into the Major's dugout where his commanding officer was seated at his tiny desk peering at a set of orders by the light of a dim paraffin lamp. He glanced up as Will entered and they both ducked instinctively as the crash of a Whizz Bang shook the ground. Major Scott brushed dust off his papers.

"Evening, Will. Divisional HQ says we're going to shell the Hun from three forty-five to five thirty Ack Emma. Then we go over the top. GHQ thinks they won't be expecting this as they've been preparing for an attack for the last three days themselves."

Will shook his head. "Any chance you can get 'em to shell their reserve trenches then, sir? They had us cold with their machine guns last time."

The Major shrugged. "I've tried, Will. Believe me, I have tried. Have a seat for a moment."

Will groaned and lowered himself on to an upturned crate. "Do they never learn anything sir?"

The Major gave a weary shake of his head and passed Will a hip flask.

* * *

The German artillery barrage slowed at three am. By three thirty it was silent. Will peered at the face of the watch he had liberated from a dead German officer. Three forty-seven. Where the hell was the British barrage? It was supposed to have started two minutes ago.

* * *

Four forty-five and the first glimmerings of dawn to the east and still not a sound from the British guns behind them – then a glint of light on a cap badge, the shuffling of boots on the duckboards and the Platoon straightened to silent attention.

"At ease. At ease."

It was a Scottish accent. Well, well, well. It was the man who had been hoping to marry Miss Aila – Mc something or other. Will saluted and led him into the relative privacy of the dugout.

"Colour Sarn't Hammond, I'm sorry to have to inform you that the barrage has been delayed on the orders of, um, the orders of…"

Will shook his head. "The orders of Captain Dudley Smythe, sir?"

The bespectacled Captain looked miserably embarrassed, peered back at the men standing-to outside the dugout and spoke in a whisper.

"He's a Major now, Colour Sergeant. Has been since May. Anyway, he was ordered to move our 6-inch Howitzers up behind the Support Trenches last night and start the barrage at three forty-five Ack Emma. He er..."

Will sighed. Good God, they'd actually promoted him again. No wonder this war would never end. "Let me guess, sir. He started drinking and eventually came up with some excuse to send to HQ explaining why he couldn't move." He stared up at the lightening sky. "He always was a coward. Always got others to do his dirty work. What was the excuse he gave, sir?"

The captain pushed his spectacles up and rubbed his eyes. "Something along the lines that his men had not been given sufficient rest to enable them to use their guns safely."

Will rubbed his jaw. "All that just to avoid the faint risk of being hit by a German shell. Does he know you're here sir?"

McDonald sighed. "We'd had a row. He was drunk. Even more drunk than normal I should have said, and I told him his behaviour was reprehensible and that he was an affront to his family. I er, I have been courting... I should say trying to court, his sister."

Will nodded. "I hope it wouldn't be out of place for me to say that Miss Aila is a fine woman and much respected in the village, sir."

McDonald nodded and smiled for the first time. "The very finest, Colour Sergeant. The very finest." He sighed again and continued. "I told him I would report him for cowardice as soon as I had got word to the infantry that there was going to be a delay. I came up to the front line to apologise. I got your name off that gunner you savaged, so I just asked for you and got directed here."

He looked at his surroundings in the faint morning light, appearing to notice them for the first time. "This how you live all the time?"

Will nodded.

"And the smell? How do you live with that smell?"

"Don't think about it, sir. Latrines overflow. Dead bodies everywhere under the mud. Germans hereabouts mostly. Our Major says it adds to the piquancy of the atmosphere, sir."

Both men paused, smiles freezing on their faces, and tilted their heads. Finally, the British barrage had opened up. McDonald listened intently. "That's not my boys. That's French 75s." He listened some more. "They're at maximum range too. Keep your head down, Colour Sergeant. God knows what's going on back there?"

A High Explosive shell landed yards away. McDonald spat mud. "What the devil are they playing at? Can't you speak to them through the telephone?"

Will shrugged. "It's in the Major's dug out, sir, but it hasn't worked for two days."

McDonald groaned. "I'd better get back and tell them."

He turned to leave only to have his arm grabbed by Will. "You'll be dead for a certainty, sir, if you try to get out now. Those idiots have either not got the range to reach the Huns from where they're stationed, or someone's given them the wrong co–ordinates."

He gave the officer a long look.

McDonald's jaw dropped. "You don't think?"

Will stepped back and shrugged. "Just wondering if that gunner decided to get his revenge on me by telling Major Smythe where you'd gone."

He stood still for a moment, hardly blinking as another shell crashed down. "I'd better go and reassure the men, sir."

His troops were getting very twitchy. Will grinned at them. "All right, boys, all right. The Captain says it's French 75s at maximum range. We're being shelled by our own side now. This is something the Major calls irony."

He glanced at his watch once more. Six minutes before five. Surely to God, not even Divisional HQ would send them over after this. It would be carnage. The barrage intensified and then it happened. One of the new recruits broke. He screamed an incoherent sentence, leapt for the ladder, raced up it and over the top of the parapet.

Will cursed and threw himself after him. At least the shelling had ended. He scrambled after the recruit, jumping, sprinting, weaving through the broken wire. The recruit was fast but no match for Will. Fifteen paces, ten seconds gone. Seventeen, eighteen, nineteen seconds. By now the Hun would be coming up now out of their cosy, bloody dugouts and preparing for an attack. Any second now they'd see him.

He grabbed the recruit's shoulder, span him, punched him full in the face, threw the half-conscious body over his shoulder and ran back, stumbling now with fatigue. Twenty-six, twenty-seven, twenty-eight. A rifle cracked behind him – then the tok–tok–tok of a German machine gun starting up. A pause. It had jammed. Seconds more of silence. Another rifle crack. He heard that bullet. Ten feet, seven – more bullets smacking into the mud. But they were going to bloody make it. They had bloody made it! He gathered all his strength and threw the private over the parapet, diving after him. Too late he saw Captain McDonald's head and shoulders come up to help him. Too late, he yelled at him.

"Get down! Get down!"

The sniper's bullet caught the officer in the throat. His head snapped back, blood fountaining from the artery, dead before he hit the duck boards below him. Will groaned and threw himself over the parapet. The sniper fired once more. He felt the agonising rip in his cheek and jaw and fell forward onto the body of the already dead officer his arm flopping over one of his riflemen. Major Scott crashed through the mud filled trench towards the troop.

"Stand to. Stand to, damn you! They're about to attack! Corporal, get Colour Sergeant Hammond into the dugout. You..." He jabbed his finger at the shaking private. "He saved your worthless hide, now damn well save his." He turned and yelled back down the trench. "Stretcher bearers. Stretcher bearers! Now!"

He stepped over the two bodies and went to the periscope, the tears in his eyes blurring his view of the grey coated troops stepping out into No Man's Land four hundred yards in front of him. "Prepare to fire on my command. Pick your targets! Pick your targets!"

He pulled his Webley out of its holster, adjusted the lanyard, and raised the heavy handgun.

STANWOOD HOUSE

* * *

FRIDAY 28TH SEPTEMBER 1917
Stanwood House

Maisie was standing in the open doorway, trembling, white faced.

"Miss Aila..." Her voice faltered and she tried again. "Miss Aila, I'm so sorry."

Aila felt the blood drain from her face.

"Who, Maisie, who?" To her own ears her voice sounded distant.

"It's Sir Alastair, Miss Aila."

Aila gasped then bowed her head utterly ashamed at the deep, deep all–encompassing relief sweeping through her that it was not Will. But poor, good, kind, modest Alastair and poor Lady McDonald.

CHAPTER TWENTY-SIX

SATURDAY 29TH SEPTEMBER 1917
First Northants Positions, British Army Front Line, Belgium

A battle's aftermath: the detritus of war. Broken bodies, abandoned weapons, water filled shell holes, tattered barbed wire bent into a thousand shapes; acres of fathom deep, fetid mud across the desolation of No Man's Land. And now it was the turn of the burial parties and stretcher bearers to make their careful way down the wrecked trenches on half–broken duck boards.

"Dead. Dead. Dead." The sergeant walked on pointing out bodies for the burial parties to remove. "Dead. No. Hang on!" He crouched and peered. "Christ, this one's still alive. Stretcher bearers?"

A stretcher bearer stopped beside the slumped figure in the dugout and stared at the body.

"He's good as dead, mind."

The sergeant glared. "Just pick 'im up, son, then we can all get out of this stinking mess."

The orderly was still muttering as they crept back down the trench. An arm flopped off the stretcher. "Told you. Waste of time and effort. He's good as dead. Anyways did you see the state of his face? Looks like half of it's missing. Who'd want to live looking like that, I ask you?"

The stretcher was dumped, with little ceremony, in the queue outside the Advanced Dressing Station. It was half an hour before a harassed doctor in a blood-stained white coat arrived and felt for the pulse in the wrist. It was faint, very faint, but it wasn't fluttering. A nurse cleaned the wound and bandaged it. The doctor injected Morphine and gave the order for an ambulance. Hours later, the body was driven to a Casualty Clearing Station behind the reserve trenches.

CHAPTER TWENTY-SEVEN

MONDAY 1ST OCTOBER 1917
Perthshire, Scotland

The weather was dreich. The Scots word summed it up so well. No other single word could capture the mood, thought Aila, as Alastair's funeral cortege turned back into the long, tree lined drive leading up to the castle. Rain dripped from branches; rain dripped from the Tonneau cover behind her seat; rain dripped from an unseen hole above the car window beside her on to the carpet by her feet. She shivered.

Once in the castle she crossed the hall to take Lady McDonald's arm and lead her through into the morning room. At least here there was warmth and light from the logs burning in the ancient grate. She found a footstool and perched on it beside the shrunken woman in the armchair and stroked the back of her hand. Alastair's mother looked down at her as Aila tried her best to help. All she could come out with though, was an entreaty to have some food. "You must eat, dear Lady M."

That, at least, produced a smile of sorts in return and the first words since the funeral service. "My dear child. My dear child."

Aila rested her head on the arm of the chair and let the older woman's fingers find comfort in stroking her hair. "You know Alastair was so very happy to have met you?"

Aila raised her head, tears forming in her eyes yet again. "And I him, Lady M. I him. Dear Alastair."

She knelt in front of Lady McDonald and they wept together. Eventually she stood and made her rounds of the relatives and friends, talking with great warmth of Alastair, endearing herself to the family by her quiet dignity. She walked back over to her devastated host once more and spoke into her ear. "May I go to my rooms for a while, Lady M? I would like to be alone."

Lady McDonald squeezed her hand. "Of course, my dear. Of course. You try and sleep."

Aila straightened once more and caught Maisie's eye. Back in her rooms she slumped into an armchair and groaned in misery. "Maisie, despite being so very fond of poor Alastair, and loving his mama dearly, I cannot bear another day here. How can I escape back to Stanwood House?"

Maisie's knelt at her mistress' side and whispered. "Well Miss Aila, you've been coughing badly in the night and I think the cold, damp weather here is affecting your health and Stanwood is much dryer and..."

The words tumbled out and Aila couldn't help herself: she laughed at her maid.

"Shhh, Miss Aila. Shhh. Someone will hear you."

In the night which followed Aila did indeed cough loudly at increasingly regular intervals. Maisie's visit to the kitchens at eleven thirty at night to request a hot toddy for her mistress was noted by the staff and relayed to Lady McDonald by her maid during her morning ablutions.

By ten thirty the Rolls was ready to depart for the long drive to the North British Hotel behind Edinburgh's Waverley station, and Aila, wrapped in coat, blankets and with a stoneware hot water bottle for her feet, left the rain drenched castle, its occupants shaking their heads over her condition.

CHAPTER TWENTY-EIGHT

TUESDAY 2ND OCTOBER 1917
Stanwood Village

The Lagonda hadn't been running well for the last twenty miles and Major Scott was glad to be able to park it by the church. It had been less than a week since the regiment had fought off the last German attack and taken back its original trenches. Of all the futile, bloody exercises... He winced at the sudden stab of pain in his right leg where he had copped a Blighty – a shrapnel wound to his thigh which had brought him at least a fortnight of home leave. He reached for his stick and called across to a passing farm boy for directions to the Hammond's house.

This was not going to be easy. He climbed up the steps that led to the front door and then paused, realising that this door would only be used for special events – like funerals. He walked round to the side of the house, took a deep breath, straightened his shoulders, and knocked on the back door. It opened almost immediately.

"Mrs Hammond?"

There was little doubt that it was Will's mother. The resemblance to her strong–jawed son was unmistakable.

"May I come in Mrs Hammond. My name is Scott – Major Scott. I've been Will's commanding officer for the last three years and I promised him I would come and see you when I next had leave."

The door opened and she stepped back. She knew. In the back parlour a frail, elderly man was seated in an armchair, a blanket draped round his shoulders, as he huddled up to the fireplace. He looked up. He knew too.

"Mr and Mrs Hammond, there's no easy way to say this, but I am afraid that Will is missing in action."

The woman lowered herself on to a kitchen chair, reaching behind automatically with her left hand to steady herself against the kitchen table. She stood up again. "Where are my manners? Can I get you a cup of tea, sir?"

The Major limped forward. "No, no, thank you, Mrs Hammond."

The woman sat down again.

"Your son, Mr and Mrs Hammond, was the bravest and the best." He shook his head. "I know that sounds like one of the silly newspapers – 'our brave boys'. You know." He lowered himself so he could perch on the windowsill. "I first met Will in 1914 at the training camp up the road beyond Finedon. He was exceptional even then and he ended up as the most valuable NCO in the regiment. You know about his medals?"

They were still staring at him, frozen in despair. "Let me tell you about how he won them."

He wasn't sure even after five minutes of monologue, whether he was making it any easier for either of Will's parents.

"Mr and Mrs Hammond, I cannot confirm that Will is dead, and I am so sorry to be the bearer of this news." His voice cracked. "Will was the only man who gave everything to all his men, all the time. I am so proud to have known him."

The old couple sat silent, lost in grief and memories of their own. Major Scott looked from one to the other then pulled an envelope from his tunic, placing it on the windowsill. "This has my name and the address of our Divisional HQ in France. I've put a stamp on it too and there's a sheet of writing paper inside. Any time you need anything – anything at all – just write to me. Divisional HQ will always be able to get a letter through."

CHAPTER TWENTY-NINE

TUESDAY 2^(ND) OCTOBER 1917
Stanwood House

By the time she arrived home, Aila was seriously ill. She was carried from the car to her rooms, with a frightened Maisie demanding extra coal for the fire, hot water bottles to be placed in the bed and a bath drawn as hot as her mistress could manage. She practically forced chicken soup down Aila's throat, hustled her into bed and sat beside her, hour after hour, watching her toss and turn, checking the pulse in her wrist, the temperature of her forehead and placing coals on the fire if it started to die back.

The next morning Maisie asked for Mr Livens to come to her mistress's room and then insisted he call the doctor. By lunchtime Aila was diagnosed with pneumonia. Maisie settled in for the agonisingly long wait, refusing help, until Aila's grandmother and her father both arrived three days later. She was ordered to bed. For six hours Lord Augustus sat beside Aila's bed, holding her hand while servants tiptoed in and out feeding coal to the fire and bringing him sustenance. But by four in the morning, Maisie was back, feeling Aila's forehead and shaking her own in concern.

"The crisis is coming My Lord. You had better let me take over."

Lord Smythe stood, tears in his eyes, and stared down at his daughter's pale, gaunt face. "What does that mean, Maisie?"

She glanced at him in surprise. He never addressed the servants by their Christian names. "I asked Doctor Cardew, my Lord..."

Lord Smythe held up a hand. "So did I, Maisie, and it meant nothing to me. Kindly explain in simple, short words."

If she hadn't been so tired and worried, she might have smiled at the thought of her being able to tell his Lordship anything. "Miss Aila has got an inflammation of her lungs, my Lord. It's a disease and the first part of it lasts between six and eight days and it's day seven today. You can feel how high her temperature is and, of course, she can't stop coughing." She leant forward and touched her mistress' forehead, shaking her own head in concern. "The trouble is, my Lord, that she's running out of strength to fight it. She's hardly had a bite to eat and she isn't drinking anything like enough. I just can't get through to her."

Lord Smythe nodded. Maisie looked up at him. "She might hear you, my Lord. Can you try and speak to her? Tell her to eat something? Anything?"

Lord Smythe stared at his daughter. Her breath was shallow. He could hear the bubbling in her lungs. Her forehead was damp with sweat. What could he say? Then he smiled and leaned forward over the bed, speaking straight into her ear. "Aila? You are a Smythe and more than that you're the best of all the Smythes. Smythes do not give up when things get difficult, they fight back. Juno is waiting for you and your poor Maisie is exhausted, but she won't leave your side until you have something to eat and drink." He bent and kissed her forehead. "I know you're listening, child. Fight back my darling, Aila. Fight back."

He straightened and stepped away from the bedside wiping his eyes. Without a glance at Maisie, he strode from the room.

CHAPTER THIRTY

THURSDAY 4ᵀᴴ OCTOBER 1917
Stanwood House

Maisie sat on the bed and lifted Aila's head, cradling it in the crook of her arm, and wiping the forehead with a cool, damp face cloth. "Miss Aila, dear, I've got some broth here and I'm going to feed it to you, and you will eat it. I think you must have heard what your father said and it's true about Juno. He misses you. I know."

She placed the spoon at her patient's lips and to her utter delight, Aila's mouth opened and she was able to trickle the hot liquid into the mouth. She tried once more, and again the mouth opened and the broth was taken: and again, and again. Maisie bent forward and kissed her mistress on the cheek.

"Darling, Miss Aila, you are going to get better. I am so pleased. So, so, so pleased."

She felt the forehead once more and was sure it was not so hot. She picked up Mr Livens' watch, felt for her mistress's wrist, took the pulse as Doctor Cardew had shown her and checked it against the chart she had been keeping. Yes. Yes! It was slower, definitely slower. She lifted Aila's hand to her cheek and stroked it.

The crisis had passed. Miss Aila would live.

CHAPTER THIRTY-ONE

FRIDAY 5TH OCTOBER 1917
Casualty Clearing Station, Northern France

The Casualty Clearing Station was a small improvement on the Advanced Dressing Station – less blood, fewer groaning bodies, more doctors, more nurses. A medical orderly untied the string on the button holding the Field Medical Card tucked into its waterproof envelope. He read the notes, looked at the cheek, shook his head, and felt beneath the filthy tunic for the asbestos–fibre identity disc. He turned it over and made out the number. It tallied with the medical notes, which helped. All too often they didn't.

Regiment: 1st Northants.
Religion: C. E.
Name: W. Hammond.

He added to the notes, glanced down at the faded stripes and crown on the arm of the unconscious soldier and crossed himself. "You're out of hell, Colour Sergeant, but all I can say is welcome to purgatory."

He pushed the gurney though into the sanitation area, pulled heavy duty, elbow length rubber gloves on and began the unsavoury task of stripping off the lice ridden uniform. He washed, de–loused and disinfected the body before wheeling it back to the ward.

A doctor examined the body and scribbled additional notes on the Field Medical Card. "Dakin's Solution on the cheek and jaw wound, please nurse. If he stirs at all, give him the standard Morphine dosage – Chloroform if there's no Morphine available. When he comes round, he'll be in agony."

He felt the pulse again. "He's a tough one, though. He should have been dead days ago. I'll come back and give him a dose of anti–tetanus serum. At least, in his state, he won't feel the pain of that."

The nurse murmured her agreement. The orderly pushed the card back into the envelope and tied it to the left wrist.

"Where to then Doc?" He waited for the response.

"We need to make sure he is stable enough to travel. Then get him onto an ambulance train to the Base Hospital in Dieppe. Put some kind of uniform on him as soon as you can. He can't travel like this."

He indicated the sheets, turned away, and paused.

"Wait just a second."

He reached into the pocket of his white coat and pulled out a label. Tie this on his chest, nurse. It may be his only hope."

The orderly peered at the card in the nurse's hand, his lips moving as he read:

'Jaw / Head Injury. Urgent. To be referred to Captain Harold Gillies (MD), Plastic Surgery Unit, The Queen's Hospital, Sidcup. Immediate'.

* * *

Three days later as the day darkened, an Ambulance vehicle crawled down the axle deep mud track from the Casualty Clearing Station. It deposited the body at the half–organised, half–dark chaos that was Amiens Station, leaving the volunteer orderlies to lift the stretcher onto a Dieppe bound ambulance train. On the siding, carriages were removed and added. Nurses made their quiet way between the recumbent bodies on the mud-spattered floors, offering water, dressings, the necessary indignity of bed pans, and comfort where nothing else would help.

A whistle blew, the dim lights dimmed even further, the train jolted, carriages bumping as couplings took the strain, and finally, and slowly, and not that he knew anything about it, Will Hammond was going home.

CHAPTER THIRTY-TWO

TUESDAY 9TH OCTOBER 1917
Stanwood House

Aila opened her eyes and yawned. Maisie's face popped up into her field of vision.

"Miss Aila? Miss Aila? Oh, you're awake at last. Thank God."

Aila peered around as Maisie ran to the window and pulled back the curtains. She blinked and squinted at the pale, winter sunshine spilling across the floor. "Maisie, I'm back home. What's going on?"

Her voice sounded strange to her – cracked and rusty through lack of use. Maisie leaned against the counterpane and took her mistress's hand, unable to keep the huge smile off her face. "You've been back home for ten days, Miss Aila. You've been so ill." She stood back. "Now, may I get you something to eat, please?"

Aila yawned again. She'd been all but lifeless for two weeks – no wonder she felt so weak. "Why am I always ill? What was wrong with me this time, Maisie? I don't remember anything after poor Alastair's funeral. Food can wait. Just tell me what I've missed." She patted the bed and Maisie plumped down beside her to explain.

* * *

TUESDAY 9TH OCTOBER 1917
The Queen's Hospital Sidcup

The move to the hut filled grounds of Frognall House that constituted The Queen's Hospital in Sidcup had taken months, using up time that could and should have been spent operating on facial injuries rather than on irritating administration. Even Harold Gillies looked tired now. Sister Amelia watched as he scribbled some more notes. She cleared her throat.

"Harold?"

He glanced at her. "Not going to nag me again, are you? Oh, and by the by, Amelia, old bean, any luck with that aristocratic cousin of yours coming here? We're still desperate for good nurses."

Amelia smiled. "I am not a bean, Harold, as I have told you before, neither am I old, much as I might be feeling it since working with you." She sighed. "Yes, poor Aila. The man who had been courting her was killed on the Somme and then she caught pneumonia at his funeral in Scotland and she's only just recovering. She'll be here, though, Harold, I promise you that."

He shook his head. "How many patients have we got currently, Amelia?"

She shuffled the mass of papers on her desk and consulted a list. "Three hundred and sixty-nine, Harold, and another train from Dieppe should be arriving at Newhaven." She peered down at the watch she had pinned on the apron of her uniform. "... right about now."

***

TUESDAY 9TH OCTOBER 1917
Newhaven Town Railway Station

Entraining fifty-four wounded soldiers at Newhaven was a slow business. The shell–shocked and the fretful were first aboard, the badly wounded next, followed by the Blighties. The barely alive or deeply unconscious were last on, the thin rain beginning to penetrate their uniforms as they lay on their stretchers at the far end of the long platform. Here they would be out of sight of the new conscripts disembarking from their trains and marching towards the ferry that would take them across the channel to war.

An orderly bumped against a stretcher. The prostate figure groaned. The orderly bent down to study the rain–spattered notes on the man's chest. He straightened, looking round for medical help and a Red Cross VAD nurse hurried down the platform in response to his waving arm.

"Says here, he's to have Morphine or Chloroform if he comes round, Nurse."

The nurse grimaced at yet another bandaged face and nodded. "Get him on the train, please. I'll find a doctor." She looked back down at the half dead soldier. "Poor boy."

CHAPTER THIRTY-THREE

SUNDAY 14TH OCTOBER 1917
Stanwood House

Within the week, Aila was allowed out of her bed so long as she promised to sit close by the blazing fire and not to try and leave her room. And it was here that she sat, struggling to concentrate on Middlemarch, when Maisie crept in. Aila glanced up and reacted, dropping the book to the floor and whispering,

"Who now, Maisie? Who now?"

Her maid walked forward. "It's Will Hammond, Miss Aila. Henderson heard from his mother, her who's landlady of The Duke in the village. She met an officer in Stanwood who'd been to see Mr and Mrs Hammond. Will Hammond's missing in action. The officer said he was a hero, Miss."

Aila could scarcely begin to react. Had all her tears been cried for Alastair? She stared at the book on the floor, picked it up, opened it, tried to read, placed the bookmark at the page she had nearly completed, closed it once more and looked up at her maid. "I don't really understand what Alastair saw in this book, Maisie. I think if I had met Dorothea Brooke, I would have wanted to slap her face for even contemplating marrying that dreadful Reverend Casaubon."

She put the book on the table beside her. "Tell Henderson that I shall want the Rolls. I shall go and visit Mr and Mrs Hammond this afternoon and take some food. Oh, and a bottle of rum. Will said his father liked the rum we gave them last time."

Maisie was watching her, worried, wondering why she was reacting like this. Aila stared at the closed book for a few moments. "Maisie?"

"Yes, Miss Aila."

"You know how I had been training to be a nurse before I was taken ill. Had you ever considered being a nurse too?"

Maisie shook her head. Aila sighed.

"I think it is time we put more of ourselves into the war effort, Maisie. Would you come with me to join cousin Amelia at The Queen's Hospital in Sidcup and be a nurse too? You have far more practical experience of nursing than me and you have such an abundance of natural kindness and goodness. I'm sure you would make the most wonderful nurse. Please, Maisie, please?"

"Of course, Miss Aila. Of course." She paused. "Sidcup's not in Scotland though, is it? I won't have to go north again, will I? I can't take the cold up there, Miss Aila, really, I can't."

Aila smiled. "No, Maisie. You can attend your classes in Voluntary Aid Detachment training in Vere Street, which is in London, so we can stay with Papa in the London House first. And Sidcup is a village in Kent, south of London. Henderson can drive us there from Mayfair. Satisfied now?"

As Maisie closed the door behind her, Aila waited for the footsteps to fade then rocked backwards and forwards in her chair, clutching her fingers to her eyes. Not Will. Not her beautiful Will. This war, this awful, awful war.

AILA'S WAR

CHAPTER THIRTY-FOUR

TUESDAY 29TH NOVEMBER 1917
Charles Street, Mayfair London W

Aila was seated in the family's London house nodding off over her revision before her final exam, when her father's valet knocked and entered.

"It is your cousin Lady Amelia, Miss Aila, speaking through the telephone and wishing to converse with you."

Aila jumped up and rushed into the hall to lift the receiver off its Bakelite stand. She had scarcely ever used the telephone and found herself shouting down it. Amelia's disembodied voice echoed back to her.

"I'm not deaf, Aila. You just have to speak normally. Or as normally as someone who has been brought up in Northants can do."

Aila blew a raspberry down the phone. She heard the responding laugh.

"Try not to be too vulgar, Aila. Telephones have ears, you know. Now listen. How far has your training gone? My crazy Major wants you here now."

Aila sighed with relief. "Oh, Amelia. That would be truly wonderful. I have completed my probationary training and I've got one more examination tomorrow; and, and, you get an extra special bonus with this particular nurse too. My dear Maisie has all but completed her VAD training and she is already so much my superior that I am very nearly ashamed. She can come too."

CHAPTER THIRTY-FIVE

MONDAY 3ʳᴰ DECEMBER 1917
The Queen's Hospital, Sidcup

Will had no idea how his world could contain such agony. He had no idea how long he'd been here, wherever 'here' was. He had no idea if he would live or die. He had no idea if his parents knew if he was dead or alive. He had no idea if he would ever be able to communicate anything to the doctors, nurses and orderlies who came to see him almost every hour of every day.

They fed him drugs, dripped nourishment into his mouth with a spout feeder and tubing and dressed his wounded jaw. His tongue felt huge, formless, his mouth and neck so bandaged that he had no idea what the true extent of his injuries were. All he knew was that his pain filled world had contracted to the dimensions of a six foot-two by two foot-six hospital bed.

And then there was the noise in his ears – that all enveloping, hissing ring that dominated and excluded every other sound. God, make it stop. And his eyes! Why was the world out of focus? His sight cleared again. Then went. Today the tall blur that was the doctor with the unfamiliar accent had come in with another blur of a doctor, a doctor who was something called an anaesthetist – whatever that was. Through the haze he watched them as the posh sounding sister who always accompanied the tall doctor lifted the dressing from his jaw

"We've got the normal problem of the airway being distorted which means that you and I are going to be in each other's way. Now I'm going to be reconstructing the Mandible first and then starting on the flaps from the neck – here and here."

He indicated the incision points. The anaesthetist nodded and stooped to study the neck and spoke almost to himself. "Standard intra–tracheal administration. Ether under positive pressure, carried by an Oxygen stream... Yes. Yes." He looked up. "Yes, I can work round you all right, Gillies. No problem."

The two men strode away and the nursing sister, bent close to his ear. "They're the best team in the world, Colour Sergeant Hammond, and when you can speak again, you'll be able to thank them."

She squeezed his hand and hurried after the two doctors. When he could speak again. If he could see again. If he wanted to live. If the pain, the awful, bloody pain would end. Just give me peace. Let me rest in peace.

* * *

A week after the next operation he managed to signal to the posh Sister – Amelia something or other – that he would like something to write on. A small blackboard and chalk were brought and held above him as he peered and scrawled laboriously: *'My ears are ringing so loudly, and I keep losing my eyesight. Everything goes blurred.'*

She stooped over him and peered into his eyes, lifting the eyelids as she did so.

"There doesn't appear to be any visible damage to your eyes, Colour Sergeant. With your ears though it's what doctors call tinnitus. I believe it's the result of all the noise in the trenches. You know, the shelling. It should reduce I think, but I'll let Major Gillies know about that as well."

He reached for the chalk board once more and wrote.

'Thank you. And please can someone make sure my parents know I am alive? God knows if the army will have told them yet.'

He scrawled the address and tried to thank the sister with his eyes.

CHAPTER THIRTY-SIX

WEDNESDAY 13TH DECEMBER 1917
West End, Stanwood

Bloody ferns hanging over the path. He stooped to brush the drops of water off his trousers, adjusted his new postman's cap, coughed consumptively, and walked round to the back door, looking at the letter in his hand once more. Poor old Alice Hammond. It looked like an official letter. They were never good news. He tapped nervously on the back door and called out.

"Post, Mrs Hammond."

The key turned in the lock. She eyed him. "What have you got there, Alan Luff?"

The junior postman saluted. "It's a letter for you, Mrs Hammond. Looks official."

He eyed her, noting how gaunt her face was, the cheeks quite sunken since she'd heard about her Will missing in action. He saluted and backed away as he heard Fred Hammond calling out from the kitchen.

Alice Hammond shut the door and walked back through the scullery into the kitchen turning the envelope over and over in her hands. She seated herself and placed the letter on the table, staring at it – willing it to tell her its contents.

"Come on, Mother, there's no point in messing about. Get a knife and open it up. It can't contain any news worse than what we've had already."

Alice Hammond reached into the drawer for the bread knife. Hands shaking, she slit the envelope and pulled out the thin sheet of typed paper and peered at it. Her left hand left the paper and drifted in slow motion to her face where it remained, her breath quivering in her throat.

"Fred? Oh, Fred. Fred, I... It's Will, Fred."

She broke, sucked in a single breath in truncated gasps until her whole body convulsed in a spasm of sobs. Fred Hammond pulled himself to his feet, picked the letter from her lifeless fingers and read.

The Office of the Hospital Almoner
Queen's Hospital
Sidcup
Kent   10th December 1917

Dear Mr and Mrs Hammond,

Your son, William, was admitted to this hospital in October with serious facial wounds and is only now able to communicate with nursing staff.

He was unsure if information regarding his whereabouts and condition had reached you from the War Office and I have, therefore, been asked to send you this communication together with two rail warrants from Wellingborough to Sidcup for you to visit him in The Queen's Hospital now that he is able to receive visitors.

On arrival here, please ask to be directed to my office as the various wards designed to accommodate our 570 patients are scattered throughout the grounds of Frognall House where we are based.

Yours sincerely,
Gertrude Bellamy
Hospital Almoner

He stared at the neat copperplate of the signature, picked up the envelope and shook the rail warrants out over the kitchen table, peering at them in wonder. He placed them in front of his wife, patted her shoulder, walked to the cupboard in the alcove by the fire and smiled at her over his shoulder. "I know you took the pledge, mother, but at a time like this I think we could both do with a tot of rum. After all, Mrs Hammond, it isn't every day your son comes back from the dead, is it now?"

Alice Hammond raised her apron to wipe away the tears and picked up the glass. "Just a sip then, Fred, just one sip. Then I'd better be getting those black ribbons down in the front parlour. Oh, and I can tell Peggy Henderson at the Duke. And I've never been on a train journey that long, Fred. And what shall I wear? I'll need to sponge your suit off too. Who's got a Bradshaw's? We'll have to get the train times right and I'll make some sandwiches. Oh, Fred. Oh, Fred."

Her husband leaned forward, smiling at her, covering her hands with his. "You calm down now, Alice love. A journey like this'll take a bit of planning. But there's no need to fret now. We've got our dear son back, Mrs Hammond. We've got our son back."

CHAPTER THIRTY-SEVEN

Friday 14TH December 1917
The Queen's Hospital, Sidcup

An orderly wheeled Will into an empty side ward the week before his next operation, where he found the hospital almoner patronising an elderly couple. He turned towards them his heart thudding, holding out his hands. His mother stood first, paused and then almost ran to the bed to clutch the nearest hand and kiss it, her tears dropping on to the bed sheets. His father moved more slowly, supporting himself with his stick, squeezing Will's shoulder and then grasping the other hand. Will's vision blurred as he managed a small gesture towards his chalk board. The almoner passed the board and the chalk to him and left the room. His father pulled the two chairs up to the bed and pushed his mother down on to one of them. She clutched at Will's hand not willing to release her grip for one second.

"Oh, Will. Will. You're alive."

Will smiled with his eyes, feeling his vision clear, picked up the board and scribbled. 'Can't hide anything from you, Ma.'

His father blew his nose and smiled at his son. "Your Major come to see us, Will. He told us you were missing in action. He said you were a hero."

Will shook his head slightly and winced. He picked up the chalk once more. *'Not me, dad. Just did my job.'* He paused and scribbled once more. *'How's everything at home?'* He winked privately at his father at the torrent of words from his mother.

"Well Peggy Henderson from the Duke sends her love and Arthur Shaw from the pub where your dad worked said how pleased he was to hear about you. He's been real good about the back rent we owe him on the house too. They stopped your wages when..."

She stopped and sniffed, reaching into her ancient bag for a handkerchief. Will directed a questioning look at his father. The frail man shook his head.

"The army stopped your wages when you was reported missing in action, son. They said we'd get a bit of a pension as and when your death was confirmed, but ain't nothing come through yet." Will eyes hardened and he looked back to his mother. No wonder she looked so thin and unwell. She blew her nose and continued.

"But we was helped out again by your Miss Aila, Will. She came round in their big car driven by that snooty Henderson boy – gives himself such airs he does – not like his mother at all. And she brought that dear little maid of hers, Miss Aila did I mean, not Peggy Henderson, of course. Brought us some food and was proper polite and nice about you too. Said how sorry she was. She thought you had passed then, of course."

Will thought about the length of the bridge between Aila and himself now and listened again to his mother as the torrent slowed to a trickle and then reached for the chalk once more. *'No rum this time, dad?'*

His father smiled at him. "Not so, my boy. She told us how you'd said I was getting a proper taste for them hot toddies and bless her heart, she brought with her two bottles of the best Lemon Hart. What more could a man want?" He squeezed Will's shoulder once more as his words caught in his throat. "Except to know his boy's alive."

Will felt the pain begin to build and reached for his board. *'I shall be sleeping soon I am afraid. These drugs, they stop the pain, but I get very tired.'* He held the board up for them to see and then rubbed the chalk dust away with the sleeve of his pyjamas. *'Are you staying nearby?'*

They both shook their heads and his mother clutched at his hand once more. "No, Will, no. The hospital got us two rail vouchers and we have to get back tonight or we'll end up paying and we don't have the money and I'm not getting sent to prison at my age. I'm not."

Will reached beneath the bedclothes, pulled out his ration tin and scrabbled with the lid. It popped open, spilling his medals onto the blanket. His father stared at them, lifting one close to his eyes to make out the wording, his lips moving as he read: 'For Distinguished Conduct in the Field'. He smiled proudly down at his son. "I told you that Major Scott of yours said you was a hero. See, mother, he's got one of them Distinguished Conduct Medals.

Will lifted the chalk board. *'If you get one of these DCMs, they give you money. They keep most of it for you, but there's £2 here'*. He passed the board to his father this time and reached into the tin. He held out the pound notes to his mother and grabbed the board for a final time. *'Take it. I can't spend it here. They feed me and give me clothes and you need it.'* He held the board up, rubbed once more and waited for the argument. His mother opened her mouth to start the tirade, but before the first sound passed her lips the almoner bustled in once more.

CHAPTER THIRTY-EIGHT

SUNDAY 16TH DECEMBER 1917
The Queen's Hospital, Sidcup

By the end of her first week at the hospital Aila was beginning to think that she had neither the stomach nor the stamina for nursing. She had tried to disguise her revulsion at the sight of the awful head and neck wounds. She was missing Maisie who was in a different ward. And she had scarcely seen her cousin, Amelia, who was the lynch pin of the plastic surgery wards.

The crisis hit at the end of her second week after thirteen continuous, fourteen-hour days. She was changing the sheets of a bed in a recovery ward, tucking in the hospital corners just as she had been taught. She realised she had been hearing sobs for some minutes although the general cacophony of the ward had muted them, but the shrieks broke through all the noise. She rushed across the ward. A young soldier was trying to tear off his bandages, screaming now at the top of his voice. She grabbed his hands and held them tight without even thinking.

"Let me go! Let me go! I don't want to live looking like a freak. Let me die! Just let me die!"

Aila leaned over his body and spoke directly into his face. "You are not a freak, Corporal. You're a man. You are a very brave man."

He stared back at her wild eyed. "But you can't even look at me. You never look at any of us. And if a nurse like you can't look at us how on earth can my best girl, or my mam, or any of my mates in the pub?"

Aila moved back from the bed and gently removed the rest of the dressing from the soldier's jaw and looked into the awful wound. "I'm very sorry, Corporal. Please forgive me. But you see I can look at your wounds. I'm looking at them now. I can also tell you that Dr Gillies has made them look so much better in your last operation." She touched the healing strips of flesh gently and smiled at him. "Very much better. You've been so brave, Corporal. Please don't lose heart now, not when your life is almost ready to begin again."

The hoarse panting subsided, the breaths slowed, the wild eyes softened. Aila stroked his hair back from his forehead and continued to smile down at him reassuringly as a wrist appeared in her vision, the hand holding a syringe. She watched while peace drifted across the soldier's face and his eyes closed. She stepped back to give Dr Gillies access to his patient, automatically smoothing the blanket and tucking the sheets back in where the wild thrashing of the soldier's legs had disrupted their pristine perfection. He listened to the chest, checked the pulse and straightened, beckoning Aila to follow him.

It was the first time that she had been asked to enter his inner sanctum and, once she had mastered her nerves, she looked around the room with genuine curiosity. She wasn't sure what she had expected but it was not this utter chaos. There wasn't a horizontal surface not piled high with paperwork. There were three full size putty models of neck operations on a trestle table, before–and–after pastels of operations stacked against a wall, and a half–open cupboard which appeared to contain nothing but a half–empty crate of champagne.

Gillies indicated a chair to her and sat behind his desk. She bowed her head and considered whether she would be in receipt of a lecture or instant dismissal. The silence continued. She looked up, wondering whether it would be better for her to start by apologising, but he wasn't even looking at her. He was tamping tobacco down into a pipe with his thumb and staring at the nearest model. He indicated the musculature on the neck and started speaking almost abstractedly.

"It's the length of time it takes for the strips of flesh to grow in, do you see, Nurse Smythe? There's nothing we can do about the time the healing process takes and it gets some men down worse than others. I mean, to be honest, you've got to be pretty brave to go through the whole shooting match: five ops, six, sometimes up to ten. Lot of pain. Lot of pain."

He leaned to one side and rummaged through the stack of pastels drawings, pulling one out and passing it to her. "This was that soldier of yours when he came in."

She studied the beautifully executed portrait and realised that she was able to look at it without any of her previous feelings of revulsion. He passed another pastel across the desk. "And this, Nurse, is what I hope he'll look like when he goes out."

Aila's eyes flicked between the two and she nodded.

Gillies finished tamping and lit his pipe. "It's far from perfect. I know that. But we're only at the beginning of what is pretty much an entirely new form of surgery." He pointed the stem of his pipe at the 'after' pastel. "So would you be able to sit in a pub with someone like that without feeling sick?"

Aila relaxed and smiled at him. "I hate to spoil the thread of what sounds like a well-structured argument, sir, but I've never been inside a pub in my life, so I couldn't possibly answer that."

Gillies looked at her and gave a sudden shout of laughter. "You'll do, Nurse Smythe. You'll do. Just like your cousin, aren't you?" He pulled his chair forward and put his pipe down. "Now, listen. What you did just now, was something special. You had the physical and emotional strength not just to admit to weakness, but to offer comfort when it was needed. You've got to remember that it's only the blind who are able to keep their spirits up through thick and thin. And you know why?" He answered his own rhetorical question. "They're the only ones who can't see the looks on other people's faces. Now, Nurse Smythe, we've been watching you and after this morning we think you're ready to step up to the tee."

Aila blinked at him. "To the what, sir?"

He sighed at her ignorance. "You'll be telling me next that you've never been on a golf course."

She stared at him expressionlessly and blinked twice. He laughed again. "Just like your cousin." He stood, put down his pipe, and walked to the window. "First, could you just stop calling me sir. The thought of an aristocrat sirring me all over the place brings me out in a democratic rash. Just call me Doctor or Doctor Gillies. The patients prefer it. Gives them the impression that we're professionals. Second, I want you to be the nurse in charge of Triage. You heard of Triage?"

Aila shook her head.

"It's just common sense really, which is a bit strange seeing as it was invented by the French. I saw it working in Paris when I was watching that genius, Morestin, operate. So, when we have a rush on, we need to assess the men as they come in off the ambulances and we need to do it quick. There will be those who are likely to live, regardless of what care they receive, those who are unlikely to live, and those who, if they get immediate attention; well, it just might make the difference between a good result and just staying alive and looking like an ogre."

He stopped talking and sat again, picking up his pipe once more. Aila realised it was her turn to talk. She arranged her thoughts. "Dr Gillies."

"Good start, Nurse Smythe. Good start. By the by, am I pronouncing that right?"

Aila gave a theatrical sigh. "I would have thought Amelia would have explained. When the name has 'y t h e' in it, it is pronounced Smythe as in 'hive'. If there is no 'e' on the end it is pronounced Smith as in a person who shoes horses."

She saw his lips twitch as he hid his face behind the pipe lighting process.

"I assume you will have a doctor nearby who can confirm if a difficult decision is right or wrong?"

He nodded and blew a cloud of smoke towards the ceiling.

"I assume also that you are aware of my inexperience and that Maisie Brown, my maid, who came here with me would be far better suited to such a post."

Gillies puffed some more on his pipe, carried out some engineering work on the bowl with a dead match and tossed it into the ashtray on his desk. He shook his head at her.

"Amelia and I both agree that Nurse Brown is ideally suited for post-operative nursing. I'm sure I don't need to tell you what a caring soul she is. The patients love her and the impact of a nurse like her on recovery has to be seen to be believed."

Aila smiled in delight. Her dear Maisie was being recognised for the heroine that she was. Gillies watched her. "You have a lot of respect for Maisie Brown, Nurse, don't you?"

Aila nodded, still smiling. "She's a saint, Doctor Gillies. She nursed me back to life after I contracted pneumonia. I know beyond all shadow of a doubt that I would have died without her nursing. She's an absolute saint."

CHAPTER THIRTY-NINE

MONDAY 17TH DECEMBER 1917
The Queen's Hospital, Sidcup

The gale driven rain lashed across the deserted terraces outside the mansion's empty conservatory. Seated in his primitive wheelchair, Will watched the workmen sheltering in the half completed, prefabricated wards and considered his upcoming operation. There was no realistic way to prepare for it. He knew now that the pain would be worse than he could imagine; the sickness from the anaesthetic dreadful; the slow recovery slower than he could bear. He sighed. At least Dr Gillies had said he would be able to start talking after it. That would be something wouldn't it? Assuming he had anything to say now.

The door half opened. A head peered round – a head he recognised. He stared in amazement as Major Scott backed in clutching an enamel mug of tea in one hand and Will's spout–pourer cup in the other. He was smiling as he placed the cup in Will's hand.

"Tea with three sugars – your normal brew. I was owed a bit of leave so when I heard how you'd managed to cheat death yet again, I thought I'd pop across and spend a few minutes catching you up on what happened after you decided to leave us. Not that there's anything much to report apart from more casualties."

Will nodded his head slowly, feeling the strips of flesh between his neck and his jaw tighten as he did so. He reached for his chalk board. *'Any idea how long it's going to go on for, sir?'*

The Major sipped at his tea, then pushed out his chin and shook his head.

Will cleaned the chalk board with the palm of his hand. *'And that barrage, sir?'*

The Major stood up, mug in hand, and walked towards the windows. "The artillery barrage was, as I think you knew, from a battery of French 75s, but was ordered up by one Major Dudley Smythe."

Will didn't move.

"I put in an official complaint as soon as the attack was over. Not a word of response of course. Divisional HQ doesn't like complainers." He shrugged and returned to his seat. "On the other hand, Divisional HQ is somewhat short of highly decorated Majors with three years front line experience."

Will reached for his board again. *'You'll never make Colonel, sir.'*

Scott smiled at their old joke. "So, I put in the complaint again and this time I got the summons. Long and the short of it: Major Smythe was blaming the Frogs for getting the range wrong. I refused to withdraw my complaint and left in a bit of a stink, but - and this is where you'll be impressed, young Hammond! I considered to myself that I was a mere half mile from the Frogs' HQ, so I toddled down the road and inveigled my way in. Took me a few minutes to convince the battery commandant that I thought Smythe had given his chaps duff co-ordinates, but then you know what?"

He paused, tilted the final dregs of the tea into his mouth and dipped his finger into the bottom of the mug to scrape up the sugar.

"He showed me the typed order that the runner had brought from Smythe. And you know what again? The co-ordinates were right over our section of the line. Chap claimed he'd queried the range and had been told just to 'aller de l'avant'. He was happy enough to give me a signed copy of the order. I toddled back to Divisional HQ, demanded to see the ADC who'd given me the brush off not an hour before, and threw it on his desk. It did not go down well I may tell you, but, and it is a big but, my complaint was reinstated."

Will held out his hand to his officer and the two of them shook. Major Scott looked down into the tired eyes of his closest friend. "Will, you sleep now. Sleep and get better. I'll come again as soon as I can." He yawned, stretched his back, patted Will on the head mockingly, and then his eyes softened. "It was hell when you were out there with me, Will. I don't know if there's anything worse than hell, but that's what it feels like now you're not there. Get well. Get well and go back home to your family in Stanwood and take care of all those horses you banged on about endlessly in the trenches."

Will clutched the Major's right hand in both of his then reached for his chalk board once more. *'I will send you a letter explaining who Smythe is, sir. It might clear a few things up.'*

Major Scott raised his eyebrows.

* * *

It had taken Aila a whole week to understand the nuances of Triage. The first morning she had had to run from the ward to weep in secret at the bloody messes being wheeled in on their gurneys. By the afternoon she had set about the bitter task of separating sheep from goats. By the Friday she started to bring in small innovations of her own to the process. Saturday was twice as busy as Friday, and there was no Sabbath break.

She had her bed moved into a tiny side room off the Admissions Ward so she could be on call at any time. One week became two and then three. And for the first time since she had heard of Will's death, she felt the energy begin to course through her veins as the constant workload put cleansing, soothing distance between her and the loss of the man she had loved.

Maisie popped in as often as possible, bringing her treats: cakes, hot chocolate, sweets, fruit; whatever she could get her hands on. Initially she had worried over Aila's commitment to her work, but as she could see how much good it was doing her, she kept her counsel and concentrated on bringing her news of the world outside her ward.

"And apparently, Miss Aila, you're going to be promoted to Staff Nurse. And three of the soldiers have asked me to marry them."

Aila stared at her with her mouth hanging open. "Which one of those statements is true, you utter minx?"

Maisie tossed her head again in the hoity–toity gesture Aila loved so much. "Both of them, Staff Nurse Smythe. Both of them."

Aila shook her head. "I am amazed that there are three such deluded men in here, Maisie. And goodness knows why they want to promote me. Seems completely unnecessary."

Maisie smiled in a superior manner and stood up, brushing crumbs from her apron. "Don't know, Miss Aila. And one of my suitors told me he'd crawl over broken glass to get to me. So there."

Aila laughed. "That explains it. They need to be in an asylum, Maisie, not here."

Maisie tossed her head again. "Oh, and they've opened another operating theatre on the other side of the grounds. It's for the men who have to go through the long series of operations. And they're bringing in new nurses all the time. I hardly know any of them. There are nearly six hundred patients here now."

Aila nodded. Her head tilted as she heard the familiar sound of tyres on gravel. The next intake of patients had arrived. She took her erstwhile maid's hands. "And you're happy you came here, Maisie, dear?"

Maisie nodded, smiling.

"And, my Maisie, if you ever decide which poor soldier to lead into a life of utter misery with you, do make sure he's house trained. Don't think for a second that you're getting out of my clutches by marrying!"

CHAPTER FORTY

THURSDAY 21ST DECEMBER 1917
British Army Reserve Lines, Belgium

Major Scott shivered and pulled his greatcoat tighter round his body. No heat at all here, although at least they had been treated with kid gloves since the Colonel had been killed in the last offensive. Strange how the death of a senior officer meant so much more than the death of a private soldier. The field telephone bell on the desk beside him pinged, interrupting his reverie.

He picked up the receiver to hear that a staff car was being sent for him. His presence was required at Divisional HQ. He rubbed his jaw, realising he would only just have time to shave, wash and put on his best uniform if the rats hadn't chewed it to bits. He yelled for his soldier–servant and the Company Adjutant.

An hour later he was standing at the window in an anteroom of the small chateau that housed the headquarters, watching the exploding shells from a German barrage as they found their range. Behind him, civilian staff rushed backwards and forwards transferring file after file from the shelves in the General's office and wincing each time a shell exploded within a quarter of a mile. He was considering at what range fighting soldiers would begin to take notice of a barrage when the General's ADC hurried in.

A Whizz Bang exploded as he crossed the room and the Major saw him jerk and then his eyes flick across to check if he had been seen.

Scott shrugged and turned back to the window. "It's about a quarter of a mile away and judging by the flash they're at maximum range now: nothing to worry about. Tell me, Captain, why is everyone rushing around?"

"We have information, Major, that the Boche are preparing to push forward in one sector to create a salient." The general had entered the room. "If they succeed in that, our current Divisional HQ would be threatened. So just in case we're moving all the important paperwork."

The Major came to attention. General Allinson walked round in front of him and leaned against the long, rosewood veneered table, crossing his highly polished boots as he did so. He had aged since their last meeting when that stupid Staff Lieutenant had insulted Will. He tapped his boot with his swagger stick and looked up again.

"How's that remarkable Colour Sergeant of yours? The one with the DCM."

Major Scott's chin went up. "In hospital in England, sir. He had half his face shot away rescuing one of his men from No Man's Land on the same night as that misdirected barrage, sir. Destroyed half his face, sir."

The General considered this and cleared his throat. "I'm sorry to hear that, Major. Very sorry." He paused, straightened, and walked across to peer at the flares and explosions in the night sky. He spoke without looking round. "So, you wish to stick to that story do you, Major?"

"Story, sir? But I gave the irrefutable evidence to your ADC here – the copy of the order including the map co–

ordinates from an artillery unit commanded by a Major Smythe to the French Commandant in charge of the 75s."

He caught the glance before the General could disguise it. That little swine of an ADC hadn't shown the General a thing.

"How did your Colour Sergeant come to be rescuing someone from No Man's Land in the middle of a barrage?"

The Major forced himself to relax and recounted the story, including the information that one of Smythe's fellow artillery officers had made his way to the Front Line to apologise for the late start of the original barrage. The General listened in silence then spoke once more.

"It strikes me, Major, that you could have mentioned your Colour Sergeant's heroism in your dispatch."

"I did, sir."

The silence was longer this time. The ADC picked up a tray of files and scurried from the room. The General straightened.

"Very well, Major. You have, as you will undoubtedly be aware, given me much to think on. However, I called you here to inform you that you had been recommended for promotion. A condition of the promotion was to be that you dropped what had been put to me as a malicious slander of a fellow officer. Your verbal report tonight puts an entirely different slant on matters, of course, and I am obliged to say that I respect your position."

He paused.

"I dislike the whole idea of a Court Martial, Major. I dislike it intensely." He studied the officer for a few seconds. "How long have you been in the Front Line?"

"Since October 1914, sir."

"Then I feel it is time you were attached to the Staff to see where and how the decisions that cost the lives of so many of your men are taken. You will report to me at wherever Divisional HQ is sited in two days' time. That is all."

The Major opened his mouth, took a breath, closed it again and saluted. "Sir."

As he turned to march away, he saw the white-faced ADC being beckoned into the General's office. The door slammed behind him.

CHAPTER FORTY-ONE

Friday 23RD December 1917
Divisional Headquarters, France

Scott yawned and wriggled his shoulders. Why was the bed so soft? He must have rolled off his camp bed into the mud. He sat bolt upright. The room was silent. It was dry. It was warm. He reached for the matches and lit the lantern, shielding it automatically with his hand until he remembered. He was out of the Trenches. He was in a bedroom. A real bedroom, in a real chateau. With a stove in the corner still pushing heat out into the atmosphere. How the other half lived. He yawned loudly and there was an immediate tap on the door. His new soldier–servant peered in.

"Did you call, sir?"

He smiled in the semi-darkness.

"Yes, yes, I did, Jenks. Any chance of a spot of hot water?"

"Well, if you're quick, sir, I could run you a bath."

A bath? A bath? "Jenks, you would never believe how quick I can be."

Jenks nodded severely and crossed the room to adjust the stove's dampers.

"Yes, sir. And I'll lay out your best uniform for the General's staff briefing after breakfast."

Scott stopped in his tracks as the thought of the meeting sobered him. He had no idea how long he would be allowed to stay here at Divisional HQ, but he knew that all this mollycoddling and soft living was designed to get him to drop his complaint against Major Dudley Smythe in exchange for a quiet life away from the Front Line. His face hardened. "Jenks, skip the bath. Just bring me water for a shave."

Jenks glanced at him. This one was a tough case and no mistake. A real fighting soldier judging by the scars he had seen on his body and the chest full of ribbons. Not like most of the cowardly slackers he had had to look after.

"Very good, sir."

* * *

An hour later and he was in General Allinson's new briefing room watching brisk young staff officers pinning up maps and arranging papers. The General walked in from his office with no ceremony and nodded to the room.

"Gentlemen, be seated. Captain Lisle will outline GHQ's plan after I have provided you with a little bit of background. Now, we believe that the German High Command will instigate a new front next Spring as they think our troops will have been exhausted and demoralised at the recent battles of Arras, Messines and Passchendaele. They're not far wrong there, are they, Major Scott?"

He glanced at Scott and continued. "We have had information that they are negotiating a peace settlement with the new Russian government and that means they will be keen to mount an attack as early as possible in the spring before any American forces arrive in Europe. Captain Lisle?"

The General stepped to one side as the shiniest of the shiny Staff Captains stepped forward, laid out his notes, and directed two Lieutenants to pin one of the large–scale maps to the vertical board behind him. Scott fought to stay awake as the reedy, upper-class voice of the captain droned on. "... We believe, therefore, that the best plan is for the First Army to adopt defensive positions here, here and here."

His cane rapped the map and the ever–present ever alert private soldiers placed pins on the specified locations. Scott stared. This could not be true. Had these men never been near the Front? He shook his head and then realised that the General was watching him.

"Major Scott, you appear to disagree with the combined wisdom of the General Staff. Perhaps you could explain yourself."

Scott detected no sarcasm in the question although the sneer on the face of Captain Lisle was unmistakable. He walked to the board, took the pointing cane from the young man and turned to the uninterested room. Fine by him! He wasn't going to get a chance to stay here anyway and the few days' rest had already done him good. If he returned to the Front as an un–promoted Major, then so be it.

"These areas here, here, and here are seas of mud, sir. The mud is deep enough for us to have lost three tanks in it with no sign of them whatsoever. Men who fall off duckboards in the trenches after a rainstorm are never seen again. As a position for attack, it is, therefore, abysmal. Defensively it is also poor. The deep trenches we have copied from the Germans simply fill with water from the river basin. The only truly defensible positions are here, here, and here."

He pushed pins into the map. "There is sufficient high ground for trenches to be dug, drained and maintained. With barbed wire across our original positions, it would be all but impossible for the Germans to mount any form of sustained attack without coming under machine gun crossfire from our positions or an artillery barrage from behind our lines."

He passed the cane back to the still sneering Captain Lisle, strode back to his seat and waited. Silence: silence for thirty seconds. Captain Lisle started to remove the new pins. The Major sneaked a glance at General Allinson who was leaning forward, elbows on his knees, hands cupping his chin, half hiding a smile. Eventually a grizzled Brigadier with a patch over his left eye, stood. "Seems to me, sir, that there's little point in bringing a fighting officer with a record like Scott's here..." He pointed at the ribbons on the Major's chest. "... out of the Front Line unless you listen to his advice. I was with my chaps there last year, as you know, sir. And conditions were pretty damn poor then." He harrumphed for a moment and then sat down.

The General stood and made his way to the board, studied Scott's proposed dispositions, and nodded.

"Lisle, I believe a trip to the Front Line is called for. Take three of your colleagues and a surveying team and let us see if Major Scott is correct in his assumptions. Gentlemen, thank you. I believe that is as far as we can take it at the present time."

He raised a beckoning finger in the Scott's direction. They entered his private office alone. Scott stood to attention in front of the desk as General Allinson rocked on his swivel chair. "So, Major. What are we going to do with you? Your first Staff Meeting and you upset a fellow officer." He looked at the Major enquiringly.

"I believe, sir, you should send me back to my regiment. I do not think I am going to be of any real use or service to you here."

The General stopped rocking. "Hmmmm. I have a copy of your dispatches from the night when your position was shelled and the original of the order to the French Commandant with the map co–ordinates for his 75s. I have summoned Major Smythe of the Royal Artillery to join us here..." He broke off at a knock on the door. "... now. Come."

The door opened and Major, the Hon. Dudley Smythe marched in. Scott observed him: a puffy, pink face supporting a broken nose already veinous and an over large stomach contained within very expensive tailoring. Arrogant, supercilious eyes glanced at him with no interest and then turned back to the General.

"You sent for me, sir."

"I did indeed, Major."

He indicated, Scott.

"Major Smythe, meet Major Scott of the First Northants. Major Scott has put in an official complaint against you concerning a barrage on the twenty-sixth of September. Do you recall the night in question?"

The puffy face reddened. "Not off hand, sir, no. And you mean to tell me that an infantry officer has had the temerity to complain about my men?"

The General shook his head. "Major Smythe, I do not think you quite heard me. The complaint was directed at you specifically."

The red face began to mottle. Veins stood out in his neck. Scott watched him. He could smell the alcohol on his breath from where he stood. And the fellow appeared to have very little control over his temper. Smythe started again. "How dare he? What is the nature of the complaint, sir?"

The General passed across the order. "Do you deny that this is an order given by you?"

Smythe stared at the piece of paper and crumpled it in his hand. "Well, you can see what the problem is can't you. It was a Frog barrage. Not my chaps."

General Allinson sat still, letting the tension rise. Scott remained silent. Only Smythe was making any noise, puffing and muttering about how preposterous the whole thing was. The General started again. "And a brother officer from your regiment was killed in the barrage too, wasn't he?"

Smythe exploded. "The damn fool took it upon himself to go up to the Front Line for reasons which have never been fully explained. I think he was not in full possession of his faculties. Some men cannot cope with the pressure, sir."

The General glanced away. "Major Scott. Your comments?"

Scott turned to face Smythe full on. "One hundred and thirty-two of my men were killed on the morning of the German attack after the barrage you ordered. They died because you deliberately sent the co–ordinates of my Company's trenches to the French as you were seeking to exact revenge on a non-commissioned officer in my Company."

Scott pulled Will's letter from his pocket, placed it on the desk in front of the General and turned back to the by now blotchy white face of the artillery Major.

"The name of that man as you well know is Colour Sergeant William Hammond, DCM, MM and bar, the finest and the bravest non-commissioned officer in the regiment. Unfortunately for you, Smythe, Colour Sergeant Hammond didn't die on that morning. He is recovering in hospital in England now with half his face shot away. The letter the General is reading provides the full background to your disgraceful and cowardly behaviour."

He hoped against hope that Smythe would attempt to hit him, but before he could move or say a single word the General raised his hand.

"Smythe, I am approving this official complaint. It will go forward to a Court Martial at the appropriate time. You may leave."

He stood and stared the other man down. With a muttered curse, Smythe saluted and strode from the room. Not before Scott had reached out and grabbed the crumpled order from his hand. The door closed and he breathed out.

"Thank you, sir. I apologise for placing you in such a difficult position. I shall collect my kit and return to the regiment immediately."

General Allinson shook his head. "You know, Major I am not often confronted by men like you."

"I'm sorry, sir."

The General sighed. "For God's sake, man, I meant it as a compliment. And don't you dare apologise again. Sit down. Now, I am recommending your Colour Sergeant for the Victoria Cross. If it goes through in time, it'll be pinned on his chest sometime in the new year. And as for you, you are going to go back to the trenches, but as a Lieutenant Colonel on the Staff and in charge of Captain Lisle's survey team. You will report back to me as soon as possible."

CHAPTER FORTY-TWO

CHRISTMAS DAY 1917
The Queen's Hospital, Sidcup

Christmas in a hospital. Aila had never spent a Christmas away from Stanwood House. She was surprised that she wasn't missing it more, but to go to Stanwood now would be out of the question. She wondered, though, if it would be possible to place a telephone call to her grandmother. She missed her more than anyone.

She washed by the light of a lantern and dressed in the darkness, smiling at the memory of how Maisie would keep on coming to try and help her. Goodness me, she was nearly twenty and there was a war on. If she couldn't get dressed now, she should be ashamed. Mind you, tying the laces in her shoes was still a chore. She straightened at a gentle tap on the door and looked up smiling.

"Come in, Maisie."

Her maid peeped round the door and cast a critical eye over the clothes, tugging the apron into position and brushing minute quantities of dust off her shoulders. Aila stood still and waited.

"It's not so dark that I can't see you're laughing at me, Miss Aila. But you simply mustn't let the hospital down today by looking a mess. I mean just look at your hair."

Aila pulled a strand round in front of her face and laughed aloud.

"You always were a tyrant, my Maisie. Anyway, what's so special about today apart from it being Christmas Day?"

Even though she was standing behind her brushing her hair, Aila knew that Maisie was tossing her head.

"Well Christmas should be enough to make it special, shouldn't it? *And* you really should have come round the wards when I asked you to, Miss Aila. They look lovely. And the village church choir is coming at twelve o'clock and they've got presents for the men. And there'll be turkey and Christmas pudding."

Aila laughed. How good Maisie was for her. "Well, I'm sorry to say, Maisie, that the German army didn't have Christmas Eve off. I've got five new admissions this morning and when they're safely settled in, I'll come and find you. Now, how are all your young men? Any more proposals of marriage?"

* * *

Aila gave the other nurses on her ward the rest of the day and Boxing Day off, smiling at their thanks, and watching them run to catch the bus to the village in the hope of finding a train to take them to their families in London. Now to find Harold Gillies and ask if she could book that telephone call to her home. She knocked on his door and opened it after hearing the yell. He looked up at her through the thick fug of pipe smoke. She waved her hand in disgust at the fumes.

"Harold, this is revolting. How on earth can you see anything?"

She ran to the window and threw it open waving the curtains as the smoke drifted out into the cold morning air. Harold Gillies laughed at her. "Morning, Aila. What can I do for you?'

She smiled back at him. "Just to let you know that I am only expecting five more patients today, Harold, and so far as I could hear through all the crackle on the telephone wire, there is nothing major, so I've let my nurses go off for two days."

He studied her through the haze. She looked thin and pale. "Sure you shouldn't be having the day off too, Aila?"

She shook her head. "No, Harold. No. I am perfectly well, thank you. And I couldn't bear to be away from here just in case. Anyway, if I run out of new patients I'll go and help Nurse Brown. At least then I could try and stop all the young men from proposing to her."

He shrugged and smiled. "All right, all right, Staff Nurse. You know best. How many is it now, by the way? Not with new admissions, with Nurse Brown's proposals I mean."

Aila laughed. "Seven and still counting. Maisie thinks it's terribly funny, so I do hope her young men do as well. The last thing you need here is duels between patients. Now, Harold, I confess I did come here to beg a favour."

He raised an eyebrow.

"May I use the telephone so I can speak to my grandmother?"

He waved an arm towards the instrument. "Unless it's private, use this one, Aila."

She smiled her thanks at him, sat down and booked the call not sure whether it would be quick because it was Christmas Day or slow... because it was Christmas Day. Then in dawned on her. It was Christmas and she had bought no presents for anyone, not even for Maisie. Not even for Harold.

"Problem, Aila?"

"Um, no. I mean, yes. I've just realised that I haven't bought any presents for anyone."

Harold Gillies laughed. "Don't worry about me, Staff Nurse. I'm not interested in presents. Though for Nurse Brown – have a look in the cupboard why don't you?"

Puzzled, she crossed the room and pulled open the door. Half a dozen crates of Champagne were stacked there. She laughed and picked up a bottle. "I'll pay you back, Harold. I promise."

The phone rang and she ran back to pick up the receiver. "Yes, this is Staff Nurse Aila Smythe speaking. Thank you."

She waited, listening to the mysterious distant clicks and faint echoes.

"Is that you, Mr Livens? Happy Christmas to you too and to all the staff. Please pass on my very best wishes to them. Is my father coming back from London for Christmas? If not, I'll try and contact him at the London house, but right now I need to know if my grandmother is available to talk to me?"

One of the servants must have already run to fetch the old lady as Aila heard Mr Livens' voice offering advice on the use of the machine. And then there was her Grandmamma's soft Highland voice.

"Aila? Aila, child? Are you there my dear wee bairn?"

She sat back on the hard chair and Harold Gillies saw a smile of deep contentment cross her weary face. He stood, raised a hand in her direction and left the room for his morning rounds. Colour Sergeant Hammond's dressings and stitches were due to come off today.

* * *

Aila yawned as her stomach growled at her. She ignored the hunger pangs and settled down to write the last of the letters to the parents of the young soldiers who had just been admitted. Even as she did so, the door was whipped open and a glowering Maisie hurried in. She placed a covered plate on the table beside Aila's sheets of writing paper and glowered some more.

"Miss Aila! You didn't come to look at my ward. You didn't come to Christmas lunch. And you haven't eaten anything at all today so far as I can tell."

She lifted the cover off the plate and Aila felt her mouth-watering at the sight of the turkey, roast potatoes and vegetables."

She smiled up at the angry young woman and bent down behind the desk. "But I did get you a present, Maisie."

She lifted up the badly wrapped bottle of champagne and held it out as a peace offering. Maisie clapped her hands with pleasure and dropped into the seat in front of the desk. "Oh well, in that case I forgive you. Champagne? I've never tasted champagne."

She placed the bottle carefully on the desk and jumped up. "You eat your food, Miss Aila. I'll be back directly."

Aila returned to the letter...

...he will be here for some months to come. Do please let us know if you wish to come and visit him and we will make sure you get rail warrants.

Sincerely yours,
Aila Smythe
Staff Nurse

She heard feet pattering back down the corridor outside and grabbed her fork as Maisie came back in followed by two other nurses carrying teacups.

"I know they're not proper champagne glasses, Miss Aila, but they are best bone china."

They all laughed and then stared at the bottle.

"Um, Maisie. I have never had to open a bottle of champagne. Any clues?"

A shake of heads: then a distant voice sounded down the corridor and Aila grabbed the bottle and hurried from the room, calling out to Harold Gillies. The nurses heard the shout of laughter, the distant pop, and the sound of Aila's footsteps coming back. There was a universal sigh of relief. Aila smiled at them.

"Now I do know you're supposed to pour it very carefully or the bubbles come over the rim of the glass."

She looked at the bottle uncertainly. Maisie grabbed it and poured while Aila wolfed her lukewarm and congealing lunch.

"Will you propose a toast for us, Miss Aila?"

Aila felt the cool bubbling liquid sooth her throat. "Of course. A very merry Christmas to all our poor young soldiers and especially Maisie's suitors. May the Good Lord restore their sanity very soon."

One of the nurses snorted bubbles down her nose as she laughed. And then Aila listened to the gossip from the other wards, none of which she had ever even visited. She told the London born girls about life in a country house and then Maisie rushed out once more and came back with a small box of chocolates to share and the afternoon sped by until the setting sun drew them back to the reality of their ward duties.

CHAPTER FORTY-THREE

CHRISTMAS DAY EVENING 1917
The Queen's Hospital, Sidcup

"Evening, Aila."

"Good evening, Harold. No more admissions. Do you think they're going to give up?"

Gillies smiled. "Not a chance, Staff Nurse Smythe." He shook his head, walked on down the corridor then paused. "Tell you what, though, one of our boys is being given the Victoria Cross. Looks like they've even got Queen Mary to come and stick it on his chest."

"Harold, you don't get Her Majesty the Queen to come and give out a medal, you humbly request and one of her Majesty's equerries graciously agrees on her behalf to accept your request. I shall have to get Amelia to train you in court etiquette."

Gillies groaned theatrically. "You're not another one presented at court, are you?"

Aila shook her head. "Not me, Harold, no. I had that fall from my horse the year I would have been presented, so I managed to miss out on all the joys of the Season."

Gillies studied her for a moment, wondering at the bitterness of her tone, but she said no more. "I'm just going across the park to his ward to tell the chap about it now. So, you'll iron your best apron and join us on parade for the ceremony?"

She sighed then smiled. "Very well, Harold. When and where? I'll come along and look soulful for you."

"It's another three weeks or more yet. Before the end of January though. There'll be a photographer chappie there too so a little bit of added glamour from a real, caring nurse would be a great help." He walked on calling out over his shoulder and then turning to walk backwards while he laughed at her. "Actually, in that case, perhaps it had better be Nurse Brown."

Aila wagged her finger at him. "Well thanks for the compliment, Major Gillies. Thanks indeed. I'll go and ask Maisie now."

Harold Gillies was still smiling as he entered Will's ward. He saw Will, half hidden by the ten soldiers who shared this cramped accommodation, practising knee bends by the window. Will stopped as Gillies tapped him on the shoulder and turned his bandaged eyes towards the doctor.

"It's only me, Hammond." Will straightened to attention.

"Morning sir. Anything wrong?"

"Not a thing, Hammond. Not a thing. Quite the reverse. Got some good news for once."

He raised his voice and turned so the rest of the ward could hear. "Seems like someone was a brave boy back in the Trenches. You've been awarded a gong, recommended by your C.O."

The ward cheered. Will shrugged slightly. "No offence, sir. But I've got two of them already. I don't mean to show off or anything. It just doesn't mean much these days."

Gillies turned and grinned at the men behind him. "This one does, Colour Sergeant." He pulled the telegram out of his pocket. "Now, what does it say? Yes, here it is. You've been awarded something for, what do they say, now... 'a pre–eminent act of valour and self–sacrifice in the presence of the enemy'. It's only a small medal apparently. It's called the er... the..." He paused for effect, pretending to peer at the telegram in his hand. "Ah yes, the Victoria Cross."

The ward burst into a spontaneous cheer. Gillies raised a hand to quiet them. "And, her Majesty, according to one of our posh nurses, has graciously agreed to attend the ceremony and present you with the medal."

* * *

"Amelia, have you heard that the Queen is coming sometime in the New Year?"

Amelia looked up from the notes on her desk and smiled, shaking her head at her cousin. "And here was I assuming that Staff Nurse Smythe, the hermit of the admissions ward would be the last one to know. Of course I know, you ass, Aila. If you ever left your ward, you'd have heard everybody banging on about it for days. I've been exchanging letters with some snooty equerry for the last fortnight as Harold refuses to deal with 'all that royalist rubbish'."

She laid on an exaggerated version of Gillies' New Zealand accent and both women smiled. Amelia tilted her head on one side and stared at her cousin. "I've been meaning to talk to you for some time, too, Aila."

Aila rolled her eyes. "Don't say you're going to be another one to tell me I look ill and should be taking a break?"

"Not a chance. I already told Harold that your branch of the family is famous for being as stubborn as mules and twice as stupid. No." She paused. "I just wanted to know what all this is about the possibility of my family inheriting Stanwood when your papa dies. One of the servants heard a whisper of it – which probably means they've been reading my revolting father's correspondence again."

The smile died on Aila's face. "Well, you know most of the long story, Amelia: the long, boring story. I told you about it when we were in Scotland. I'll tell you the bits I missed out when you have some time and I can face it."

Amelia looked down at her work and then back up again. "You don't have to tell me anything more, dear. It's just surprising – that's all."

Aila nodded. "I know. I know. I know why and I cannot pretend to like it. If you're willing to accept the premise that even a man like Dudley is worth more than the best woman in the world then it will make sense of a kind once you hear the whole sorry saga. Oh, look, before I forget, Harold wanted me to attend this VC ceremony, but I said if they wanted a truly beautiful nurse, they should ask Maisie. Is that all right with you?"

Amelia laughed. "Maybe your side of the family isn't that stupid. So you get out of standing in the freezing cold and escape the boredom of having to talk to a procession of senior army officers and minor royals, most of whom we've spent our earlier lives trying to avoid."

"I most certainly do, and also, cousin Amelia, it will be you who has to ask Maisie. For your information, she will undoubtedly be more than a bit excited."

CHAPTER FORTY-FOUR

SUNDAY 6TH JANUARY 1918
The Queen's Hospital, Sidcup

On this first Sunday of 1918 Will managed to avoid church and walked, tapping with his cane, along the gravel path towards the conservatory.

He stopped. The whinny of a horse. Near too. He turned to where he believed the sound had come from, lifted the bandages from his eyes and squinted into the pale light of the winter morning. A big hunter was watching him from a paddock beyond the untended lawns of the country house.

Will stumbled against the edge of the grass and then walked towards the fence calling out in his cracked voice the soft and gentle words he had always used with horses as they flooded back into his mind. The horse watched him, whinnied, turned and galloped away, pausing only when it felt safe in the middle of the field. Will walked towards it, talking all the time in his calm, conversational voice, squinting against the light and holding out his hand. The horse whinnied once more, came up on its rear hooves, slashed at the air in front of it, came back down on to all four legs and galloped straight at him.

Will moved not an inch. He continued his one–sided conversation with the lonely, scared, angry animal until it skidded to a halt, inches away from him. The horse whinnied at him again, baring its teeth, shaking its head, attempting to crowd and intimidate him. Will kept talking, holding out his hand, speaking the soft words that he had known all his life were what horses wanted to hear. The panting stopped. Will took a step closer, half seeing the rolling eye. He stroked the forehead. "Never fret, my boy. Never fret. You and me, we're going to be friends, aren't we?'

The horse shook its head again, but by then Will was beside it, stroking it, running his fingers through the mane and patting the cheek. The horse breathed out and now he could stroke the velvet muzzle. The horse nodded its head, and snorted gently. Without warning, the tears rolled down Will's cheeks and he sobbed and sobbed, dampening the horse's mane. "I'm sorry boy. I'm sorry. I didn't mean to cry like this. I don't want to scare you. Just that me and you, you know, horses, we just go together, and I've missed you all. I've missed you so much."

He looked at the animal's gentle eyes and realised his own vision was blurring once more. A cry sounded from the far side of the paddock and the horse's ears pricked up and back. It looked down at him, seeking permission to leave. He patted its jaw once more and spoke softly, his voice coming more easily now. "You go, boy. You go. But I'll see you again, won't I, boy?"

The horse whinnied deafeningly and backed away, turning to gallop across the wet grass. Will listened until he could hear the beat of the hooves no more. How could he have forgotten all that horses meant to him and he to them? Perhaps there was something to live for. Perhaps. He turned, pulling the bandages down over dimmed, wet eyes, and made his cautious way back to the conservatory.

CHAPTER FORTY-FIVE

Saturday 19TH January 1918
The Queen's Hospital, Sidcup

A sudden influx of casualties cut Aila off from the increasing hysteria surrounding the impending royal visit. By the day of the ceremony the flow of casualties had lessened and she went in search of her one–time maid. She hurried round to Amelia's office, knocked, entered, and laughed. Maisie was standing motionless while Amelia prowled round her, brushing specks of dust off her shoulders. Maisie looked distinctly ill at ease. Aila put her arm round her and smiled. "Maisie, you look perfect. Now, isn't it time you were on parade? I meant to ask, Amelia. What did the chap getting the medal do to earn it?"

Amelia grimaced. "He's a Colour Sergeant. Already had a D.C.M. and an M.M. His Commanding Officer told one of the nurses that he was the bravest man he'd ever met and really cared for his men. Apparently, he was shot in the face after rescuing one of his men's lives. So very brave."

"Poor boy. And what's his name, Amelia?"

"Hammond. Colour Sergeant Will Hammond."

Aila felt the blood rush from her head and the world span. She just caught a glimpse of Maisie's shocked face before she sank to the floor in a dead faint. For a moment it was blackness and a singing in her ears. She felt hands lifting her onto the sofa, the throat–catching whiff of smelling salts and her heart stopped its fluttering. She opened her eyes and stared around her. Harold Gillies stooped over her, his fingers feeling for her pulse, Amelia was putting the cork back in the sal volatile bottle and Maisie was wringing her hands in anxiety. Aila pushed Harold away.

"Now stop it, all of you. There's nothing wrong with me. It was just a huge shock hearing that someone I thought was dead is alive and not only that, but he's here. Please get out there on parade: all of you. Now. And please, not one of you tell Will Hammond that I am here. Wait, though. He'll recognise Maisie."

Harold Gillies put a soothing hand on her shoulder. "No, he won't, Aila. His eyes are bandaged to protect them from the light. And if Nurse Brown here can be persuaded just to whisper to him throughout the ceremony, there will not be a problem."

"Maisie, promise me you won't say anything."

Maisie nodded. "Go on now, all of you. Shoo! I promise I shall explain later."

The door closed behind them and she lay back with a groan, putting her hands to her face. She pulled herself to her feet, peering in Amelia's mirror to see a thin, white face with brown smudges beneath her eyes. She whispered at her reflection. "Will, you're not dead. You're not dead. But whatever will you think of me now? Look at me – worn out, barren and a bastard. Oh, dear God!"

Why did she only feel terror at this news? Why wasn't she overwhelmed with joy? The man she loved was alive. He was near to her. She spoke to her reflection. "You're nothing but a coward, Aila Smythe. A coward. You never had the nerve to tell him you loved him when you were together in Stanwood. You could have written to him and told him you would wait for him. You could have told your grandmother and your father about him. You could have stood up for yourself. But how can I make this up to him? How can I help him?"

She took two deep breaths, rinsed her face in the wash basin, wiped her eyes, pulled her cape close round her body and walked out into the bitter winter morning.

* * *

The nurse detailed to be at his side must have been even more nervous than he was. Will had tried twice to make conversation, but she had only replied in whispered monosyllables. Still, he didn't need to be told when the Queen had arrived. The noise of the rubber tyres on the gravel, the skirl of the pipes, the roared order of the Sergeant Major bringing the honour guard to attention.

The nurse gripped his arm, whispered in his ear, and led him forward to the presentation platform. And he recognised the voice of the General introducing her Majesty to his Commanding Officer, no longer Major, but Lieutenant Colonel Scott. And his C.O. explained to the queen how Will had been wounded. And then Will answered the Royal questions as best he could and thanked her Majesty for taking so much trouble over him. And he felt the pressure on his arm from Lieutenant Colonel Scott and heard the kind words from the General as the photographer fussed in front of them. He felt the magnesium flash as the photograph was taken and the Royal party moved on. And he was alone.

He stood in the cold, waiting for a hand to help him, thinking about his supposed bravery in the war. If he did want to live... If! Well, if he did, he would have to overcome what he saw as his present cowardice. Whatever lay beneath the bandages, he had to look at it. To look and to see if he was a monster or a man. An orderly took his arm and led him inside to face the cheers and congratulations of his fellow patients.

* * *

Aila stood alone at the edge of the Parade Ground, not even realising she was shivering with the cold. She had watched the ceremony, recognising Will's tall, lean body and wide shoulders as Maisie led him to the podium. She turned, hearing running feet and managed to smile. "Maisie, you looked utterly lovely. Did Will...? Did you...?"

"No, Miss Aila, I didn't speak above a whisper and he didn't know me, I'm sure. What are you going to do?"

She took her mistress' arm and walked her back into Frognall House where the remnants of the Royal party were sipping tea and making small talk with Amelia, Harold, the army contingent from France and the big wigs who had financed the purchase of the country house. Amelia crossed to her side.

"Aila, you're shivering. Come and stand by the fire for goodness' sake and talk to me. Apart from the rather handsome Lieutenant Colonel Scott, the rest of them are utter bores. Oh good, he's coming across."

Scott smiled down at them. "May I fetch you another cup of tea, Sister? And one for you, Staff Nurse."

Amelia laughed. "If you would just stand between me and that young baronet who is trying to work out where he last met me, I would be deeply grateful, Colonel. I became a nurse primarily to escape from the boredom of conversations with the likes of him."

CHAPTER FORTY-SIX

MONDAY 21ST JANUARY 1918
The Queen's Hospital, Sidcup

It was remarkable how much illicit booze could be sneaked into a hospital. It was less remarkable how many men would drink themselves into oblivion at the slightest excuse.

Will slipped out of the ward that housed the bacchanal and walked back to his own empty ward, counting the steps and tapping his cane against the corridor corners as he had taught himself over the last weeks. He walked through to the side ward in which Major Gillies had removed his stitches and switched on the single electric bulb. He began to unpin the dressings from his lower face, took a deep breath and peered into the mirror, his breath hissing between his lips as he took in the savage scarring, the deformed cheek, the hole in his flesh. And this is what Dr Gillies had called 'pretty messy'. God in heaven! What must it have been like when he came in?

He raised his hand to his cover his left cheek and the old Will Hammond looked back at him. Lower the hand and a monster was there in the mirror. He paused. Wait. An artist had painted him when he first came in. Or had he dreamt that? No, no, he was sure of it. Major Gillies had mentioned it one day. And where would that painting be? He thought for a moment, turned off the electric light and made his way across the ward in the darkness and into the corridor that led to Major Gillies' hut.

He took a deep breath and turned the doorknob, half expecting, half hoping it would be locked. It wasn't. He stepped into the darkened room and felt his way back to the untidy desk where he knew there was a lamp. He scrabbled for the switch, found it and leapt back with a strangled sob of fear at the sight of a ghastly, ghostly head. He squeezed his eyes shut, then opened them again. The head was still there, but now it was just a putty model with the bones, muscles and veins exposed. He patted it.

"Well at least you look a sight worse than me, old chap."

There they were, stacked three or four deep along the floor, pastel paintings of the results of the snipers' deadly work. Will squeezed his blurring eyes tight shut, counted five and opened them again. That worked. He knelt in front of the pictures and forced himself to look at face after shattered face, feeling sick to his stomach at the damage done to so many of his comrades. After three agonising minutes, he found himself, recognisable only by the colour of his hair and the set of his eyes. He lifted the pastel out and laid it on the desk beneath the light. His vision blurred. The monster in the picture disappeared. Will sat back, pressed his hands over his eyes, then leaned forward to stare down at the wreck that had been his jaw and cheek.

"I didn't think you were ready to look at that, Colour Sergeant."

Will leapt to his feet. Major Gillies was standing in the doorway watching him, compassion evident in his eyes. Will drew a deep sobbing breath and managed to speak, his voice still hoarse from lack of use and wracked with emotion.

"Why?"

Gillies shut the door and walked across the room. "Why what, Hammond?"

Will straightened his back and pointed to the pictures on the floor. "Why let us live? Why not just let us die?" He stooped and picked up two of the paintings, thrusting them in front of the doctor, shouting in his face. "Look at us! Look at us! We're monsters!"

Gillies seated himself behind his desk and struck a match, sucking the flame into the tobacco, making it glow red, blowing a thin cloud of smoke through the light of lamp. "Have you heard of the Hippocratic Oath, Colour Sergeant?"

Will lifted his eyes from the pictures once more and shot the other man a hard glance. "Don't patronise me, Major. I know why doctors do what they do. But have you thought, really thought, about what our lives are worth now? When I first came here, I didn't understand why so many of the patients couldn't wait to get back to the war, but I do now." He nodded and looked across the desk to the stacked portraits. "They want to get back to the thing that created them. To the place where no one cares what they look like because over there it is hell, utter hell, and monsters like us would rather live in hell and die in hell."

He stared through and beyond the doctor, his vision blurring once more, seeing only the wreckage of men and machines in the wire–entangled sea of shell–holed mud that was No Man's Land. Gillies felt a shiver run up his spine at the depth of the young soldier's feeling.

"And I don't even get the chance to do that — to die where I belong, because..." His gaze refocused on the doctor. "... because I couldn't guarantee to see even twenty feet into No Man's Land. I couldn't lead my soldiers. I'd be a liability to my own men."

He pulled the Victoria Cross medal off his tunic, threw it on the desk and walked towards the door.

"Wait."

Will felt his shoulders drop, his emotion spent for the moment.

"You are more than halfway through your course of operations here, Will. Within months you will be able to face the world without shame, without fear of the look on the faces of the people you meet."

Will shook his head and made to move.

"Listen to me, Will." Gillies picked up the medal and let it swing from his fingers. "You didn't get this for killing hundreds of 'the Hun' in some crazed battle frenzy. You got it because you saved someone's life in that 'hell' you were just talking about. If someone like you can do a thing like that, it cannot be hell can it?"

Will listened.

"You and I have one thing in common. We save lives. That is all I meant about the Hippocratic Oath. When I first saw what the French were achieving with the earliest attempts at plastic surgery, I realised it was something I had to do as well. I had to do it, Will. Not just splinting bones and sewing up flesh, not just repairing, but re-building, re-creating. Will, do not give up now. Too many people care for you and about you. Please."

Will paused by the door. The passion had passed. The rage had died back. "Is it too much to ask if I could have a small room on my own, sir, until I can... until I can..."

Gillies spoke quickly before the bitter anger returned. "Yes. Yes. I shall give the order tomorrow morning. For tonight sleep in the side ward and lock the door."

Will nodded and fumbled for the door handle.

CHAPTER FORTY-SEVEN

TUESDAY 22ND JANUARY 1918
The Queen's Hospital, Sidcup

Only five people remained awake that night, re–living the day, reviewing their pasts, re-evaluating their futures.

Aila knew there was nothing she could have changed about her past life. She wondered again when the memory of meeting Will as a boy in the stable yard at the pub in Raunds had resurfaced. She smiled to herself as she pictured his demeanour on the day when her half-brother's horse had gone wild – what was the horse's name? Prancer, that was it. Mr Chant, the vet, had eventually managed to convince Dudley that the horse had an injury and could not be ridden. She hoped the poor thing had ended its life somewhere where people were kind to it. And then she could see Will again as a young man digging in the front garden of his parent's house in Stanwood. How strong he was, with those muscular arms and wide shoulders, how tall, how he walked with a natural grace, how he smiled so readily at her, how his brown hair tumbled down across his forehead.

"Oh, Will."

And what would his life be now? She had bullied Amelia into talking to that nice Lieutenant Colonel and finding out as much as possible about what had become of him in the army. Not that Amelia had needed much bullying – if she hadn't known her severe older cousin so well, she would have sworn that she had been flirting with the Staff Officer. She stared at the dark outline of the window.

"What can I do for you, Will?"

* * *

Lieutenant Colonel Scott found that his normal ability to sleep anywhere at the drop of any kind of headgear had deserted him. That Sister was rather smashing. He smiled at the ceiling. He'd only heard that word recently on the lips of one of the sillier young Staffers, but he liked it.

"Sister Amelia is smashing." He spoke the words aloud, laughed at himself, then sat up cursing. He had no idea what her surname was. He'd have to find out. Mind you she was probably too aristocratic to be interested in him. She had even known the Queen. He thought about the ceremony and then about Will. Sister Amelia and that surgeon chappie had been very defensive of him, almost if Will were some kind of hospital mascot. What would become of him? And how could he help? He'd better ask the surgeon.

And why hadn't he asked Sister Amelia for her surname? Idiot!

* * *

Sister Amelia Burkett–Smythe turned over again and punched her pillow. It was strange. She stared up into the blackness over her bed. Strange. Why? Strange because she had never been remotely attracted to any of the men she'd been forced to meet during the Season – braying asses all of them. And it was so blindingly obvious that their mamas only wanted them to have her hand in marriage because she was the daughter of an earl. She sat up and shook the feathers of her pillow into a different configuration and flopped down again. Why hadn't that handsome Colonel Scott asked for her surname? Wait, though. He'd be staying up in Frognall House, wouldn't he? Of course. So, if she happened - she smiled - just happened, to be calling in there at about breakfast time she might – just might – bump into him again. She sat up, set her alarm clock for six o'clock and lay back down. The pillow felt just right now.

* * *

Major Harold Gillies sat up far into the night staring at the putty model on his desk, sketching pictures of Will's jaw and wondering if there was anything he could do to improve his work. At two in the morning, he threw his pencil down and reached for his address book, muttering to himself as he did so.

"Underwood; Vernon; Webb; where is it? Ah, yes, there we are."

He reached for his pen and unscrewed the inkpot.

Captain Francis Derwent Wood
Royal Army Medical Corps
Masks for Facial Disfigurements Department
3rd London General Hospital
Wandsworth

Dear Wood,

I was delighted to hear of your promotion and trust that all goes well with you and the chaps in your Tin Noses Shop. I am writing this time to ask if you could pay us another visit at your earliest convenience.

I have another young fellow who would benefit from one of your masks. I think he will, eventually, come to terms with his disfigurement, but right now he is as low as anyone could be – I am afraid that he sneaked into my office and found the pastels of his 'before' face done by old Tonks – and I am well aware of the limitations of our surgery in injuries of the kind he received.

I should tell you that he is a war hero. In fact by the time you receive this missive you may have seen his picture in the Daily Herald and read a few quotes from yours truly there too. Her Majesty was here today (I should say yesterday as it is now two in the morning) and pinned a VC on his chest for a particularly outstanding piece of bravery in rescuing one of his men from No Man's Land.

In the meantime, I will carry out another operation on him.

This letter comes with my very best wishes,
Sincerely yours,
Gillies

* * *

Will sat on his bed, a blanket wrapped round his body, the bandages still off his eyes and stared out at the still moonlit night. Any foolish dreams he had been holding close to his chest about the possibility he might meet Miss Aila again and tell her... Tell her what? That he, an unemployed, monster faced labourer had fallen in love with her? He groaned. But did that mean he regretted looking at his scars? He thought about this as the early morning minutes ticked into hours. No, he didn't. He was a man. He had killed. He had led men to their deaths – which was yet more killing of a different kind.

But now that his war was over, did he want to live now? To see pity or disgust in the eyes of everyone he met until the day of his own death? What reason could he give himself to keep on living?

His parents. That was the only reason. They would see beyond the scars, but above all they would need the tiny war pension he would get if he stayed alive. If he committed suicide, the pension would disappear. So... A bitter smile twisted the broken face beneath the bandages. So, kill yourself, but make it look like an accident. That could work. Then his mum and dad would get the pension all right. The Major – sorry the Lieutenant Colonel – had always said he had an eye for tactics. So, find a way to kill yourself that would convince everyone it was an accident.

CHAPTER FORTY-EIGHT

TUESDAY 22ND JANUARY 1918
The Queen's Hospital, Sidcup

Amelia shook the rain off her cape and peered around Frognall House's entrance hall. She jumped as the front door slammed back and then relaxed as the postman placed the mail sack on the side table, touching his cap in her direction as he departed. That would do. Perfect excuse. After a brief struggle she managed to unbuckle the strap, groaning as the small avalanche of mail swept over the tabletop and down to the floor, engulfing her shoes. Nothing else for it then. She was still kneeling among the letters, sorting them alphabetically, when the Lieutenant Colonel's voice made her start.

"And there I was assuming that the Sister Amelia I met yesterday was the lynch pin of the entire nursing establishment and now I discover she is little more than a mail room assistant."

He smiled at her. She smiled back, delighted to have found him so soon.

"Well, Colonel Scott if you would consider the possibility of getting the knees of your frightfully smart uniform dusty you could help me find if there's a letter from my little brother, Huon, who is somewhere in France with his RFC squadron."

He knelt beside her and cocked an eyebrow in her direction. She wrinkled her nose at him. "What, Colonel? Why are you failing to scrabble amongst the correspondence?"

"For the very simple reason, my dear Sister Amelia, that I have no idea what little brother Huon's surname is?"

"Well, my dear Colonel Scott, the general idea is that if you want to know, you ask."

He cleared his throat. "Sister Amelia, I would be deeply honoured if you could see fit to impart to me your family name."

"Burkett–Smythe, spelt with an e both sides of the hyphen."

"And are you frightfully aristocratic?"

"Of course. Could you not tell from my deportment and diction?"

"Me? No. I fear that I am entirely class blind. If I like someone I couldn't care less if they turn out to be the daughter of a lord or an assistant postwoman?"

"In which case, as I am both, you have double the reasons to like me. Excellent."

They searched through the letters contentedly.

"Sister…"

"Colonel…"

They spoke simultaneously and laughed at each other. He placed the last bundle of letters on the table, levered himself upright, dusted off his knees and held out his hand to help her up. She took it and they stood, looking into each other's eyes for a few seconds until voices from the landing above heralded the arrival of the General and his ADC. She shook her head and lowered her eyes,

"It seems odd to me, Colonel, that I know your surname but not your forename while you knew my forename but not my surname."

He pointed at his chest quite unable to keep the smile off his face. "Iain – with an i either side of the a."

Laughing, Amelia turned to curtsey to the officers coming down the stairs. "Good morning, General. You will have to forgive Colonel Scott his dusty knees, but he had offered to help me in my attempt to find a letter written to me by my younger brother in France. Alas, without success."

She curtsied once more and allowed Iain Scott to hold the door open for her. She smiled up at him, pulling her cape closer round her shoulders as he stepped out behind her and glanced up at the rain filled sky.

"May I write to you, Sister Amelia Burkett–Smythe?"

Her eyes sparkled. "You'd better, Colonel Iain Scott." She turned and ran in the direction of the admissions ward.

She was seated on Aila's bed still smiling when her cousin walked back in from her morning ablutions.

"Amelia? What are you doing round here so early?"

She glanced at her cousin who blushed. Aila prodded her in the stomach. "It's that colonel, isn't it? It is. Amelia Burkett–Smythe, you like that colonel. I knew you did. What are you up to?"

"Little cousin, you can mind your business."

Aila smiled, enjoying the possibility of her cousin falling in love, made a mental note to tell Maisie, tied her shoelaces after two efforts and then made feeble attempts at brushing her hair. Amelia growled and took over the brush.

"Right young Smythe, it's time you and I had a talk. You never completed your sad tale at that ball in Scotland and I want the full and complete story of why on earth my family may be getting richer at your expense." She held up her hand as Aila started to protest. "And then we can discuss Will Hammond. And when we have discussed him, you and I are going to visit Harold to see what he can do to help."

Aila seated herself on the edge of her bed and started from the beginning. "Amelia, Will Hammond has been part of this story for many years. I met him first when I was nine and he must have been ten or thereabouts…"

The story moved from 1903 to 1913, to her 'fall' and rescue by Will, to Will's beating by Dudley and his thugs, to his enlisting. She didn't expect much by way of a reaction. Her cousin was no more prone to displays of emotion than she was or, for that matter, any other member of their family. She was wholly surprised, therefore, when Amelia jumped up and began to pace round her tiny room.

"Aila, this is bloody awful – terrible. If I didn't know you were as sane as anyone who has been born and brought up in Northamptonshire can be, I would be calling for the mad doctors. So, this is why grandmamma wishes to disinherit Dudley and let the title pass to my side of the family?"

Aila nodded.

"And your papa agrees?"

Aila nodded.

"And none of this bothers you? I mean having to pass Stanwood House over to outsiders." She waved her arms in the air. "Don't they know we're in the twentieth century? Haven't they heard that women can inherit? What is wrong with men? What are they so scared of? Not content with thousands, no, millions being killed in this war because of their stupid decisions, they try and destroy the lives of their very own families – the ones closest to them – the ones they're supposed to love, to care for."

She deflated and looked across at her cousin seeing the pain in her eyes. She reached out towards her, but Aila lifted her hands out palms forward to keep her at bay.

"Amelia, there is one other thing. It's something which explains why I could not inherit."

She let her hands drop to her sides, took a deep breath, and looked her cousin in the eyes. "Papa and my mother never married. So, you see I am not even a proper Smythe. I'm nothing more than a half–sister and a half–daughter! And even worse, my mother ran away soon after I was born and has never been seen since. According to my grandmamma she is probably still alive, but I can't even look for her, Amelia. I don't where to start. I don't know how to start. And with this awful, stupid war I do not even have time to start. And she may be ill; she may be living in direst poverty; she may be in somewhere awful like a mental institution. And I cannot help her. I cannot help her."

Her voice rose almost to a scream. Amelia grabbed her hands, held her close and listened to her cousin's whispers through her sobs.

"Amelia, all I can do for now is to try and make myself give up caring about things and places and just care for the two people I do know I can help. My Maisie and Will Hammond. But my poor mother, Amelia. My poor mother."

And then she did allow her cousin to pull her into her arms. Eventually she pulled back.

"Amelia, I'm sorry to have snivelled all over your uniform. Now listen, please. I don't think I slept for more than an hour last night, but during the time I was awake I made up my mind what I was going to do. Will Hammond saved my life. My family destroyed his. I want to be allowed to care for him here, now, without him knowing who I am. How can this be arranged?

CHAPTER FORTY-NINE

TUESDAY 22ND JANUARY 1918
The Queen's Hospital, Sidcup

A quiet day, thank God. No new admissions. Harold Gillies made his morning rounds, cajoling, congratulating, comforting. He found an orderly and gave instructions regarding Will Hammond's new room. The deputation he had half expected was awaiting him in his office. No jokes today. No humour. He watched the cousins and waited. Amelia leaned forward, but before she could open her mouth Aila had started addressing the Head of Surgery.

"Harold, I am very sorry I fainted yesterday, it was nothing to do with fatigue, it was utter shock. I think you've probably worked it all out anyway, but Colour Sergeant Will Hammond comes from our village. I had been told he was dead. I had visited his parents to offer condolences. Will Hammond was the man who found me when I had my fall from my horse, Juno. He saved my life."

She looked down at the fingers of her hands that she had knotted in her lap. "Now I want to save his, Harold."

Gillies nodded. "Well in order to ensure that I am being completely open with you, I can tell you your job is going to be a sight harder today than it would have been yesterday."

He reached behind him and found the pastel of Will's pre–operative face and passed it across the desk. "He let himself into my office last night and found this." He sighed. "It nearly broke his spirit, I think. He had removed his dressings earlier and looked at his face in the mirror."

Aila winced. Gillies continued. "You said yesterday that you didn't want him to know you were here. I think I understand why, and I can tell you that the one thing in your favour is the problem with his sight. He asked me this morning for heavily smoked glass goggles or spectacles to wear as he claims he can see shapes perfectly well at night. I have agreed. Last night, by the by, he put me in my place and richly deserved it was too I can tell you. I had the temerity to ask him if he knew what the Hippocratic Oath was. I shan't be forgetting his answer for a long while."

Aila nodded. "Will Hammond is never to be underestimated, Harold. He sees through things that others don't even notice. He knew someone had tried to kill me when I had my fall from my horse. He knew it long before I realised. Now I know you think I'm just a stupid woman from the land-owning class, but I am right about him. And remember I also understand horses."

Gillies winked at Amelia. "Goes with the territory, Staff Nurse."

Aila hmmphed. "If you want to see what Will Hammond is capable of you have to watch him with horses. You're a clever man, Harold, a very clever man. I think Amelia would agree that we have never met anyone to match you. But your education will not be complete until you have seen Will Hammond with horses. He can calm the wildest, the most enraged animal. He is special and I want to save him from his despair."

Gillies smiled. "Well, it might interest you then, Aila, to know that your Colour Sergeant asked for permission to visit the stables on the far side of Frognall House."

CHAPTER FIFTY

MONDAY 11TH FEBRUARY 1918
The Queen's Hospital, Sidcup

Aila stared blankly out of the window in the direction of the mansion's red brick façade. It seemed eerie and forbidding in the morning mist.

The sun had already risen to its zenith, the pale, misty globe hanging low over the park, offering little warmth to the midwinter morning. The mist soaked her shoes, the droplets hanging off the shoulders of her cape before sinking into the wool, adding what felt like pounds to its weight.

She turned two corners of the house and found the stables. Deserted. She would have sworn he would be here. And then in the distance the whinny of a horse – she raised her hand to shield her eyes against the pale light – a horse was cantering across the paddock towards a tall figure wearing an army uniform. It was Will. Without giving herself time to think she hurried across the wet grass towards them. The horse saw her first and raised its head in her direction. She saw Will's shoulders tense and then, still talking to and stroking the horse, he turned his head in her direction. The bandages hid his lower face effectively, the black glass goggles covered his eyes. She bit down on her fear and, scarcely thinking, spoke to him in the voice and accent of her grandmother.

"What a bonnie, bonnie horse. I heard him whinny so I thought I'd come and look for him. What's his name?'

She would have sworn her voice wavered. "I don't know his name, Miss."

The voice was cracked, but recognisably Will's. She held out her hand to him. "My name's Heather McBride. I'm one of the nurses at the hospital. I was just exploring."

He ignored the hand. Of course, he couldn't see it. The horse nudged his back, making him stumble slightly and he turned back to it, reaching out to scratch its jaw, resting his head against it in a way that was so familiar to her.

"Where did you learn to ride, Sergeant?"

The head turned again. "How did you know I'm a sergeant?"

She smiled and tapped his arm. "It's the three stripes here and the wee crown above them that gave your rank away... Staff Sergeant, I should have said, shouldn't I?"

That brought a small grunt of amusement. "Colour Sergeant, Miss, not Staff Sergeant. I'm in the infantry. Have you come to take me back to the hospital?"

"No. I had no idea anyone was here. I was just wandering round the mansion being nosey and I heard the horse whinnying." The Highland accent was coming to her easily now. "I'm sorry, Sergeant. I didnae mean to intrude."

The horse peered at her over Will's shoulder, nodding its head, attention seeking. She laughed. "Isn't he a beauty, Sergeant? May I stroke his muzzle?"

Will moved aside. "I wouldn't know, Miss. I can't really see him."

Aila babbled on. "Well, he's a bay hunter. Eighteen hands I should think, and he's a big, strong boy, aren't you?"

She patted the side of the jaw and stroked the muzzle. Will had gone quiet. She glanced sideways. His left hand was still stroking the horse's shoulder. The black glass lenses turned towards her. "You know a lot about horses, then, Miss."

She needed to be careful now. One wrong move and he would clam up and perhaps never forgive her for seeing him like this. "I grew up in the country, Sergeant. I know horses. And you, what do you know about them?"

Anything to stop him asking more questions any one of which might give her away. He stood silent for a moment then rested his forehead against the side of the horse's jaw once more.

"I grew up with horses too, Miss."

She breathed out. A crisis seemed to have been averted. "I'd better get back to my ward, Sergeant. I hope you don't mind if I come and say hello to your friend again."

He nodded. She seemed to have passed a test of some sort.

"Goodbye, Miss. Miss?"

She waited, nerves on edge.

"You sound tired, Miss."

She forced a little laugh. "Well, it's a long enough journey from Fort William to Edinburgh Waverley station and a much longer journey from there down to the village of Sidcup, Colour Sergeant, and you don't get much sleep in Third Class."

He nodded and turned back to the horse and started speaking to it once more in that beautiful way he had with the creatures. She turned her back on him and walked across to the gravel path, pondering over what this meeting might mean to him... and to her.

* * *

Will stepped back from the horse. "She seemed nice then boy, didn't she? Something familiar about her too, but I don't think I ever met a Scots nurse before. Maybe it's just that accent – same as those Argyle and Sutherland Highlanders in the Trenches with us last year."

He didn't see the Scots nurse the next day which, to his surprise, he found disappointing. He rode the hunter bareback for a while, walked him back to the stables, rubbed him down and wandered away from the house. He needed to make a proper plan for his death. He had already found he couldn't think about it when he was in the presence of that horse: back to the river that skirted the edge of the park.

Maybe a trip and a tumble into the water would work. He crept across the long grass on the riverbank to reconnoitre the possibilities. He reached for what he thought was a sapling, discovered too late that it was a thistle, jerked his hand away, lost his footing and slid, cursing, into the flowing water.

The base of his back cracked against a half-submerged rock. He struggled to get air into his lungs, half panicking, half recognising that for all the pain he was only winded. He slid further down, gasping in mud and water, finally managing to lift his body out of the flow. He coughed water, spat gravel, and hauled himself onto the bank by the sheer strength of his upper arms.

He spat again and rolled onto his back, staring up into the blue, blue sky. The mist had cleared then, from his eyes as well as from the sky above. Did this mean he could see again? A Robin hopped nearer to him and paused to sing its winter song. He listened to the familiar sound and the mist fell over his sight. He groaned and scrabbled in the shallow water to find his black glasses.

Only then did it sink in. He had just been given the perfect opportunity to kill himself, to rid himself of a future of pain, pity and mockery. And what had he done? He had struggled and fought for life like any other animal, wild or tame. Not once had the thought of using this fall as the perfect vehicle for his death, crossed his mind. He stared down at the stream through the darkness of his lenses. The mud and gravel he had disturbed seemed to have settled; the silhouettes of the sedge leaves were waving once more beneath the surface at the edge of the bank as the water flowed clear once again. All that was left of his fall was a broken thistle. He shivered, turned away, took his bearings, and stumbled towards his room.

By the time he arrived there he was shaking with cold, drenched as he had been from his fall and bruised in both his body and his spirit. He unlocked the door, pulled his clothes off and hauled himself into his bed, clutching the blankets close and curling into a foetal ball.

He was still in this position two hours later when Aila, diverting from her duties once more, passed the half open door and peeped in. She hesitated, picked up the clothes, felt them, realised they were soaking, and crossed to the bed to examine the naked man. He was asleep, shivering and muttering to himself. She felt his forehead. It burned. She changed the damp sheets and ran for Harold Gillies.

* * *

Gillies took his fingers away from the pulse. Too fast, too weak. "Nurse, would you get some Bayer's Powder. We've some left in the dispensary and the next batch should be through soon." He turned to Aila. "You'll have to wake him and force him to drink it though. You prepared to do that? There are no new admissions today, so you'll be all right here. You'll need to put light bandaging on his eyes before he wakes, and change the dressing on his jaw."

Aila nodded. She was ready for anything. After Gillies and the other nurse had left the room she stirred the aspirin powder into the water, seated herself on the bed, and dropped into her Highland accent.

"Staff Sergeant? I mean, Colour Sergeant, I've got some medicine here that will bring your temperature down, but you must drink it." She put her arm beneath his head and lifted it off the pillow. "Come on now, drink."

She tilted the spout of the cup to his lips and was relieved to see them open slightly, ready to receive the medicine. He must be half conscious then. She tilted and poured. He half sipped, gagged, then sipped again and swallowed. She sighed, checked the time on her watch, made a note on the chart and sat down to wait, stroking the hair back from his forehead and listening to his tortured breathing.

* * *

"Who's there?"

She jumped and opened her eyes. She must have fallen asleep on the chair beside his bed. Oh, goodness, it was getting dark. She'd been here for three hours or more.

"It's only me, Colour Sergeant, Nurse McBride. We met the day before yesterday. You'd left the door of your room open and I found you on the bed with a fever. What happened?"

He lay still for a moment, staring up into the nothingness of his bandages. "I didn't die. That's what happened, Nurse McBride. Or didn't happen. Is it the same day?"

"Yes."

A pause. She risked a question. "You wanted to die, did you?"

Another pause. He raised a hand and touched the dressings over his jaw. "Would you want to live if this had happened to you, Nurse McBride?"

Aila thought about this. "I think I would, yes, Sergeant. In any event, I would be too scared to try and kill myself."

He gave a short, harsh bark of laughter. "Death means nothing. Not when you've seen as much of it as I have. In the Trenches, you make death your friend. If you think of it like that you lose your fear of dying."

She waited. Silence. "And, Colour Sergeant?"

"And nothing, Nurse. Death is just easier to manage than life."

He shivered and she reached out and laid her hand on his forehead more than half expecting him to shake her off.

"Your temperature is going up again. I'll give you another dose of the Bayer's Powder and then I hope you can sleep again."

He allowed her to hold the spout to his mouth. She reached for a damp washcloth to cool his face and neck. He made no effort to move to help her.

"How come, Nurse McBride, I have never seen you before and now I meet you twice in three days?"

But she was ready for that. "How come, Colour Sergeant Hammond, that you leave the door to your room open with a pile of wet clothes on the floor?"

"This is when I think posh people say something like touché. Are you posh, Nurse McBride?"

She smiled to herself. "Posher than you, that's for sure, Colour Sergeant Hammond. Not that that's saying much. Now if you'll promise to go to sleep, I'll leave you alone." She stood and smoothed down her apron. "And if you promise not to try and kill yourself when you've recovered, I'll come and take you round to see that bonnie horse again. I want to know his name."

Will grunted in as noncommittal a way as he could manage. He heard the door close and, as the drug began to take effect, he thought once more through ways in which he could end his life. But as his eyes closed, he found he was thinking about that horse – and that annoying Scottish nurse. He slept.

He didn't hear the door open two hours later. He didn't feel the fingers on his wrist feeling for his pulse. He didn't feel the hand on his forehead feeling for the fever.

CHAPTER FIFTY-ONE

THURSDAY 7TH MARCH 1918
Divisional HQ, Belgium

The General's eyes were drawn to the map pinned on the wall of Iain Scott's office. He studied the Northeast corner of the defensive positions. "That's where they'll come through. If they do anywhere, that is."

Scott nodded. "I'm recommending that we have artillery here and here, sir. A battery of eighteen pounders back here, for their range, and French 75s here and here. The Boche hate 'em as you know, sir."

"Good work Iain. Good work."

The General slapped him on the shoulder and continued. "Now. The court martial of your friend Major Dudley Smythe will be in three weeks' time, not entirely sure when yet. And there's one thing you won't have expected. You will have to prosecute the case. So, once you've finished the staff briefing you had better sort out your witnesses and all that stuff. I mean to say, it's bad enough having one of my staff officers involved in a court martial of an officer from another regiment, but if you lost the case, I'd be bloody furious. Understood?"

Scott winced. "Yes, sir."

"Very well, Colonel, I'll leave you to it. By the by, I am not being sloppy when I shorten your rank to Colonel.

You've been recommended for promotion yet again. Goodness knows why!"

Scott's jaw dropped. General Allinson raised an eyebrow. "There you are, that'll be something to share with that pretty young nursing sister you've been courting, won't it?"

Scott closed his mouth. How the hell did the General know about Amelia?

CHAPTER FIFTY-TWO

Friday 8TH March 1918
West End, Stanwood

"Mr Hammond?"

Fred Hammond watched the big man at the back door of their end terrace house. "Who wants to know?"

The big man smiled. It wasn't a nice smile. His few remaining teeth were broken and brown from years of neglect and pipe smoking. "Me, Mr Hammond. I wants to know. I'm what's called a bailiff, see, and you, Mr Hammond, are late with the rent again. 'Fraid your landlord wants payment now. You're in something called arrears." He pulled a grubby piece of paper out of his coat pocket. "You are in fact three months in arrears."

He held his hand out. "Pay up, Mr Hammond." He leaned forward, towering over the small man. "Pay up or get out. Your choice, see? Your landlord's a very fair man."

"What's he saying, Fred?"

Mrs Hammond pushed her way past her husband, squared up to the bailiff and then wrinkled her nose in disgust. "You stink, Mister, whoever you are. Anyways, Arthur Shaw at the pub would never see us thrown out. And we ain't three months late with the rent neither."

The bailiff glared at her. "What I smells like is up to me, Missus. What's up to you is to pay your bills. And who said Mr Shaw is your landlord?"

The couple eyed him in silence.

"Sold up, he did. Got a real good offer. And smelly old me, Missus, I works for the new landlord. And he tells me you owe three months' rent. And he wants you to pay up. Like I said to your old man, pay up or get out."

The old woman stared at him, sick with horror. "And who is this new landlord you work for?"

He leered at her. "Chap by the name of Smythe – Dudley Smythe."

She gasped, her hand coming up to cover her mouth in shock. As the bailiff leaned back to laugh, she slammed the door in his face and threw the bolts. She bustled back into the kitchen, pulled the thin curtains across the window, and then scrabbled among the cards and letters in the small brass letter rack on the mantelpiece. Her husband watched her from the door.

"Quick, Fred. Quick. Where's that envelope from Will's commanding officer, the one with his address on. Aaah. Here it is."

She waved it in the air, pulled out the kitchen drawer, and scrabbled once more for a pencil. She had never written a letter before, but that was not going to stop her. She chewed the end of the pencil, wrinkled her brows, practised on a crumpled copy of the Daily Herald and, after many crossings out, wrote.

Dear Sir,

This letter is from Will Hammond's mother. My husband Fred and I have just had a visit from a horrible big stinking bully of a man. He said that Dudley Smythe has bought our house from our landlord and that unless we paid three months' rent, we would be thrown out.

Please can you help? We still have money from Will, but I am sure that we do not owe three months on the house. I pay every week and tick it off on the calendar in the kitchen.

Yours respectfully,
Alice Hammond

CHAPTER FIFTY-THREE

Saturday 9TH March 1918
Queen's Hospital, Sidcup

Will came to the surface. He could hear movement in his room and a quiet woman's voice singing the Skye Boat Song. He lay still, listening to the pleasing voice...

"Carry the lad that's born to be king, over..." She paused halfway through the line. "I know you're awake, Colour Sergeant. Your breathing changed. So, if you'll just get dressed now, and eat the spot of breakfast that I've brought in, we can go and visit that horse again, can't we."

He heard the rustle of her skirts as she came close to the bed.

"Your clothes are right here on the back of the chair. Come on now, quick, quick. You've been in bed for almost a week, but your temperature is right down and it's a bright and bonnie day. I'll be back directly to see to your dressings."

The rustle faded and the door clicked behind her. Annoying, bloody woman. It was bonnie this and bonnie that! He growled, swung his legs out of the bed and sat up, stretching his arms and bending his back, feeling for his clothes, and then realised that he was humming that damn song. Aila, her ear pressed against the door, heard the humming and did a little dance down the corridor. How many admissions today? When would she be able to get back to him?

An imperious voice called her from the entrance door at the far end of the corridor.

"Oy, Nurse Mc-Whatever-you-call-yourself."

She put her finger to her lips and hurried down the corridor towards him. "Shhh, Harold, he might hear you."

He waved a dismissive arm. "Pah! Now listen, Aila, I've got that fellow Francis Wood coming across from the Masks for Facial Disfigurements Department. Stuff he does is quite spectacular. I think he's the chap for our Will Hammond. He'll make a tin cheek for him. Quite amazing how good they are. No idea how long they last, but should be plenty long enough for him to gain some self–confidence. Wood's written stuff about it. Have a look in one of your spare moments between admitting wounded soldiers, impersonating Scottish nurses and healing war heroes."

Aila laughed, took the manuscript, returned to her room and browsed. First make a plaster–of–Paris cast of the face; then chalk the mould. Then press clay or plasticine into it. That gave them a model of the healed wound and surrounding skin which could be worked up into a new cheek, eye socket, nose or jaw. How long would this take, and could she keep Will alive to see the result?

The last of her patients was triaged. She glanced at the clock, grabbed an apple from the remains of the basket sent to the hospital from Stanwood House, slipped another into her apron pocket for Will and hurried across to the hut where he had his room. She knocked and waited. Nothing. She knocked again, opened the door, called his name and glanced round the empty room.

He'd better not be trying to throw himself into that river again. She sighed as she ran. Ah, finally, there was the river. And no sign of Will, thank God, or maybe he had just thought of another way to end it all. She ran on, panting now, the knitted bones in her hip protesting at this unaccustomed exercise.

Where was that horse? Aaaaah – a deep, sighing breath. There was Will, seated on the hunter, bareback, trotting across the field and steering it with his knees. How had he been able to see well enough to mount let alone see where he was going? She called out, nearly smiling at the way she sounded like her grandmother on the warpath.

"Colour Sergeant Hammond! What are you doing?"

His head went up. The horse's ears pricked forward and at a word it slowed to a walk and turned towards her. Will was an intimidating figure, high above her, but Aila had lived round horses all her life. She stepped forward, gripped the halter and spoke in her most severe voice.

"Colour Sergeant Hammond, what do you think you are doing? Are you trying to ensure you have a fall? Is that today's silly game? And has anybody changed your dressings?"

She stamped her foot. The bandaged and impossible to read face stared in her direction through the black lenses until, with a click of his tongue and a nudge with his knees, he turned the horse, urged it to a trot, a canter, and finally a full gallop, heading towards the hedge on the far side of the paddock. No! No! He was going to try and jump it. She froze as muscles bunching in its haunches, the horse soared above the hedge.

She gathered her skirts and raced across the dew-wet grass. How dare he behave like this? How dare he? She stumbled to a halt. The hunter and its rider were walking back through the open gate in the corner. She waved her arms at the horse and waited for it to come up to her, her anger dissipating with every step it took.

"Do you feel better now, Colour Sergeant Hammond?"

He didn't answer, just swung his leg over the horse's back and dropped lightly to the ground. "It depends on what you mean by better, Nurse McBride. And instead of shouting at me perhaps you might consider that I had assumed you were busy and not wanting to be a further trial to you, I decided to make my own way here."

"Hmmph!"

He turned back to stroke the horse. "No use glaring at me, Nurse. I can't see you."

Aila changed tack. "He'll need a rub down now. You've made him sweat."

The dark glasses turned in her direction once more. "You really do know an awful lot about horses, Nurse."

She snorted in irritation. "I have already told you, Sergeant, I grew up on a Manse. Now come along. We have to find his stable. And then I need to change your dressings. You hold on to his headstall and I'll lead him by the halter."

He shrugged and did as he was bid. The pain in her hip was bad now. She hadn't tested it at all during the months she had been at the hospital. She pressed her hand against it and walked on trying not to limp too obviously.

"You hurt your leg, Nurse?"

How could he have seen? "Yes, Colour Sergeant. Thanks to you. I tripped on a molehill running to try and find you. And how could you know I had hurt myself if you can't see?"

There was a long silence and then he spoke again more hesitantly.

"I can see shapes and movement. At night I seem to be able to see quite clearly, although because it's dark I can still only see shapes and movement."

They walked on together in a silence that was a lot more companionable than she could have hoped for. She made a sudden decision. "Colour Sergeant, if you don't want me to come back again, I won't."

She peered round the horse's head but again could read nothing in his masked–off face. "We're at the edge of the grass now. There's a small step down onto the gravel path."

He nodded without speaking. She tried again. "I think that must be the stables about a hundred yards ahead."

Again, he nodded. Again, she spoke. "I'll help you rub him down."

The same nod. Aila shrugged, half annoyed, half concerned he would refuse to let her see him again. She found combs and brushes, pushed a set into Will's hands and started on her side. They worked together in what she assumed was a friendly silence until Will spoke.

"Is that the only song you know?"

She paused. Yet again she'd been singing the Skye Boat Song without even thinking about it. "My granny taught me it." Her voice caught in her throat. "My wee granny."

She missed her grandmamma so much. How absurd. She worked on in silence.

"I er, I didn't mean to upset you, Nurse McBride. I'm sorry."

She smiled, wiped tears from her cheeks and peered round the horse's head again. That was the old Will for sure – gentle, caring.

"I shouldn't have snivelled, Sergeant, so it's me who should be apologising. It's not your fault that I miss my granny. Do you not miss anyone in your family?"

He shrugged off her question and worked the currycomb in strong semi–circular motions. He was twice as fast as her she realised. She had barely finished her side of the horse before he had completed combing out the mane and the tail. He ran his hands over the horse's coat and patted its rump. "You'll do, old fella. If the wee Scots nursey can find you some bran, we'll have you settled in no time at all."

The horse nodded its head and snorted gently. Aila snorted, a lot less gently, and watched the tall man standing close to the animal lost in some form of silent communion with it. She reached out, took his arm and led him away and back to his room. He said not a word as she changed his dressings, his eyes hidden behind the black lenses. She placed the apple in his hand and they parted in silence.

CHAPTER FIFTY-FOUR

MONDAY 11TH MARCH 1918
GHQ France

"Mail for you, Sir."

Scott nodded and continued to study the photographs taken by those brave chaps of the Royal Flying Corps. He placed the magnifying glass over the aerial photograph of the German Forward Trenches again, studied it, and yelled for a subaltern. He glanced up as a young officer entered the room, saluting and removing his cap. Good, it was one of the brighter ones. Scott beckoned him closer to the table.

"Take a look at that, Gerald, will you and tell me what you see?"

The subaltern stooped and squinted down through the magnifying glass. After ten seconds, he straightened and passed the glass back to his colonel. "Looks to me as though they've got something big there under a camouflage net, sir."

Scott nodded. "And to me too. Be a good fellow now, Gerald, and pop over to the RFC Army Wing and show it to the chaps in the photographic section. Tell the liaison officer that you and I both think it's important and see what he says."

The subaltern replaced his cap, saluted, and marched out. Scott smiled dourly: too bloody keen by half some of these young chaps.

He reached for the letters and smiled with pleasure. That one was from Amelia. There was another from his mother, and one... he stared at the envelope. He recognised that writing. He looked closer and half smiled. He damn well should recognise it – it was his own. Now who the hell had he given this to? He reached for the paper knife, promising himself that he would read Amelia's letter this evening. Thirty seconds later and he was striding up and down his office, running his fingers through his pomaded hair until it stood out in bizarre shapes. He smoothed his hair into some semblance of order and started to think. He knew of nobody in the Royal Horse Artillery who might be willing to help. Wait a second: Jenks. Hadn't his soldier–servant been in the artillery? He sent a runner for him and hunted out the Divisional copy of the Manual of Military Law.

By the time a worried Jenks arrived, Scott was reading Section 4: Offences in Respect of Military Service. This had to have something that included Smythe's behaviour. Deserting one's post, convincing a superior officer to surrender, throwing away one's arms in the presence of the enemy, assisting the enemy, corresponding with the enemy, and the catch all: showing cowardice in the face of the enemy. If nothing else that one must cover his behaviour.

"Jenks, I am not going to insult your widely acknowledged low cunning by assuming you know nothing of the upcoming court martial of Major Dudley Smythe."

Jenks nodded, trying to see where this line of questioning was leading. "Yes, sir."

Scott stood and stretched. "You were in the Royal Horse Artillery?"

"Yes, sir."

"Did you know Major Smythe?"

Jenks hesitated. Scott snapped. "Come on, man this isn't a trap. Did you or did you not know him?"

Jenks swallowed. "Sir, nearly everybody knew Captain Smythe, sir. He was a Captain when I was there, sir."

"And?"

Jenks' eyes darted round the room. "Permission to speak freely, sir?"

So, something was going to come out. "Permission granted, Jenks. This will go no further than me. Carry on"

"Well, sir, put it this way, sir. He drank a lot."

"While on duty?"

"Oh, all the time, sir."

"And?"

"It was where he went drinking, sir, you see."

"Meaning?"

"Well, sir, he'd always go to one of the really rough bars – you know, those Estaminets, the ones that sell that Absinthe muck. Thing is, sir, there were some real devils there too. I mean I grew up with some right villains, but these ones are proper nasty. You know, sir, thugs, killers. You name it."

Scott sat on his frustration with the convoluted tale. "Meaning?"

"Well, sir, when he was just a Lieutenant, he got a right bollo... er telling off, sir, from his Company Major. Next thing we knew was the Major was in hospital. Been badly beaten about. Lieutenant Smythe had been in the Mess all evening of course, sir."

"Circumstantial. Any other instances?"

Jenks was loosening up nicely now. He licked his lips and continued.

"Several, sir. There was this Farrier Sergeant Major. Great big bloke, twenty-five years in the army, Military Medal and all. I'd been detailed to help him with some shoeing once and happened to mention Captain Smythe's name. 'Hmmm', he said, sir. 'Would that be a Dudley Smythe?' I said yes it would and he just says. 'Just let him know that a certain Will Hammond told me about him when I was in a training camp in Northamptonshire.' Well, I didn't know what to make of that, sir, and I don't exactly mix with officers if you know what I mean, but I did mention it to his soldier–servant, sir, in confidence like. Next thing, that Farrier Sergeant Major is found half dead in a ditch. They tried to say he'd been drunk and fallen over but his face, sir, you don't get a face like that unless someone's given you a right kicking."

The subaltern knocked on the door and Jenks jumped to attention. Scott nodded.

"Right you are, Jenks. I might visit that Estaminet place tonight if you'll let me have the address. And if you think of anything else, please let me know immediately."

Jenks went to open his mouth in protest at such a course of action, thought better of it, saluted the two officers, and left. Scott held out his hand for the photographs.

"Now, let's see what you learnt from those photographer chaps."

CHAPTER FIFTY-FIVE

MONDAY 11TH MARCH 1918
An estaminet somewhere in France

The Estaminet offered a selection of wines of dubious origin, bottles of the illegal and lethal Absinthe gut rot and a champagne with a label he didn't recognise. He pointed at the champagne, paid the exorbitant price, indicating that he would open the bottle himself. At least that would mean the barman wouldn't shake the bottle to ensure the maximum spillage. He found a seat at a small table in a dimly lit corner far from the bar.

Half past eight was probably too early for any activity, but at least it gave him time to read Amelia's letter in peace. He slit the envelope and started to smile.

My dear, dear Iain,

I have still not fully recovered from that most wonderful meal in Simpson's. What a treat for a poor nurse who has had nothing but hospital rations for the last three years.

'Poor nurse'. He smiled and read on.

How I wish, though, we had had more time together. I am sure you will be relieved to know that the train was delayed by a mere twenty minutes although I still had to walk home. (Oh, look at me

calling this hospital 'home'), from the station in the dark. Anyway, this is the merest scribble as I am on duty again in five minutes, but I wanted you to know that I miss you and cannot wait to see you once more.
Your very own,
Amelia

By the time he had read the letter three times the bar was more than half full. He sipped the indifferent champagne and looked around. Not a face was looking in his direction. He had chosen his corner well. He unfolded a piece of Army regulation paper and started his reply to Amelia's letter, thinking again about their day together in London. He started to write.

My Dearest Amelia,
This letter is being written with the doubtful assistance of a leaking pen on a wobbly tabletop in a seedy Estaminet somewhere in France, fortified by sips of a singularly uninspiring champagne. But it does come to you with all my love. Why am I here? Well contrary to what you may be thinking I am not seeking solace in the arms of women of loose virtue. I am here to help my dear, wounded colour sergeant...

A commotion by the entrance distracted him and there was Major Dudley Smythe, surrounded by four seedy looking officers, followed by two thuggish NCOs and a handful of civilians. It was more of an entourage than a group of friends. A man whom he assumed must have been the owner of the bar stepped forward, pushing three women in front of him, one of them scarcely more than a child. He herded the whole group to a big table at the far end of the bar. Absinthe was poured, water added, and the cloudy, pale-yellow mixture thrown down waiting throats with practised ease. A shadow blocked his view and he glanced up, ready for trouble, wishing he had transferred the Webley to his trench coat pocket.

"Jenks! What the hell are you doing here? Sit down for God's sake before you draw attention to yourself."

He studied the three men behind his soldier–servant warily. "And who the devil are these men?"

Jenks leaned forward in what could only be described as a conspiratorial manner and proceeded to murmur behind his hand. If Scott hadn't been quite so on edge he would have laughed at the absurdity of the situation. The blubbery bar owner arrived, spotting men in his establishment without alcohol. He leered in Scott's direction.

"You gentlemen drink, non?"

Scott pulled out a wodge of notes and pushed them into the waiting, dirty nailed, fingers and turned back to Jenks.

"It would seem, Corporal Jenks, that your villainous appearance has led mine host to the assumption that we are using his establishment for purposes of a nefarious nature. Not that I am anything but insulted to be mistaken for a criminal, but it would appear to be of some use in this instance. Now, may I please get to the bottom of why you are here? Would I, for instance, be correct in thinking that you are the Farrier Sergeant Major who was beaten on the instructions of himself?"

A nod from the massive figure on Jenks right, "Yes, sir."

"And you chaps?"

He looked first at the small man perched on the edge of his seat.

"Sir, I was servant to Captain McDonald. Him that was courting the Major's sister. He was the officer as went up to the Front Line to say sorry for the barrage being late."

"And?"

"Well, I know the reason it was late, sir."

Scott sat on his impatience yet again. Dragging information out of 'other ranks' was never a job he relished. Jenks came to his rescue.

"Just tell the Colonel the whole story, Bert."

"Well, we knew there was to be an artillery barrage, sir. Orders had come through from GHQ. Captain McDonald was in the office with the adjutant when I went in with a cuppa for him. Must have been almost eleven in the evening, sir. And the Captain was going on something hard about how the battery should have been moved up into position by now and what the hell was happening. Begging your pardon, sir.

"Adjutant just sat there sipping at a brandy and shrugging so the captain goes storming over to the Major's hut and starts hammering on the door and threatening to kick it in if the Major didn't come out and give the orders.

So, the Major comes out. He's half-dressed and obviously well gone, sir. With the drink I mean. He yells right back at the captain, tells him that he was just about to countermand the orders because the men are too tired from the previous engagement to operate the eighteens safely and goes to slam the door in his face. But the Captain he stands his ground, tells the Major he is a disgrace to the regiment and that he himself is going to go up to the Front

Line to apologise to the First Northants for the lack of artillery support. And off he goes."

He paused and took a huge swig of beer. Scott moved not a muscle.

"The next thing is, sir, the Major comes out and rushes off to the adjutant's office and then the pair of them come back and unlock his hut and go back in. And they locked the door behind them."

Another group of officers entered the bar and Scott saw Smythe waving a welcoming arm across the smoke-filled room. The little soldier–servant followed his gaze, peering over his shoulder and tensing.

"That's the Adjutant, sir. Him and the Major are as close as that, sir." He crossed two fingers on his left hand and raised his glass with his right.

The Farrier Sergeant Major placed a heavy hand on the little man's shoulder. "Don't you worry, son, I'll get you out of here alive." He tilted his chin in the direction of Smythe's table. "There's no one there would give me much of a problem."

Bert swallowed nervously and continued. "Anyway, they come out again, sir, and this time they're carrying something rolled up in a rug. I could tell it was a body, sir. Weren't heavy though, so I thought it had to be one of the whores that the Major was keen on and that she was dead drunk or something. So, I followed them, sir. They put the body in the back of the Major's staff car and went to crank it up. And they didn't notice as how the rug had slipped and I could see a face. And it wasn't one of the whores, sir. It was a young lad. From the nearby village. He was dead, sir.

His eyes were open and there were bruises, sir, all over his face. And his neck was swollen like."

He paused once more, picked up his third bottle of beer and poured it out, his hand shaking. Scott nodded at the Private and turned to the final soldier.

"And you, Gunner?"

"I signed up young, sir."

Scott snorted. "You and half the damn army, Gunner. How young is young in your case?"

"Sixteen, sir."

"And they let you come out here?"

"Yes, sir. They stopped being fussy after all the losses on the Somme."

"Go on."

"I was seconded to the Major's company in the cookhouse. They knew I was too young to be out here, sir. Anyways, Major Smythe, he saw me one day. Wouldn't stop looking at me. It was odd, sir. Next thing I knew I was ordered by the adjutant to report for duties as a Mess orderly." He hung his head. "If it wasn't for a Company Bombardier sir, I don't know what would have happened. The Major... He tried... He tried to. He had his thing out, sir. He was really nasty drunk, if you know what I mean, sir. But he tripped over a rug trying to get to me and I ran, and the Bombardier covered for me. I got transferred the next day."

Scott put his elbows on the table and rested his chin in his hands. "Won't he recognise you, Gunner?"

"No, sir. Looks like he's got someone new to play with tonight. It don't matter if they're male or female, sir. He just likes 'em young. The younger the better, I dare say."

"And are any of you willing to testify at the court martial?"

The Farrier Sergeant Major raised a hand. "I would, sir, but I couldn't prove for definite that the Major was involved."

Scott nodded, turning the stories over in his mind. "You knew about Will Hammond didn't you, Sergeant Major?"

"Yes, sir. And I know what Major Smythe's bullyboys did to him back in 1914 before the war, sir. I only knew him for a few weeks at the army training camp, but I can tell you, sir, that I've never seen anyone to touch him for handling horses."

The Colonel grunted. "So of course, he ended up in the infantry. Now listen."

The men all leaned in over the table.

"I received this letter today. It's from Will Hammond's parents."

He pushed it across the table and the Farrier Sergeant Major read it first by right of rank. He passed it on and looked up, his face sombre.

"One of the men who set on me, sir, all I knew was he stank something rotten."

Colonel Scott smiled. "I think it's time we left this establishment. Try your best to look furtive as you leave. Jenks, just look like you normally do. I've got a staff car waiting at the end of the street. Meet me there."

The men laughed at Jenks' attempt to look hurt. They left separately, the Farrier Sergeant Major bringing up the rear to ensure they were not followed. It was a three-minute walk back to his staff car which gave the Colonel sufficient time to marshal his thoughts. The men watched him.

"Right. S'arnt Major, is there any chance you can get a forty-eight-hour pass starting from tomorrow morning? If you could, then my proposal is that you travel to Stanwood in Northants and see what you can do about this bullying bailiff."

The Sergeant Major grinned. "Be delighted to do so, sir. It would be a real pleasure."

"Good man. I'll give you some cash for tickets and food and things."

The grizzled warrant officer looked deeply affronted. "No, you won't sir. Like I say this will be a real pleasure."

The colonel turned to the other three men. "I'm not going to ask you to testify, men. All I want you to do is turn up in court on the first day. I'll have you listed as witnesses, but I promise on my honour that I won't call you. I just want you to be there for Smythe to see. The Sergeant Major here should be back from Blighty in time to act as your bodyguard and Jenks will arrange accommodation and additional physical assistance. Jenks?"

Jenks straightened to attention. "Sir."

"You will act as liaison with to keep everyone informed about the starting date and time. Don't let me down, men. We need to put a full stop to Major, the Honourable Dudley Smythe, once and for all. Jenks, wait for me here. I'm going back to the Estaminet to get that poor young girl out."

There was a sudden silence.

CHAPTER FIFTY-SIX

FRIDAY 15TH MARCH 1918
The Queen's Hospital, Sidcup

Amelia passed the letter from Colonel Scott to her cousin and waited. Aila read the first page in silence then looked up. "Goodness, Amelia, your Colonel... He's wonderful."

Amelia smiled smugly. "But of course, why else would I let him court me? And at least he's not a common NCO."

Aila tossed her head in a reasonable approximation of Maisie's hoity toity gesture. The smile dropped from her face. "Amelia, may I borrow this letter? It's just that I think we need to, what's the word, co–ordinate, what's going on. I mean this threat to Will's parents. It's awful. And Dudley. I mean. This is awful."

Amelia patted her on her head. "Yes, dear."

She glanced back as she left the room. Aila was already busy with a double foolscap piece of cartridge paper, a ruler and a pencil. She looked up. "Amelia, can you find out when the court martial is going to start? I have an idea."

* * *

Will removed his dark glasses and stared out at the night sky. January had been bitter cold, but February had ended bitter cold and wet - February fill dyke. He touched his jaw where the stitching from the last operation would be coming out tomorrow. It didn't hurt now, or not much anyway. Only one more operation, Major Gillies had promised. So, this was going to be it. Whatever he looked like after this one he would get no better.

Which led him to think about that Scottish nurse. He almost smiled. She appeared to have adopted him as some kind of pet, never missing a day to visit him, or walk with him out to meet that horse. At least they now knew his name, Casper. The nurse had managed to speak to its owner, or rather to the owner's daughter, the owner being on a battleship somewhere in the Mediterranean.

Right, time to work on the plan. He pulled his army cape closer round his shoulders, tilted his cap forward and strode over the grass in the direction of the copse. Within moments he had found his cache of tools and had dropped into the hole he had dug over the last fortnight. It was five feet deep now and he was beginning to have trouble disguising the mound of earth and stones he had dug out.

He worked on for an hour then climbed out, as satisfied with his work as he ever would be. All he had to do now was go for one of his late-night walks and disappear. It would take them days to find that opening. Days in which he would have breathed his last and then the hospital, his fellow soldiers, and his family, all could mourn his accidental death.

* * *

Aila waited five minutes before moving. The candlelight in Will's bedroom snuffed out leaving only the faintest of afterglows. She hurried to where he had been digging and after five minutes of muddy scrambling, crouched back on her heels and chewed her bottom lip. The distant clock struck once. Half past three. Well at least she knew about it. You can try whatever you like, Will Hammond, but I'm still going to keep you alive. She yawned and squelched her way back to her room. Three hours sleep again. She couldn't carry on like this, not with all her nursing duties. She hung her wet clothes up, set her alarm clock for six o'clock and was asleep within seconds.

It felt as though she hadn't slept at all. She peered blearily at the figure kneeling at the foot of the bed.

"Maisie? Maisie, what on earth are you doing?"

The blonde head popped up into her field of vision and frowned at her.

"I'm trying to dry out your shoes, Miss Aila. You should have put newspaper in them last night before you went to bed. And they're coated in mud. Whatever were you up to?"

Aila yawned hugely. "Don't ask, Maisie dear. Don't ask."

Maisie hmmphed. "Well, I bet it was something to do with Will Hammond."

Aila just smiled, grabbed her towel and ran to wash, turning to call out over her shoulder. "May I borrow your cape, please, Maisie? Mine's still soaking wet."

Maisie shrugged. "But I'm shorter than you." As the door closed on her complaint she murmured. "And I have a bigger bosom."

The door opened again and Aila peered round. "I heard that, Maisie Brown! I believe the difference between us is that I am tall, willowy and elegant and you are short, common and big in the chest region. It's a matter of class."

They both laughed.

By eight Aila had received the first list of today's arrivals. She checked it and wondered why there was still no word back from Amelia's Colonel as to when the court martial would start. She counted off the days on her wall chart. The Farrier Sergeant Major should be in Stanwood tomorrow. She stared at the chart until her eyes watered: all the people, all her hopes, everything, converged on the first day of the court martial at GHQ in France. She shook her head, checked the clock, grabbed another apple, hurried to Will's room and listened through the door panel. She heard his voice clear and loud from inside the room.

"You know the funny thing about thin doors is that you can hear people on both sides of them. Do come in, Nurse McBride."

She shrugged and entered, grabbing his hand and pushing the apple into it. "And, Colour Sergeant Hammond, you will not give this one to Casper like you did with the last one. You will eat this one yourself. You're looking far too thin."

The dark glasses turned in her direction. "You know I'm pretty sure that Colour Sergeants outrank common–or–garden nurses so I believe I shall continue to do as I like, while thanking you for the apple, of course."

She snorted. "Come on. Casper will be waiting for you."

"Don't you mean waiting for us?"

"No, I do not, Colour Sergeant. Much as Casper may pretend to enjoy my ministrations, he is only interested in you. As you well know! Now, are you going to try and ride him again today? I'm not going to have to get severe with you, am I?"

She guided his hand to her shoulder and led the way out into the cold morning and shivered. "At least it's not raining."

His hand moved on her shoulder. "That's not your normal cape, Nurse."

She thought quickly. "Don't be silly, of course it..."

She stopped and pulled the cape off to peer at the label in the collar. "Oh dear, I do seem to have picked up the wrong one." She glanced at him, trying to see if that had convinced him, but could, as ever, read nothing behind the black glasses. "Och well, Nurse Brown, you will just have to take mine. Come along do, Colour Sergeant, you really shouldn't keep Casper waiting."

* * *

Twenty minutes later she was leaning against the gate in the field watching as Will worked his magic on the horse, guiding him only by the strength of his knees and the gently spoken words. Surely this was a good sign. Surely. She saw him turn towards the fence on the far side of the field again. Oh no! She opened her mouth to shout and then stopped. Whatever Will might try to do to himself he would never run the risk of harming a horse.

She forced herself to turn away and hurry across the park towards the stables. She was sure she had seen a saddle hanging over the half–door on one of the stalls. Yes! There it was, but it was too bloody heavy to carry. She smiled at her bad language and dragged the heavy saddle off the door. Bridle? Bridle? She grabbed a bundle of tack, found a wheelbarrow and pushed it in the direction of the paddock.

CHAPTER FIFTY-SEVEN

TUESDAY 19TH MARCH 1918
Wellingborough Railway Station, Northamptonshire

The asthmatic steam locomotive wheezed and gasped its way up the incline and ten minutes later Farrier Sergeant Major Ernest Trubshaw found himself standing on the platform contemplating his next move. He could, according to the ticket office clerk, either wait an hour for an unreliable connection to Finedon or walk the seven odd miles to Stanwood village. He thought for a moment, rubbed the bristles on his jaw, asked for directions, swung his kitbag on to his shoulder and set out. Seven miles – shouldn't take him more than three hours and he could do with some exercise.

He hummed an infantry marching song to himself as he left the last of the town's houses behind him, breaking into a tuneless bass rumble as the threatening rain clouds drifted away and the early spring sun slanted through the branches of a copse east of the road.

... If you want to find the old battalion
I know where they are.
They're hanging on the old barbed wire.
I've seen 'em, I've seen 'em
Hanging on the old barbed wire...

It was fully midday by the time he arrived in front of the village church. And there was that pub the Colonel had told him about. The landlady looked up at him warily as he came through the door, but he just nodded in her direction, gazed round the room, smiled in satisfaction, placed his kitbag on the settle by the fire, and crossed to the bar. She waited for him to speak. He touched his forelock. "Afternoon, missus. I'd be grateful for a pint of your best beer and bit of bread and cheese if you have such a thing."

He pulled coins out of his pocket to show willing and smiled at her. She looked back at him for a long moment. What a fine-looking woman; strong minded as well, judging by the set of her jaw – and plenty of flesh on her bones too. He stopped his eyes from roving as she finished drawing him a pint of beer from one of the barrels lined up behind her and left the room. He glanced at the black framed photo of a middle-aged man on the wall. A widow too. He sat by the fire and closed his eyes until the swish of skirts roused him. He jerked into wakefulness to see her smiling down at him, a plate of fresh bread and cheese in one hand.

"Now I don't what it is about the atmosphere in here, but you're not the first soldier to take one look at the fire and nod off."

Trubshaw relieved her of the plate. "Well, you know, Missus, I think it's just that a place like this is what we soldiers dream of, but don't really believe exists. So the minute we find ourselves in it, we fall asleep and then you know what? We dream of the army!"

She laughed and seated herself on the other settle, watching him. He chewed a hunk of bread, nodded approvingly and glanced across at her. "You had any smelly men in here, recently, Missus?"

"I've got a name, Sergeant Major: Mrs Peggy Henderson. So that's what it's about is it? Yes, I have, and I don't like the look of him one bit."

Trubshaw sipped the beer. "Him and four of his mates set on me a while back, on the instructions of someone who you'll know all about, and left me in hospital. Now I understand he's giving some problems to Will Hammond's parents. So, I've took a bit of leave and come here to see what I can do to help." He reached into his tunic pocket. "Missus - sorry, Mrs Henderson - I'm guessing you'll know the person who wrote this letter. Miss Aila Smythe?"

She glanced at him in surprise and scanned the letter. "Well, well, well, Sergeant Major Trubshaw, you do move in high circles, don't you; a set of instructions from Miss Aila?" Her face softened. "She's such a dear, good soul too. You wouldn't believe she could be related to that brother of hers, Dudley Smythe."

A pair of farm labourers entered the bar before he could respond and she bustled over to the bar to serve them. Other men entered, all too old for army service, most glancing at the big, tough soldier seated by the fire, all leaving him well alone. The lunchtime stream of customers dwindled to a trickle and as two o'clock struck on the village church clock, Peggy Henderson pushed the bolts across the door and carried the last tray of glasses out to the kitchen to be washed. Within five minutes she was back on the settle opposite the soldier. He waited for her to explain.

"It'd be best if I take you down West End and introduce you to Fred and Alice Hammond. If another hulking great brute turns up at their back door unannounced, they'll be proper terrified."

Trubshaw smiled. "I'll try my best not to hulk too much then."

She came to her feet. "Now we don't have any proper accommodation for guests since my husband passed, but I can put you up on the big ottoman in the back room if that would be sufficient."

He stood up too, towering over her. "That is right generous of you, Mrs Henderson. I got some money for this trip so I can pay you proper, mind."

She tied up her bonnet and opened the door. "Come on now. We can talk on the way."

She led the way down the lane, talking as she walked. "You're in luck with what Miss Aila is asking for. My son is the chauffeur up at the big house and he did say he'd call in later this afternoon, so I can give him the message for you."

CHAPTER FIFTY-EIGHT

TUESDAY 19TH MARCH 1918
West End, Stanwood

Alice Hammond had almost stopped shivering when she looked at the Farrier Sergeant Major. Fred Hammond had a half–smile on his face as he listened to him finish his story.

"So, Mr and Mrs Hammond, I've a mind to camp out here for tonight by the fire if you'll let me and I'll have words with the smelly gentleman if and when he arrives."

Fred Hammond laughed and wheezed. "Oh, he'll be here alright. He must stand outside somewhere 'cos when we puts the lamp out, he starts knocking on the doors and windows and calling out. Neighbours ain't best pleased, but he's put the fear of God into them too."

Trubshaw nodded. "He alone?"

The old couple shook their heads and Alice Hammond spoke for them both. "We think we've seen a couple of people out there with him, but it's hard to see in the dark."

He turned to the pub landlady. "Would it be possible for Mr and Mrs Hammond to stay up at your place this evening, Mrs Henderson? Reckon I might have my hands full and I wouldn't want them to worry."

He helped them into their overcoats then ushered them out of the back door and stood watching as they walked carefully down the path to the steps that led to the lane below. Peggy Henderson paused, put down her baskets and ran back up the path. She went up on tiptoe and kissed him on the cheek.

"You're a good man, Sergeant Major. Thank you for this. And you take good care of yourself."

He found he was grinning stupidly at her departing back. He rubbed his jaw, glanced at the Westering sun and went inside murmuring to himself. "Well, I never. Well, Mrs Peggy Henderson, I never did."

The ancient Vienna Regulator clock ticked its irregular way through the afternoon hours as the Farrier Sergeant dozed away the hours until the darkness of early evening. He made himself a cup of strong tea, banked down the fire in the grate and watched the clock. If he lit a candle after eight, it would still be burning after closing time and that would provide him with just enough light to see who he was hitting.

* * *

The clock's spring whirred and the arm struck the bell once for eight thirty. Trubshaw yawned, stood, stretched until his joints cracked, and drew the curtains. It was time. He buttoned up his greatcoat and slipped out of the back door, past the outhouse privy and on to a brick path that ran through the neglected vegetable plot. He seated himself on an upturned bucket and waited in the blustery rain, reflecting that soldiers were good at waiting. Half of army life involved a wait of one sort or another. Mind you, it also gave you the chance to think about handsome widows who ran pubs in little tannery villages.

The light in the kitchen flickered. He closed his eyes, tilted his head and listened. Nothing for a minute, or another. Wait. That was no animal. He peered through the dripping twigs of the gooseberry bush in front of him. Someone was trying to peer into the kitchen through the crack in the curtain he had deliberately left there for just such a time as this. So, according to Will's father there should be one other chap somewhere else. Yes, there he was, coming round the side path to join his mate. Time to act.

He crept back down the path – five paces behind them, four, three... One of the men glanced round, opened his mouth to yell and the Farrier Sergeant Major took one long step forward. Two powerful arms and shovel like hands extended and slammed the men's heads together with a crack that might have been heard in the pub.

He dragged the two bodies back up the path through the vegetable garden, dumped them on the compost heap, rubbed his hands together, and smiled. Peggy Henderson may have wanted to reconsider her belief in him being a good man had she seen that smile. He pulled the collar of his greatcoat up, grabbed the worn, greasy cap from the head of the nearest body and made his way back to the window. He leaned against it, pretending to peer through and listening intently for the sound of footsteps. But it was the smell that reached him first, then the sound of the slightly slurred, rough voice just behind him.

"Where's Nobby, then? Where's the little bastard hiding?"

Trubshaw smiled to himself and straightened, lifting the cap off his head and throwing it in the other man's face. He waved his hand in front of his nose.

"Blimey, you really do stink, don't you? Remember me? The soldier you and your chums beat up across the Channel a few months ago? You probably don't 'cos scum like you never remember anything about putting a man in hospital. Anyway, your little friends are having a nice sleep on top of the compost heap and maybe I'll let you join them there, and then again maybe I won't."

The 'bailiff' took a step back, squinted at the silhouette in front of him in the darkness and threw a haymaker of a punch. Trubshaw's hand whipped up to block the fist. The smack of knuckle hitting palm echoed off the outhouse wall. Trubshaw tightened his grip. Twenty-five years of hammering horseshoes in army forges across the world had left him with fingers that could bend nails. He squeezed and squeezed until the crack of small bones signalled the end of that hand as a weapon of any sort. He opened his fingers and pushed the arm away.

"Want to try with your other arm now?"

The thug was panting in pain. He turned and ran for the steps leading down to the lane below the terrace. Trubshaw laughed and went after him, waiting until the other had reached the bottom step before throwing his fifteen stone off the top step to crash on to the body below him. The thug hit the stone surface of the lane with a bone shaking crunch and a whoof of expelled air. Trubshaw straightened and waved his hand in front of his nose once more.

"You know, I think it's time you had a proper wash."

He reached down, grabbed the coat collar and dragged the unconscious body up the lane to the horse trough by the pub. With a grunt, he lifted the body and threw it in to the cold water. The thug came round spluttering wildly, tried to stand and got the full force of Trubshaw's left fist in the centre of his face. He left the body slumped in the water and strode back down the lane. It had crossed his mind that digging the compost over the other two men might keep them warm for a while. He doubted they would have come round yet.

CHAPTER FIFTY-NINE

TUESDAY 19^(TH) MARCH 1918
The Queen's Hospital, Sidcup, Kent

Aila paced across Harold Gillies' empty office, massaging her hip almost unconsciously, waiting for the operator to contact her. She paused in front of the stacked pastels of the 'befores' and flicked through them until she found Will's shattered face. She lifted it from the stack and walked back across towards the telephone holding it in her left hand. The bell on the machine rang and she jumped, nearly dropping the picture. She picked the receiver off its hook and spoke into the mouthpiece.

"This is Staff Nurse Aila Smythe speaking to you."

"One moment, Miss. I shall connect you now."

Aila seated herself, clutching the telephone to her ear.

"Miss Aila? Are you there, Miss Aila?"

She relaxed. "Good evening, Mr Livens. Yes, I am here. Now is Henderson there yet?"

"Yes, Miss Aila, and may I say what a pleasure it is to hear your voice."

Aila shook her head. This would have to proceed at Mr Livens' pace. He was an elderly man now, of course. "And yours too, Mr Livens. Please pass on my very best wishes to all the staff and let them know that Maisie is getting along famously. I trust you all saw her photograph in the newspaper when she met her Majesty."

"We did indeed, Miss Aila. It was most gratifying. Henderson is here now, Miss. He has a military man with him too."

She heard the murmur of voices which was probably Mr Livens instructing Henderson in the protocol of telephonic communication – and then Henderson's nervous voice. "Um, good evening, Miss Aila."

"Good evening, Henderson. Now pay attention. You are to take Farrier Sergeant Major Trubshaw wherever he instructs you. He may well have a prisoner."

"He does, Miss Aila."

"Excellent. In the near future, Henderson, and on the assumption that my father is still at the London house, I shall also require you to bring the Rolls to this hospital. I may need you for two or three days. Now please pass the telephone receiver to Sergeant Major Trubshaw and then ask Mr Livens to see if my grandmother is able to talk to me."

More murmuring and then a deep voice.

"Ma'am?"

"Sergeant Major. Did you have any trouble?"

"Trouble? No, bless you, ma'am, no trouble at all. The gentleman in question is sitting outside, as he's somewhat on the damp side having taken a bath in the village horse trough. Made him smell a bit better too, ma'am."

Aila laughed. "Colonel Scott said that you had been looking forward to this meeting for a while, Sergeant Major."

"I most certainly have, ma'am. And once we've given him an even longer wash and some new clothes, it will be my pleasure to take him wherever you want."

Aila checked her notes and gave exact instructions. "Now if that is all clear, Sergeant Major, is my grandmother there yet?"

"Yes, ma'am, she is."

Aila pressed the receiver close to ear once more.

"Aila? Are you there, Aila, child?"

And that did it. Aila sobbed into the telephone speaker incoherently for a full ten seconds before pulling herself together once more.

"Oh, Grandmamma."

She let the dear Highland voice wash over her while she snivelled and hiccoughed her way to being able to put her questions to her grandmother. And finally the operator informed her that she had to clear the line.

Aila wiped her eyes and stared at the pastel picture of Will resting on the table where she had placed it during the phone call. She moved her hand across the jaw and stared into the cool blue eyes. That Lieutenant Tonks was a fine artist. He had captured the essence of Will in just a few strokes. She moved her hand and stared at the shattered jaw. On impulse she leaned forward, kissed the broken cheek and then sat back laughing at her ridiculous behaviour.

She thought back to the day she had discovered his name when she had been recovering in bed from her fall. She smiled at the memory of how she had thrown the pillow at Maisie which had hit the vet, Mr Chant. What had he said about Will? She stared into space. Oh, yes. That was it. He'd repeated the words that he had heard Will speaking to the stable boy after Will had sewn up Juno's face:

"A scar on the face means nothing. It's what's inside that counts and this is a good horse, gentle, kind and willing. If a man had a scar like that, would you send him to a knackers' yard? Well, would you?"

No, Will. No, you wouldn't. She straightened. Yes. Of course. How stupid not to have thought of that before. She ran round the desk, seated herself in Harold Gillies' chair, grabbed a sheet of headed notepaper, dipped a pen into the ink pot and began to write, the words flowing fast off the pen onto the paper.

'Dear Mr Chant,

Forgive my writing to you out of the blue and after so long an absence. You may be aware that I have become a nurse at The Queen's Hospital in Sidcup where they specialise in what is called facial reconstruction or plastic surgery.

You may also have seen in the papers that Will Hammond is a patient here and has been awarded the Victoria Cross for gallantry. His facial wounds are very bad and I fear for his future as he is a proud man and having to live with these scars is a most daunting task.

Mr Chant, I want you to come here to Sidcup and see Will and I want you to offer him a job with you at your veterinary practice. You know how wonderful he is with horses and how skilfully he stitched up dear Juno. I will guarantee to pay any additional costs that you may incur and I enclose a cheque for a guinea to cover your travel and disruption.

There is one thing though. I do not wish Will to know that I am behind this. He does not know I work here as a nurse and if he did know I think it would upset him.

Please use the telephone to inform me if this is acceptable.'

Aila added the exchange and number of Harold Gillies' telephone, skim read the letter once more, addressed an envelope to the vet at his Raunds address and returned to her room to write out a cheque.

CHAPTER SIXTY

SUNDAY 24TH MARCH 1918
Dover, Kent

"This is as far as I can go, Miss Aila."

Aila gnawed a knuckle and peered through the condensation on the Rolls' side window at the chaos of the South Eastern & Chatham Railway's Dover terminus. The ferry to Calais must be somewhere nearby. She stepped onto the running board.

"Very well, Henderson. Find a porter will you. Come along, Maisie."

Henderson held the door as she stepped out into the cold morning, pulling her nurse's cape tight round her and making sure Maisie did the same. They hurried towards the probable shelter and possible warmth of a First-Class Ladies Waiting Room. A tiny coal fire flickered in a tiny grate. Maisie knelt to offer first aid and within minutes a blaze was warming them as they stood before it, their capes opened to absorb the heat. Aila glanced at the Union Flag drooping on the flagstaff above the platform.

"At least it should be a quiet crossing, Maisie. There's not a hint of wind."

She saw Maisie shiver. She knew her companion had never been so far from home, let alone on a Cross Channel ferry and that the thought both excited and scared her. Just a metal plate between them and cold wet oblivion with German U Boats being reported up and down the Channel. A knock at the door and a peaked cap above a very youthful face poked round.

"Miss Smythe? Sarn't Major Trubshaw sent me to escort you to your berth on the ferry."

He stood to attention as they hurried towards him, Maisie casting a sorrowful glance back at the now blazing fire.

The ferry was packed, but to Aila's relief the immense presence of Farrier Sergeant Major Trubshaw ensured not just their safety, but a reasonable level of comfort. She perched on her steamer trunk in the small cabin and read through her notes once more. "Maisie, can you read out everything on that list so I can check I've done it."

Maisie picked up the page. "Colonel Scott witnesses?"

Aila moved some papers, shuffled three pages and counted. "Yes, he has three willing witnesses who will testify to Dudley's bad character if required. And I asked him to find the family of the Belgian boy Dudley killed to confirm that he has been missing for months."

She picked up another page and smiled to herself. "And thanks to Sergeant Major Trubshaw he also has one unwilling, and somewhat less smelly than he was, witness."

Maisie glanced at the list again. "French artillery officer who had the command to fire from Major Smythe."

Aila ticked again and raised an eyebrow at her maid.

"Oh. Yes, sorry, Miss Aila. Er, Adjutant?"

Aila nodded. "Yes, I suggested that to Amelia's Colonel. If he attends the hearing, Colonel Scott could get testimony from Mr Smelly and then call for the Adjutant to take the stand."

"Lord Augustus, Miss Aila?"

Aila tapped her teeth the pencil. "Well... I spoke to my grandmamma and told her what was happening. She said she would speak to my father on my behalf so something may come of it. I'm not sure what though."

"Miss Aila? Are you sure Will Hammond will be all right with you not keeping an eye on him?"

Aila pursed her lips and stared at the bulkhead, drumming her fingers on the lid of the trunk. "Well, I've got Ruby watching him during the day and I'm paying that kitchen orderly a fortune to stand outside his window at night." Her jaw came up. "And I warned him that if anything happened to Will, he would pay with his life." She smiled. "I have to say that I didn't realise I could be that fierce. Poor boy looked terrified. So, the answer is, yes, he will be all right. I shall use the telephone to contact the hospital when we arrive at Étaples though, just to make sure they both know I am watching from afar."

The distant sound of the ship's siren made them both look towards the porthole. Maisie's eyes sparkled, making Aila smile. "Come along, Maisie dear, we can go on deck and watch them cast off."

Aila held Maisie's arm feeling how her maid surreptitiously tried to move her as close to one of the lifeboats as possible. But as the ferry nosed out into the channel and started its slow roll and pitch, she began to smile. Aila watched her out of the corner of her eye with great affection as two spots of colour appeared on her wind-blown cheeks.

Maisie was the best possible person to have on an adventure like this – irrepressible, interested in everything and always ready to help. And by the time the boat was nosing into Calais harbour she had also become the centre of male attention. Aila looked up from her notes and smiled. She knew they had nothing to fear in the presence of Farrier Sergeant Major Trubshaw. If any one of the young soldiers got too close to the line a deep growl would come from his throat.

The train journey from Calais to Étaples, the site of the massive army base near Montreuil–sur–Mer, home to the British Army's GHQ, was miserable. Munitions trains had priority. Troop movements were constant and what should have been a short and simple trip took over four hours. Staring listlessly out of the carriage window, Aila could see that the journey by road would have been even slower. Horses drawing guns plodded along behind tired infantry, staff cars pushing through the mass of men, Klaxons blaring importantly. She glanced at Maisie and smiled again. She was watching the scene with fascinated amazement. She felt Aila's eyes on her and turned.

"I've never seen so many men, Miss Aila. And those poor horses look so tired. And those guns! They're huge."

She shivered. In an adjacent carriage singing had started. Maisie tapped her foot to the rhythm.

Mademoiselle from Armentières, parlez vous
Mademoiselle from Armentières, parlez vous
Mademoiselle from Armentières
Hasn't been...

She saw Sergeant Major Trubshaw striding down the corridor. The singing stopped. It didn't take much imagination to work out what the next word would have been. Maisie, she noticed, had her head down and was smiling at her lap. What a lot they had learned about adult life in the last eighteen months.

The grey, early afternoon blurred imperceptibly to evening. The train jerked. The couplings snapped taut, and they ran into Étaples station.

CHAPTER SIXTY-ONE

MONDAY 25TH MARCH 1918
The Queen's Hospital, Sidcup, Kent

"Sit still, will you, young man! I thought infantry soldiers knew how to control their movements and making sure this is the right fit is essential, otherwise it will be rubbing against your cheek bones and then you'll be back blaming me for the bad fit."

Will lifted the hand away from his face. "Captain Wood. You seem to be mistaking me for a Guardsman. If an infantryman remains still for too long in the trenches he gets shot by a sniper. And the skin where you're touching is very sensitive. It makes me jump." He looked the other man in the eye. "Don't think I don't appreciate what you are doing for me, sir, but over the last three or more years in the trenches I have developed a strong objection to being shouted at for no good reason."

The captain sat back, stunned into silence by this speech. He opened his mouth to point out to this soldier that he was a famous sculptor, remembered the story he had been told by that staff nurse and shut his mouth. Suddenly the sacrifice of giving up his chosen path seemed singularly trivial when compared to the help he was able to give to people like this remarkable young man.

"You're quite right, Colour Sergeant. Forgive me. It has been a long day. What do you think of your tin face?"

Will picked it up, holding the delicate tin against his face and peering into the mirror. "It's quite extraordinary, sir. You may not think of it as such, but for me it's a work of art. I have periods where I can't see well, but my sight's clear at the moment." He turned the mask over and over in his hands. "The varnish makes it look so like... well like the grease on my face."

He rubbed his thumb down the unscarred side of his cheek and stared at it. He looked up at the sculptor. "I'm sorry for being rude just now, sir. It's just that I'm not sure if I'm being a coward for wearing it. Whether I should just face up to my scars right now, face up to being a monster I mean, if I'm able."

He passed the tin plate back to the sculptor and closed his eyes. "It's something I think about a lot, sir."

Nurse Ruby Pearce, listening through the thin door, felt tears come to her eyes. She peered at her watch and hurried down the corridor and across the park to the nurses' office to wait for the telephone call from Staff Nurse Smythe in France.

* * *

Étaples Army Camp, France

Maisie was still in shock. She had never, ever seen so many men in one place.

"I mean, I know London's huge, Miss Aila, but this whole camp has been built just for the war. It's scary."

Aila nodded. The atmosphere was very bad. "Not just twenty or more hospitals here, Maisie. It's a training camp as well, and a supply depot. And there are prisoners of war, thousands of them." She shivered. "I just hope we don't have to stay here too long. Colonel Scott says he'll be here this evening, but he hasn't got a time for when the Court Martial will start. So, in the meantime, shall we walk over to that hospital tent? I need to book the telephone call to Ruby in Sidcup. I'll let Sergeant Major Trubshaw know where we've gone."

Maisie kept her lips firmly closed. She would happily have sat at the window of the small hut, near to the stove and to the kettle, for the rest of the day. She looked up at the leaden sky and then down at the massive encampment and her face softened. "And the poor souls are all in tents too, Miss Aila, and it's not yet April. They must be freezing."

* * *

The Queen's Hospital, Sidcup, Kent

"There's a visitor for you, Colour Sergeant."

Will peered at the young nurse who seemed to have taken over his care from Nurse McBride. She blushed and ran out of the room almost bumping into the bulky figure who was standing in the doorway smiling at him. Will squeezed his eyes shut, opened them again and removed his smoked glass goggles.

"You're Mr Chant, the vet."

"I am that."

"What are you doing here, Mr Chant?"

"Come to meet a war hero, lad. You're the talk of Northamptonshire."

Will gave him a sidelong glance and put his dark glasses back on again. "I'm not a performing monkey, Mr Chant. People don't line up to look at me through the bars of my cage."

The vet gave a short, comfortable laugh. "That nurse said you could be a bit sharp, but that I wasn't to mind as you're quite nice underneath. Now, I've come all the way down from Northants to offer you a job. What do you think of that then?"

Will removed the dark glasses once more. "Could you say that again, Mr Chant?"

"I said, Will Hammond, that I've come to offer you a job. I've lost two of my young chaps to the army and now they don't want to come back and work in a vet's practice. They're saying horses are a thing of the past. But I reckon if you'd come and work for me that'd be fine, 'cos you'd do twice the work in half the time. So, how about it?"

He stood and looked down at the young man who was still staring at him. In silence.

"But..."

Will stopped and went to replace the glasses on his nose. It gave him a moment to think. He twisted them in his fingers. Was this a future? Did he want a future?

"But what, lad?"

"But why me?"

"I'm getting old. I've only got daughters and I wouldn't let one of my sons-in-law near a cat let alone a horse." He stepped up close to the young man and peered at his eyes.

"I was told about your eyes. They're on the mend now, though, aren't they? Can you see me?"

Will nodded uncertainly. "I can see for longer periods now, but then everything gets blurred again. And you didn't answer my question, Mr Chant."

Chant cocked his head to one side. "Who was it who said *'a scar on the face means nothing. It's what's inside that counts and this is a good horse, gentle, kind and willing. If a man had a scar like that, would you send him to a knackers' yard? Well, would you?'*?"

Will shook his head in confusion as Chant bent nearer to him. The older man reached out to his bandages. Will's hand shot up to stop him.

"Stop messing about, lad. After I saw your name in the paper getting one of them Victoria Crosses, I wasn't able to stop thinking about you and the way you stitched up Miss Aila's colt. Let's see if the doctors have done as good a job on you as you did on Juno."

He pushed Will's hand down, removed the bandages and studied the repairs, murmuring to himself as he tilted the jaw this way and that. He lifted the chin and whistled. "So that's how they do it. My, oh my! Whoever did this to you was a clever man, a very clever man indeed." He stepped back and squinted. "A year or two more and no one will even notice the hole. The layers of flesh are a bit crude, though. Don't suppose you can grow a beard either, can you?"

He smiled at Will's discomfiture. "So, you ready to face the world like that or are you going to hide behind that tin mask there for a while 'til you get a bit of confidence back?"

He indicated the beautifully executed tin cheek plate on the table. Will stopped staring and started to laugh, stopping only when the stretching of the new flesh on his cheek started to hurt. It was, he realised, the first time he had laughed properly since he had woken on the platform at Folkestone station. It was a pity that Scottish nurse wasn't here. She'd probably start singing the bloody Highland Boat Song again in celebration. The vet smiled at him in satisfaction.

"Now. You worked out who said that thing about a scar on the face?"

Will shrugged.

"'Twas you, lad. I was there in the stable the morning after you'd stitched Juno up and I heard what you said to Jimmy, the stable boy. Never forgotten it. I told Miss Aila what you said too. She was mightily impressed."

Will stuttered. Mr Chant peered at him. "Maybe I'm making a mistake now. Maybe you've lost your touch with horses."

Will's head came up. He jumped to his feet. "You think so, do you, Mr Chant. You think because I've lost half my face that I lost my way with horses. You just follow me."

He strode from the room followed by the amused vet. Minutes later Mr Chant was watching in admiration as Will called Casper across, helped him to kneel, swung himself up bareback and then put the hunter through a complex series of steps. He jumped back down and walked across the paddock with the horse breathing over his shoulder every step of the way.

"Still think I've lost my way with horses, Mr Chant."

The elderly vet laughed and clapped Will on the shoulder. "Not I, but did you always rise to the bait so easily though?"

Will deflated. "Sorry, Mr Chant. Made a fool of myself there, didn't I?"

Casper nudged him in the back, pushing him forward. He turned and scratched the horse's face. "Stop it, you silly old thing. I'm still paying attention to you, aren't I?"

The horse snorted at him, nodding its head and then moving round between the two men, staking its claim to Will in no uncertain way. Both men laughed at its antics and Will spoke over the horse's back.

"Casper's owner's back on leave next week so I won't be seeing so much of him for a while. There's not much hunting going on here though, mind."

Mr Chant nodded. "Nor in Northants neither, Will. Terrible thing, war."

Will thought about replying, but as so often when dealing with the happy ignorance of civilians, he kept his counsel.

* * *

The dim corridor light was switched on making him blink. Interesting. A week ago, he wouldn't even have been able to see the difference. He sat, unmoving, on the hard chair outside Major Gillies' office listening to the doctor's firm stride as he neared the door.

"It's open, Colour Sergeant. You could have waited inside."

Will followed the doctor into his office. "Once was more than enough thank you, sir."

They watched each other across the desk. Gillies reached for his pipe and started the complex procedure of reaming the bowl on to a set of notes on his desk. Will cleared his throat.

"A chap came to see me today. A vet."

Gillies encouraged him with a nod.

"He wants me to go and work for him near where my parents live."

Gillies stood and pulled his tobacco jar down from the mantel. He tamped the shreds down, struck a match and proceeded to draw smoke into his mouth. The burning tobacco hissed as he watched Will through the haze.

"And you don't know what to do especially as you've been spending every spare minute trying to work out how to end your life."

Will blinked. Gillies struck another match, sucked at the pipe once more and then pointed the stem in Will's direction.

"Thing is, I'm not sure you're even ready to leave here."

Will looked down at the back of his hands. "But you said that was going to be my last operation."

Gillies waved a hand dismissively. "That's not what I was talking about, old chap. Your face is going to be as good as I can get it. I grant you that it's still a mess by normal standards, but it's a damn sight better than it was. Even you would admit that. No. It's nothing physical, Will. It's something else. Look, you're full of anger. Full of it! If someone said the wrong thing to you at the wrong time, you sure you'd be able to stop yourself from striking him? No. No. You're best off here for the moment."

"If I was full of anger, sir, I'd be over that desk right now, punching you in the face for patronising me again... Sir."

Gillies smiled. "Touché."

Will thought for a moment. "That's what I said to that Scottish nurse the other week. Do you discuss my case with her, sir?"

Gillies shrugged. "She's part of my medical team. I discuss all my patients with the relevant staff. Why?"

"No reason, sir. Just that she suddenly appeared from nowhere, spent hours of her time on me, then two days ago she just disappeared."

Gillies blinked at that. "What do you mean, 'disappeared'?"

"She hasn't been to see me since the day before yesterday. Normally I have to put up with her 'bonnie' this and 'bonnie' that morning, noon and night."

Gillies reached for the telephone receiver and asked for another extension. "Amelia? Yes, I know it's late. Colour Sergeant Hammond has just told me that your Scottish nurse, Mc–something or other, has disappeared? That right? Oh. No, no, there was no reason to tell me. Thank you, Sister. Yes, yes, I do realise you're only a corridor away and that there's no need for me to shout."

He put the receiver back in its hook. "Apparently her grandmother has been taken ill and she's rushed off home. And apparently also the scheduling of nursing staff is nothing to do with me."

He studied Will closely, put down his pipe and came round the desk, gripping his jaw in the possessive manner that only a surgeon could assume.

"You can see me, can't you, Will? You haven't had blurred vision for the duration of this meeting."

He grabbed a magnifying glass from the chaos of his desktop and peered into both eyes in turn. "Well, well, well. Is it like this in full daylight too? What can you see? I need to write this up for my colleagues at the Craiglockhart hospital. Goodness me!"

He grabbed a notebook from the corner of his desk and started to scribble, firing questions at the Colour Sergeant as he did so. As Will responded a corner of Gillies' mind still considered why his admissions staff nurse had disappeared and where she had gone. Amelia had been less than forthcoming on the matter. What had those two been planning behind his back?

CHAPTER SIXTY-TWO

MONDAY 25TH MARCH 1918
Étaples Army Camp, France

It took Colonel Scott over an hour to find his way round the base to the empty hut that should have housed Aila and her maid. He slammed the door on the empty room and then, to his relief, caught sight of Sergeant Major Trubshaw striding towards him. He grunted in irritation. "I thought you were keeping an eye on the ladies, Sarn't Major."

"I was, sir, yes, but Miss Aila wanted to be taken to have a look at one of the hospitals and while she and Nurse Brown were in there nattering away to the matron, there was a new intake of wounded. Next thing I saw was Miss Aila with a nurse's apron on rushing around inspecting wounds and telling orderlies where to take the men. She said it was called tria... something or other. And then Nurse Brown disappeared into one of them operating theatres to assist. That was three hours ago."

Scott sighed. "The Court Martial starts tomorrow, nine ack emma at GHQ. That's an hour's journey away in Montreuil–sur–Mer and I need to talk to her first. Can you find her?"

Trubshaw grimaced again. "I know where she is, sir. Um, sir?"

Scott raised an eyebrow.

"It might come better from you, sir."

Ten minutes later Scott was standing near the entrance to the General Base Hospital tent – marquee would have been a better description – watching the groaning mass of bodies being sorted into a semblance of order. The elegant figure of Staff Nurse Aila Smythe was the still eye at the centre of this storm. Scott watched in admiration as she examined wounds, directed orderlies and comforted men. It was all done with a degree of calm, caring efficiency that was a pleasure to watch. After half an hour the flow of new arrivals dried up and the movement of bodies into wards was completed. Aila was left supervising the sterilising of gurneys and the washing of floors, grabbing a mop herself to encourage the tired orderlies and cleaners. He watched as she straightened up to ease her back and rub her hip.

"Miss Aila?"

She glanced up, smiled, and walked towards him. "Colonel Scott. How good of you to come and find me. Do we have a time yet for the start of the court martial?"

He bowed and led her towards a chair. "We do indeed, Miss Ai..."

She raised a hand. "Colonel, do you address my cousin as Lady Amelia?" He shook his head. She smiled at him. "I didn't think you did, so I would be grateful if I could just be Aila, please. And whether you like it or not I am going to call you Iain. In fact as I have had to put up with Amelia rambling on about 'Iain this' and 'Iain that' for the last three months I really don't care if you do object to the familiarity."

He smiled back at her. So, Amelia had rambled on about him, had she?

"Aila it will be. Yes, we do, and it's at nine o'clock tomorrow morning at GHQ in Montreuil–sur–Mer so you will need to leave here at seven to be sure of arriving on time. The roads are often blocked. Now, may we discuss the plan?"

She nodded, serious again. "The wonderful Sergeant Major Trubshaw has my papers."

She indicated the NCO standing under a tent flap, holding a file and watching them. "Have you received the sworn deposition from Colour Sergeant Hammond?"

The Colonel produced his own briefcase and glanced at the approaching soldier.

"Any chance you can commandeer a table for us, S'arnt Major?"

Within minutes they were seated at a slightly damp, slightly blood-stained table laying out pages and considering the task ahead.

* * *

The hammering at the door woke both Maisie and Aila at the same instant. Maisie ran to open it as Aila struck a safety match, lit the lantern and checked her watch. Three thirty-eight in the morning. The hint of lightening in the sky silhouetted the anxious orderly.

"Sorry, Miss, but there's a train load of wounded just arriving from the front and Matron asks if you could spare an hour or so to help?"

They scrambled for their clothes. Maisie just had enough time to smile at the realisation that Aila was now able to tie her own shoelaces before they scurried down the path in the bitter cold.

* * *

TUESDAY 26TH MARCH 1918
GHQ, Montreuil–sur–Mer, France

Colonel Scott woke at his normal hour of six a.m. and allowed himself the luxury of five minutes of lingering in his bed while he considered the information that Amelia Burkett–Smythe had been 'rambling on about Iain this and Iain that.' A tap at the door announcing the arrival of his early morning cup of tea interrupted his reverie. As Jenks pulled back the curtains the sight of his Number One uniform hanging in front of the wardrobe sobered him. It was far from certain that Major Smythe would be found guilty. The only strong evidence was the order sent to the French Commandant in charge of the 75s. If Smythe could wriggle his way out of that, his case would come crashing down.

And all that he had learned of Field Courts Martial did little to reassure him. Too many stories of bored officers curtailing evidence and sentencing men to the most extreme penalties having paid little attention to witnesses and argument. The trial would probably not last more than a day and the bias would always be towards the officer class. He stropped his cutthroat razor and wondered again about Aila's revelations of her half–brother's past behaviour and her insistence that she take the stand as a character witness. Why was that so important? He lathered his jaw and peered in the smeared mirror. Concentrate now. No nicks or cuts today.

* * *

TUESDAY 26TH MARCH 1918
Étaples Army Camp, France

It was two trainloads, not one. Every hospital at the camp was receiving its allocation. Aila dismissed all thoughts of the court martial from her mind and concentrated on organising the orderlies and nurses under her command reflecting that she was becoming as domineering as her grandmother. She groaned at the lack of organisation.

"Proper paperwork is essential, Nurse. Essential. If you don't have a record of who this man is and which regiment he is from, how is the army going to be able to inform the hospital in England of the history of his case, let alone tell his mother or his sweetheart that he is alive?" She patted the soldier on the shoulder. "And that, after his operation, he's going to as good as new."

An eye opened in the white face beneath her. "Depends which sweetheart you mean, mind, Sister. Got to be careful there."

She shook her head, smiling, as the laughter followed her down the reception ward.

And in what seemed like a matter of minutes, the wounded men were sorted, categorised, their notes completed and she could sit back, absentmindedly wiping blood from the table top and wondering if it was time for breakfast.

"Miss Aila! Miss Aila, look at the time."

A bloodstained Maisie was hurrying through the beds towards her. Aila pulled her watch out of the pocket of her tunic and yelped. Eight o'clock already. She grabbed Maisie's hand and they ran back up the path to search for the staff car and driver. Aila stared round wildly. Where? Where? Oh no. Maisie squeezed her hand. "Look, Miss Aila."

She pointed down the hill at an ambulance being cleaned by an orderly outside the hospital tent.

"I bet you can drive it Miss. It's just like your father's Rolls Royce."

CHAPTER SIXTY-THREE

MONDAY 25TH MARCH 1918
Queen's Hospital, Sidcup

He could see now. Maybe not quite as well as he had done before he was shot, but well enough. He hadn't had what he termed a blurring session all day either. It was a pity that Nurse McBride had disappeared. He'd have been interested to see if her face was as gentle and attractive as her voice.

He jumped down into the deep pit beneath the fallen tree and stared round at the muddy walls, patting each side, remembering the sheer effort he had put into digging it out; the blistered palms, the sore back, the bramble torn forearms. He pulled the spade out from its hiding place and leaned on its handle. He liked it here. Here he could think without the distractions of a horse or of a kind nurse, or of memories of Miss Aila whom he loved now as passionately as he had ever done. "Aila Smythe... Aila Hammond." He glanced round, realising he had spoken aloud. He came to his feet, staring at the walls of what he had built to be his grave. A slant of moonlight touched the edge of the pit and he looked up into the night sky.

Death, his friend death, was the meaning of this place. It was why he had moved the fallen tree to the edge of the hole where the slightest jerk would bring it down on him, trapping him into eternity. A cloud passed over the moon, the sky darkening to black, revealing the uncountable number of stars in the galaxy revolving above his head. He stood and turned round in a slow circle, his eyes still raised to the night sky. And the moon reappeared. And the stars faded. And the world still turned. And he had no fear of death. The pain that would come before death could be no worse than the pain he had endured over the length of his endless operations. And everything that he knew about death welcomed him. What had life got to offer him now? He leaned back against the wall of his grave, still thinking. Well... Now he could see again. Now, if he wanted, he could go back to his regiment, back to the madness and the killing.

A month ago, that had been a hope beyond hope, but now? Now, he had the offer of a job. And not just any job; a job he could scarce have dreamt of before the war. He seated himself back on the spade and let his mind drift where it would. There was no one here to make his decision for him. No doctor to tell him that he wasn't ready to leave; no commanding officer to offer him understanding; no nurse to tell him he should choose to live; no mother to cry over him; no Miss Aila to love and be loved by in return. He leaned back against the damp earth and watched the moon sail high above the shredded clouds. And the world still turned. And he knew that he had found his peace, here in this grave he had dug for himself. His eyes closed. He slept.

* * *

It was the snort of a surprised vixen that woke him. He opened his eyes. She was watching him from the far side of his pit, not five feet away. She wasn't spooked, just cautiously interested. Will's spoke quietly. "Morning, Missus. I'm not ready to be eaten yet. Sorry about that, but you'll need to look elsewhere for your cubs' breakfast."

He watched the intelligence in the vixen's eyes as she listened, her ears cocked forward until, with a swish of her brush, she turned and trotted away. He stood, easing the crick in his back and staring down at the bandages from his jaw lying in the mud beneath his feet. When had he taken them off? He touched his chin, running the fingers over the ridges of flesh, familiarising himself with the contours of his new face. And it sank in. He had made his decision.

He pulled himself up out of the pit and kicked at the base of the fallen tree. It creaked and with a slithering rush spilled down into the pit, wholly obscuring its existence. It would have worked then. He smiled sourly, feeling again how the skin stretched over his operation scars as he did so.

"Not angry now, Doctor Gillies. Not angry at all. I got a job to go to."

Sod 'em all if they laughed at him behind his back, or worse, if they felt pity. He put the spade back in the gardener's bothy and headed for his room. Today he would try and get into one of the bathrooms and shave whatever part of his face he could find hair on. Then find a clean uniform, the one he was in smelt distinctly agricultural. He sniffed at his armpit. Maybe it was the person beneath the uniform too. He wondered if he should do what Mr Chant suggested and use Major Gillies' telephone to tell him he would take the job. He'd never used one of course, but somehow it felt right.

The bushes shook, separated and the half-frozen orderly peered out. He beat his arms against his chest and stared down at the tree filled hole. That Staff Nurse Smythe had certainly made him work for his money. He yawned and ran in the direction of warmth and food.

CHAPTER SIXTY-FOUR

TUESDAY 25TH MARCH 1918
GHQ, Montreuil–sur–Mer, France

Where the hell was Aila bloody Smythe? Colonel Scott ceased his pacing and looked at his watch for the umpteenth time. Eight forty-five. What the devil had happened? He shaded his eyes to peer up the road through the drizzle to see if Trubshaw was waving to indicate good news, but the massive figure could have been carved from stone for all the movement he made. With a clenched, "bloody hell" of frustrated anger he indicated to the Sergeant Major that he should return to guard the witnesses, turned on his heel and strode into the hall.

* * *

"What's the time, Maisie?"

Maisie peered at her mistress's watch. "It's fifteen minutes before nine, Miss Aila."

"Hell and damnation! How much further?"

"The man we asked back there said it was only a few miles. If we can just get beyond this group of men, we could probably see it from the brow of this hill."

Aila relaxed her hold a minute amount and smiled. "It's a company, Maisie, not a group. A company of soldiers, or a platoon, or a brigade, or... well, it's definitely not a group!" The worry returned. "Use the Klaxon again, will you. They should move out of our way. After all we are in an ambulance."

Maisie pressed the horn. The sergeant marching alongside the company glanced back and bellowed an order. With a sigh of relief Aila watched the men move into the edge of the road and she accelerated past waving her thanks at them and praying there would be no more troops between the car and Montreuil–sur–Mer. But even as she prayed the car touched the edge of the rough road. There was a sudden explosion and the steering wheel jumped in her hands. It took her a matter of seconds to realise that it was a flat tyre. She wept in frustration and hammered the palms of her hands on the steering wheel. Maisie flicked a glance at her mistress, jumped out of the car and ran back towards the troops marching up the hill, waving her arms at them frantically.

* * *

Colonel Scott completed the rearrangement of his paperwork and looked up at the rapidly filling hall. Major Dudley Smythe had arrived looking serenely confident, his fleshy jowls freshly shaved, his uniform pressed, his boots gleaming. Scott opened the lid of his watch, shrugged off his concerns about the non–arrival of Aila and stared at the second hand. Two minutes to nine. One minute. He raised an eyebrow in Trubshaw's direction and the NCO slipped out of the room as unobtrusively as a fifteen stone, six-foot five-inch man could.

A throat was cleared in front of him. Scott glanced up to see the seedy looking Adjutant standing in front of his desk.

"I'm acting as Prisoner's Friend, Colonel, although of course Major Smythe is not a prisoner in any sense of the word. There's still time for you to withdraw these charges. You must recognise that you haven't got any evidence."

Scott tilted his chair back and drummed his fingers on the tabletop. He spoke clearly and loudly enough for half the room to hear.

"You know I find being in the presence of scoundrels brings me out in a rash. Aaah. The first group of my witnesses has arrived. Excuse me."

He pushed past the shocked officer and guided the young gunner, the lance bombardier who had been Sir Alastair McDonald's soldier servant, and Trubshaw, to three reserved seats. Two tough looking military policemen stationed themselves behind the fourth chair in which was now seated the manacled and once smelly bully with the badly broken nose and plastered hand.

Urgent whispering emanated from Smythe's coterie. Even as his Adjutant stepped forward, the Corporal of the Guard called the Field General Court Martial to attention and the two presiding Generals and three Colonels entered. Scott stepped back behind his desk, trying to assess the quality of the panel. One of the two Generals had the high colour and gooseberry eyes of the true huntin' shootin' 'n fishin' country gentleman. And the others? Brighter definitely, but of an identical class to the defendant. He risked a quick glance in Dudley's direction. The blotchy face had become blotchier while his entourage were making infinitesimal body movements, distancing themselves from their leader.

The room remained at attention as the Court Martial Officer proceeded with the formalities. He flicked a glance in Dudley's direction and began to read the charges.

"Major, the Honourable Dudley Alfred Smythe you stand charged on one count of behaving in a scandalous manner unbecoming to the character of an officer and a gentleman, one count of assisting the enemy and one count of cowardice. How do you plead?"

Smythe's pompous voice echoed round the room. "Not guilty on my honour. Not guilty. This is a travesty and an insult to..."

The Court Martial Officer raised his hand, removed his spectacles, stared at Smythe in amazement at this outburst, then nodded at the seated Adjutant. "You are the Prisoner's Friend are you not, Captain?"

The Adjutant stood and cleared his throat. "I am, sir."

"Perhaps you have not informed Major Smythe of the process of a Field General Court Martial. Major Smythe will have a chance to respond to these accusations at the appropriate juncture."

Scott was not alone in hearing the sotto voce exchange between the huntin' shootin' n' fishin' General and one of his fellows on the panel. "Chap's got a right to be annoyed though, what? Blackening his family name before the whole damn world. Eh? Eh?"

He harrumphed into silence. The Court Martial Officer glanced in Scott's direction. "Colonel Scott?"

He took a deep breath and stood. And once he was on his feet all the nerves dropped away and the structure that

Aila had proposed made complete sense. This was no more difficult than presenting strategy to a Staff planning meeting. He lifted his papers and approached the panel.

"If I may, sir? In order to demonstrate the veracity of the accusations of assisting the enemy and cowardice, I would produce my initial evidence in the form of a letter written by a Colour Sergeant under my command who had been in the trenches with me for over three years and had already been awarded the DCM and an MM and has, for actions on the morning of the misdirected barrage, been awarded the Victoria Cross. First, however, I shall explain the immediate circumstances that led to this letter being sent to me."

He stepped back to his table and recounted in detail the story of the shelling, his discovery that Hammond was still alive and the visit he had made to his hospital. It took him almost an hour. He reached for another file, clicked his fingers at Jenks and took a sip of water.

"There is, gentlemen, one more piece of paper which does, I believe confirm the second accusation – that of 'Assisting the Enemy'. I have here..." He passed six pieces of paper to the Court Martial Officer. "... a somewhat crumpled original and five certified copies of the order sent by Major Smythe to a battery of French 75s located at..."

He turned to where Jenks had pinned the detailed map and tapped it with his pointer.

"You will note from the order that the co-ordinates provided by Major Smythe are not the German lines or their reserve trenches as requested by Divisional HQ. The co-ordinates on the order signed by Major Smythe, were, in fact, of the trenches of the First Northants where I had the privilege to be the officer in command."

It took him a further half hour to demonstrate his case using detailed maps, pins and a pointer.

"The French Commandant has also provided a sworn affidavit that this was the order he received, and I have here the copy of the request he sent back asking for confirmation. It is beyond doubt that the giving of this order directly resulted in the deaths of one hundred and thirty-two men of my regiment on the morning of the German advance."

He paused, took another sip of water from the glass on his table, and studied the panel. The huntin' member was heading towards what was probably his normal late morning snooze. Scott cleared his throat loudly. The General jerked back to wakefulness.

"The final charge is of behaving in a scandalous manner unbecoming to the character of an officer and a gentleman. I have a wealth of evidence to attest to this, plus a large number of witnesses to this behaviour over a number of years."

He glanced at the door. God, Aila where are you? The General in command of the panel leaned forward and studied Scott through his monocle. Scott realised that he was being assessed.

"Very well, Colonel Scott, it being twelve we will pause here for luncheon and then return to hear the remainder of your evidence at one fifteen."

Scott stepped outside and peered up the road towards Étaples once more, but some kind of massive hold up in the far distance caused by what looked like a broken-down ambulance meant that it was impossible to see if Aila was anywhere in sight. He walked back into the courtroom.

CHAPTER SIXTY-FIVE

TUESDAY 25TH MARCH 1918
Queen's Hospital, Sidcup

The phone rang and Amelia picked the receiver off its arm. "This is Sister Amelia Burkett–Smythe speaking to you."

Will watched and waited. She glanced up at him. "They're making the connection to your vet. Ah. Yes, he is here."

She held out the phone receiver and indicated where he should speak. Will nodded his thanks.

"Mr Chant? Are you there, Mr Chant?"

A crackle and a distant high–pitched whine came through the receiver to him and then he heard the vet as clear as is he had been standing in the room.

"... your mind if you're going to come and join me, Will?"

"Yes, Mr Chant. I shall come."

He heard the delighted laugh. "Good lad. Good lad. I shall write you a letter to give you all the details."

Will realised he was thanking an empty line. He shook his head in bemusement and handed the telephone back to the sister.

CHAPTER SIXTY-SIX

TUESDAY 25TH MARCH 1918
GHQ, Montreuil–sur–Mer, France
1:30pm

"Colonel Scott, will it take long to produce the rest of your evidence?"

The hostility from the senior officer on the panel was visceral.

"No, sir."

"Very well. You have fifteen minutes."

So this is how it went. He looked at Smythe. The man was almost laughing.

"Thank you, sir. I wish to demonstrate that the actions of Major Smythe on the night of the misdirected barrage were not a sudden demonstration of aberrant behaviour but part of a long-held plan to destroy the life of Colour Sergeant Will Hammond. I would now like to call Farrier Sergeant Major Trubshaw to the stand to testify."

The huntin' General snapped out of his reverie.

"What? What? T'isn't right that Other Ranks should be allowed to give evidence against an officer."

The Court Martial Officer leaned across the panel's table and spoke quietly but forcefully for thirty seconds. The harrumphing died away to silence. The Sergeant Major marched to the stand, saluted the panel and took the oath.

He was an impressive witness in every way. In a court room full of soldiers, Scott knew he had no need to make anything of the Military Medal and campaign ribbons. The panel would all know that this was a respected professional.

His testimony about his trip to Stanwood was terse but damning. Scott glanced at his hunter watch, open on the table in front of him. Seven minutes gone. Still no sign of Aila. He gritted his teeth, pushed the sworn deposition from the man he referred to internally as Mr Smelly to one side and summoned him to take the oath.

He was a dreadful witness, too stupid to be coherent, too frightened to be believable. After two minutes during which he had, at least, incriminated Smythe for being responsible for Trubshaw's beating and indicated that it was the Adjutant who had ordered him to go to Stanwood, Scott told him to stand down and called the Adjutant himself to the stand wondering if the Court Martial Officer would stop him. He glanced in his direction and was surprised to see the suspicion of a nod. He hardly dared look at his watch.

"Captain, could you please confirm that you gave the order to the last witness to go to the village of Stanwood."

The Adjutant stumbled over his reply. Scott pressed home his advantage. "And what, Captain, was the purpose of this order?"

"Er, Major Smythe had acquired some property in his village and he asked me as a favour to find someone to go and check on the state of the property of one of the tenants to make sure they were fulfilling their side of the contract."

"And that man was the previous witness, Captain?"

A nervous nod.

"And his official position was as a...?"

"I don't understand."

Scott sighed loudly. "I have a sworn deposition here from Colour Sergeant Hammond's parents, who are the tenants of the house in Stanwood, to the effect that the previous witness informed them that they were in arrears on their rent and that their landlord was going to evict them. He also informed them that he was a bailiff."

The Adjutant stumbled through an even more unconvincing answer. Scott dismissed him with a flick of his wrist. He stared at his papers. Bloody Aila, bloody Smythe. Without her testimony... The chairman of the panel cleared his throat.

"Whilst I am informed by the Court Martial Officer that enlisted men should be allowed to give evidence against officers, I have to say that it is not a course of which I can wholeheartedly approve and in any event the information from the witnesses you have called seems to have little bearing on this case."

Scott bowed his head. He had failed; failed Will, failed his own General, failed to bring a case against a vile and cowardly man whom he knew had killed for pleasure as well as for personal gain. He straightened his shoulders.

"I apologise for my inadequate presentation, sir, I had been expecting to be able to present a final witness to the court, but..."

The General shook his head. "Too late, Colonel. You have had your chance. Now, if the... What the devil is going on back there?"

Two young dishevelled nurses, bloodstained aprons over their uniforms, had pushed their way into the back of the court. The taller of two limped her way forward, curtsied gracefully to the panel and spoke in a perfectly modulated, aristocratic voice.

"I do humbly apologise, sir, and I would be most grateful if the court would indulge me for one moment. I am the witness that Colonel Scott was expecting to be able to present. I was due here at nine o'clock this morning, but in the middle of last night I was asked by the Matron at Number 24 General Base Hospital at Étaples to assist with a sudden influx of wounded men from the front line as I have experience in the analysis of complex wounds. To compound this delay, the vehicle I was driving from Étaples to Montreuil burst a tyre and broke an axle and that is why I am so late attending your court. But please forgive me, General, I intended no disrespect to you, your colleagues on the panel, or to this court, no disrespect at all."

She swayed on her feet. Maisie ran forward to help her and under Iain Scott's guidance she was led to the witness chair and seated. The background mutterings from Dudley Smythe burst out into a full-blooded roar of fury.

"What the hell is going on here? How dare you bring that... that bitch into this courtroom? She is a disgrace to my family."

He was on his feet, pushing aside the Adjutant who was making a desperate attempt to tug him back by his belt. Scott turned to face him, but even as he went to step forward, he felt a kick on the back of his ankle. He glanced round as Aila stood, moving him to one side, facing her half-brother showing no hint of fear. He raised his fist to strike her as she lifted her jaw and stared him straight in the eye. He hesitated for a second and Sergeant Major Trubshaw's hand caught his forearm. Dudley's whole body rocked as the grip tightened. Trubshaw released the arm, saluted the panel and marched back to his seat.

The silence was palpable. Dudley stared about him wild eyed, then stumbled to his seat. The panel president breathed out. "Colonel Scott, in the light of the arrival of your witness I am prepared to extend the length of time allocated to the prosecution of this case. Kindly inform the court of your witness's full identity."

The Colonel bowed his head and raised his right hand, palm sideways, towards Aila. She nodded and addressed the panel. "My name, sir, is Miss Aila Smythe and I am half-sister to Major Dudley Smythe. The man to whom I was expected to be married, Captain Sir Alastair McDonald, was killed in what I understand has been termed the 'misdirected barrage'."

Scott watched the panel. Postprandial snoozing was now a thing of the distant past. They sat forward watching the witness in fascination. He raised his right hand again. "Perhaps, Staff Nurse Smythe, you would be so good as to inform the court of your knowledge of the background to this dreadful event."

Aila bowed her head. "Colonel Scott has informed me of the case he has presented to you, gentlemen. I am here to confirm that not only do I believe my half-brother to be more than capable of committing such a heinous act, but to confirm that he has committed similar attacks in the past including one on me and one on the life of Colour Sergeant Hammond."

She cleared her throat, took a sip of water and started her story with the day of her fall from her horse, the day

Will Hammond carried her home, the day he was dismissed by her half-brother. She paused, rested her chin on her hand for a moment her eyes gazing abstractedly at the floor, then spoke once more.

"The strange thing about my fall from the horse during the hunt was that I had retained disconnected memories of other riders nearby when it happened. After nearly four months when I was able to walk using sticks, I went to visit Will Hammond and thank him. On the night of my fall, my horse had apparently become entangled in a coppiced tree and had received a terrible gash on its face. Mr Hammond told me that this was unusual – strange. Even more strange was his discovery of my half-brother's blood-stained riding crop at the place where my horse was found."

Scott had never thought that he would hear a communal gasp from a room of professional soldiers. Aila shook her head and continued. "I made my father aware of this and it shocked him deeply. It was as a direct result of this that Dudley was ordered by my father to join the Northamptonshire regiment. Within weeks he had transferred to the Royal Horse Artillery."

She looked up at the panel president, tears running down her pale cheeks. "It is me who is guilty, sir. It is me. I was the cause of Colour Sergeant Hammond losing his job as a ploughman, then being beaten by my half-brother's thugs. Finally, sir, I am guilty of causing the death of the gentleman who had been courting me together with the deaths of one hundred and thirty-two British soldiers and the destruction of Colour Sergeant Hammond's face. All this happened because my half-brother wanted me dead or at the very least to ensure that there was no chance of any issue from me that could possibly interfere with his inheritance."

She raised her bloodstained apron to her face and wept in silence. Iain Scott glanced at Maisie, indicating with his head that she should come to Aila's aid. Maisie helped Aila to her feet and led her to a seat at the back of the courtroom with her arm wrapped round her. Scott returned to his table and looked across at the panel president. "The prosecution has further witnesses to very recent behaviour by the defendant should you wish to hear them, sir."

He indicated the three soldiers sitting beside Trubshaw. The General studied the men. "I do not believe that will be necessary, Colonel."

He stared across the floor at Smythe and spoke to his Adjutant. "Do you wish to start the defence, Captain?"

The Adjutant came to his feet. He was shaking. "No, sir, I do not. I was not aware of any of this information, and I would now be more than happy to add my knowledge of other events and facts."

Dudley glared at him, his face pale with fury and fear. He opened his mouth, stuttered, and went silent once more. The panel president watched him. "I think, given the circumstances, Major Smythe, that silence would be your best option. The panel will now adjourn to consider its verdict."

He stood as the room came to attention. "Corporal of the guard?"

A military policeman stamped his boots. "Sah?"

The president pointed at Dudley. "Two men, Corporal."

"Sah."

As the panel left the room, a buzz of awed whispering broke the silence. Iain Scott seated himself behind his table, shuffling his papers into some semblance of order. Thanks to Aila – and bless her for what she had done – his case had been made. He looked over to where she sat, Maisie's arm still wrapped round her, staring at the floor, lost in thought. He had better tell Amelia about this now. He pulled a clean piece of paper towards him and started to write.

'My dearest Amelia,

Your cousin Aila has behaved in the most exemplary manner at this court martial. I do hope that it has not taken too much out of her. She looks dreadfully ill and I am deeply relieved that her Maisie Brown is with her.

Everyone is right about Maisie. She is a saint...

The doors at the rear of the court opened, followed immediately by the roar of the Corporal of the Guard bringing the room to attention. Scott glanced at the still open hunter watch on his table. Less than fifteen minutes. Was that a good or a bad thing? The senior officers seated themselves and nodded to the Court Martial Officer. He went through the preliminaries. The panel president placed a finger on the pad of paper.

"The prisoner will stand." Dudley climbed to his feet. "On the counts of cowardice and assisting the enemy we do not accept that Major Smythe's behaviour demonstrated that he was deliberately assisting the enemy or that any cowardice was involved on his behalf."

Dudley started to smile. The general continued.

"However, a direct result of his behaviour was that one hundred and thirty-two men were killed purely so he could pursue a vendetta against a non-commissioned officer whose courage was a byword throughout his regiment."

He paused again. Scott realised his nails were biting into the palms of his hands. He forced himself to relax. The panel president resumed. "Thus, on the count of behaving in a scandalous manner unbecoming to the character of an officer and a gentleman we find Major Smythe guilty as charged. This decision was reached not solely on the evidence we have before us here, but also in sworn testimony provided by the defendant's father, the Right Honourable Lord Augustus Smythe. This testimony was made available to the Court Martial Officer on condition that it would only be opened and read if the court was minded to find against Major Smythe."

Scott glanced towards back of the court and caught Aila's eye. The Court Martial president continued.

"It is the sentence of this Field General Court Martial, therefore, that Major Smythe should be dishonourably discharged from his regiment and that the various sworn testimonies provided in evidence during Colonel Scott's prosecution should be handed to the civilian authorities for them to prosecute as they see fit. Finally, we wish to thank Colonel Scott for bringing this matter before the court and the concern he has shown for the men under his command."

He nodded in Scott's direction. The Colonel stood to attention and in the breathless hush that followed, the two MPs each grabbed one of Dudley's arms and all but lifted him out of the room.

CHAPTER SIXTY-SEVEN

THURSDAY 18TH APRIL 1918
The Queen's Hospital, Sidcup, Kent

So that was it: the remains of the worst two years of his life tucked into a half full kitbag. He looked round the bare room, picked up his tin cheek, peered in the mirror, fitted it, and stared at his reflection. His very own tin cheek, covering his very own shattered flesh and bone. He smiled and the symmetry of the face was ruined. How could this ever work? He shook his head, swung the kitbag onto his shoulder and closed the door behind him. But as he rounded the corner of the corridor outside Major Gillies' office his confident stride failed him. He stumbled to a halt, his kitbag falling to the floor. "I can't bloody do it."

The whisper of skirts made him look round half hoping it would be his gentle Scottish nurse. It was Sister Amelia.

"I think you've forgotten, Colour Sergeant, that three years in the trenches is a great deal more terrifying than walking out of a hospital. You can do this. You will do this."

She pushed his kitbag in his direction and led him by the hand towards Harold Gillies' office. "And Will, I have checked on the times of your train and made myself available to walk you to the station." She looked back over her shoulder. "Whether you like it or not."

She knocked on the door and entered without waiting, waving her hand at the pipe fug and rushing across to open the window. Harold Gillies looked up smiling.

"Morning Amelia. Morning Will. Let me have a final look." He pored over the scar tissue and nodded. "Some of my very best work, you know. Let's see how the tin cheek fits then."

He took it out of Amelia's hand and fitted it again, looping the thin elastic across the back of Will's head and stepping back to get the full effect. He nodded once more. "Damned good work, you know. Damned good. That chap Wood deserves a knighthood."

Will managed a one-sided smile beneath the tin. The Major's good humour was infectious.

"I just wanted to thank you, sir. And I wanted to say how sorry I am for all the trouble I caused you. And if anyone deserved a knighthood, sir, it's you for what you have done for all of us here."

Harold Gillies looked embarrassed. Amelia laughed. "Well, I can tell you, Will, it's a rare moment when Doctor Gillies is lost for words."

Gillies winked at Will. "Since she's been courting an officer, she's become unbearable you know."

"Hah! For your information, the officer is courting me, not the other way round. Now come along, Will, I don't want you to be late for your train."

Will held out his hand, uncertain of the protocol at such a juncture. The Major grasped it in both his and shook it vigorously. "You come back if you have any worries of any sort, Will, you hear? Oh. Wait just one second."

He ran round behind his desk, rummaged in a drawer and pulled out a small metal cross attached to a ribbon. He walked back to Will, holding the medal out in front of him.

"You may not want to wear this for yourself, Will, but I want you to wear it for all of us – all of us who work here or are patients here. We are all so proud of you."

He pinned the medal on to the broad chest in front of him and coughed, tears forming in his eyes. Amelia grabbed Will's hand and practically ran him to the door. "Come on, Will. We'll be late."

In the doorway, Will turned once more and looked back at the Major. "Thank you, sir. Thank you."

* * *

The station wasn't as empty as Will had hoped. There were a couple of consumptive commercial travellers and a farmer buttoned up in his best suit, now far too small for him. To his horror, a crocodile of school children arrived, two by two, hand in hand, led by a sweet faced, young female teacher. Amelia smiled at them and started chatting to the teacher. Will tried to pull away and turn his back, only to discover the strength in Amelia's hand and forearm as she held him rigid against her.

The children, attracted by the sight of a uniform, crowded round Will asking him where his rifle was, how many Germans he had killed and how long he had been in the trenches. Will wondered when the first child would notice his tin cheek, but it was another piece of tin that one of the children recognised. A young boy spoke from below his chest.

"Mister, that's a Victoria Cross that is. They give that to heroes they do. I saw a picture of one in my dad's Daily Express last week."

Almost immediately Will was wholly immersed in children.

"Are you a hero, mister?"

"What did you get the medal for, sir?"

"Did you go up in a flying machine, sir? I really want to do that."

Amelia clapped her hands and the children fell back into their lines as they recognised the voice of authority.

"Colour Sergeant Hammond is indeed a war hero, children, but, being a true hero, he doesn't like to talk about it. Very quickly now because your train will be here soon, he ran out into what they call No Man's Land to rescue one of his soldiers and carried him back to the trenches with the Germans shooting at him the whole way back. He got shot in the face at that time and hides the scars behind this tin plate."

Before he could stop her, Amelia lifted off the tin cheek. The children crowded round to examine the wound, exclaiming as Amelia showed where the bullet had gone in, and how his face had been re–built. Not one of the children showed the least inclination to vomit or be repulsed. To the contrary they were delighted with the whole experience, demanding that the tin cheek was taken off and put back on to satisfy their macabre fascination. And as their train pulled out, they hung out of the windows cheering Will for all they were worth. He seated himself on a milk churn and looked at Amelia from under his eyebrows. She shrugged a casual dismissal and leaned against the station sign.

"You knew those children would be here didn't you, Sister?"

She waved a hand airily. "I might have done, Will Hammond, I might have done."

He shook his head. "You take a lot for granted, Sister."

"It's my upbringing you see, Will. Daughters of earls are just plain naughty."

He grunted with amusement. "Should I call you My Lady, then?"

"Don't you dare!"

"Sister, your surname?"

"What about it?"

"Are you Burkett–Smythes related to a Lord Augustus Smythe?"

She bit the top of her thumb thinking fast, staring at him wrinkle browed. "Northamptonshire somewhere?"

He nodded.

"Some kind of cousin, I think. Why?"

He shrugged. "I met his daughter." He grunted again. "And his son."

She watched him closely, hoping she was showing none of the anxiety she felt. He glanced up and gave her one of those penetrating gazes she had seen from him so often. Yes, she really could see what Aila saw in him. He was a remarkable man.

"There's one other thing, Sister."

He held out an envelope to her. She glanced at the neat copper plate writing on the cover: Nurse McBride. He looked uncertain.

"It's not a love letter or anything stupid like that, Sister, but I thought Nurse McBride was somebody rather special and I wanted to thank her for what she did for me. I hope her grandmamma is well soon."

The train puffed in, tooting importantly. She stepped forward, hugged him, kissed him on his broken cheek and stepped back, surprised to find that she was crying as he swung himself up into a third-class carriage, giving her a quick salute as he sat down.

CHAPTER SIXTY-EIGHT

WEDNESDAY 5TH MAY 1918
Stanwood House

The weeping wound of the bullet hole in the soldier's cheek was huge, distorting his face, growing and growing. He was laughing now, a hyena like braying right there on the edge of hysteria. She reached out to touch the hole with her fingers, to show him she cared, and her fingers went through and in and in and in. Then her hand, her arm. She screamed and screamed again. And Maisie was there, holding her close, rocking her in her arms whispering to her.

"Shhh, Miss Aila. Shhh. It's only one of your nightmares. I'm here now. I'm here."

She took a deep shaking breath and regained control. "I'm sorry, Maisie. I'm so sorry. I didn't mean to scream."

"Don't be silly, Miss Aila. You know I don't mind. Which dream was it, anyway? Judging by the noise it had to be the one about you putting your fingers in the bullet hole under the soldier's eye."

Aila shuddered and nodded, gulping back tears. A half-expected knock on the door and Maisie jumped from the bed, hurrying to answer it.

"That'll be your grandmamma."

She opened the door and curtsied as the old woman walked straight in tapping her stick, her hair hanging down in a neat plait over her dressing gown. Maisie smoothed the eiderdown for her to sit on her grandchild's bed and watched as she reached across and stroked Aila's cheek.

"Well that, my dear wee granddaughter, is that. Your father and I talked through the telephone this afternoon and agreed that if you had one more nightmare, we were going to pack you off to the south of France with Maisie Brown here, where you will have what is called a holiday."

Aila opened her mouth to object, but the grand–maternal finger pressed against her lips. "Silence, child. This isn't a suggestion. It's an order. Your father and I will start making the arrangements tomorrow."

Aila removed the finger from her mouth. "Grandmamma, Cousin Amelia is still working at the Queen's Hospital. All the other nurses who shared Maisie's dormitory are still there. I cannot be the only one who is too weak to continue. It's my duty to go back and help."

Lady McBride shook her head. "My dear, your beloved Dr Gillies sent me a letter earlier this week saying that you had done the work of three people while you were there and that he would lock you in the cupboard in his office if he saw so much as the tip of your nose peeping round a corner. You are going to recover your health, child. No more argument."

She turned to include Maisie in the conversation. "And you, young lady, will be in charge of the money. From what I have seen, your mistress can't tell a penny from a florin, let alone a French franc from a pound note."

She held out her hand to Maisie and pulled her down on to the bed beside her. "Aila, child, you have exhausted yourself. You do understand what you have done to yourself don't you? The battle with your brother, your battle to stop your marriage, Alastair's death, your illness, Dudley's court martial, your nursing. Maisie has told me some of what you both had to witness at that hospital. Your war is over now, Aila. If you want to get beyond the age of thirty it's time to rebuild your strength."

But it still took four weeks to arrange the trip.

CHAPTER SIXTY-NINE

22ND JULY 1918
Cannes, France

"Miss Aila your hip isn't going to get better if you keep rushing up and down the cross–it at this speed."

"For the hundredth time, Maisie, it's the Croisette, not the cross–it."

Maisie wrinkled her nose. "Well, if we'd stayed in Nice – and they can't even pronounce that right – we'd have been walking along the Promenade des Anglais and at least I know what that means."

Aila walked on, smiling. "Well, I'm sorry to tell you, dear, that I much prefer the Carlton Hotel here in Cannes to the Grand in Nice, whether Queen Victoria stayed there or not. There aren't so many of those pushy French officers on leave from the Front here. I mean they wouldn't leave us alone for a minute."

Maisie looked as innocent as she could. "I know, Miss Aila. I hated every second of it."

Aila stopped dead and rounded on her maid. "Maisie Brown, you should be ashamed of yourself."

"Oh, but I am, Miss Aila. I truly am."

"Hah! I knew I should have come here alone wearing mourning dress. That way I'd have been left well alone and wouldn't have had to put up with your lewd, lascivious and licentious behaviour. Now come along or we'll be late for luncheon."

Maisie laughed in delight. She'd never been called lascivious before, let alone lewd or licentious. As they walked into the hotel foyer, she studied her mistress out of the corner of her eye. Her colour had come back, her face had filled out again, the dark rings under her eyes had gone, her limp was scarcely noticeable. Maisie sighed with relief. No wonder all those French officers had swarmed round them – bees round a honey pot as her older sister would have said.

"I know you're looking at me, Maisie Brown. What is all the sighing about?" She slipped her arm through her maid's and dragged her towards the dining room. "Come on Miss Lascivious, I'm starving after all that rushing around on the cross–it."

The Maître d' hurried across to find them a table, ignoring the outraged family of a wealthy banker. Waiters pulled out their chairs for them, the sommelier was bowing beside them ready to recommend his favourite Provence Rosé and all the limitless spécialités–de–la–maison were offered to them on silver platters. There were times, Aila considered, when it was almost impossible to remember that the war–to–end–all–wars was being fought out in the filthy trenches of Flanders. She opened her bag and passed a letter across the table to Maisie.

"It's from my grandmamma, bringing news of the village. Will Hammond has opened a branch of Mr Chant's veterinary practice in the village. He's training a couple of young lads."

Maisie glanced at the letter and raised her eyes to watch her mistress who was picking at the bread on her side plate.

"I don't know what I'll say to him, Maisie. I don't even know if I can face him."

Maisie shook her head and straightened her lips into a firm line. "Yes, you do, Miss Aila. You will see him. And if you don't, I'll go myself and tell him the woman who saved his life and who loves him is too scared to meet him. Honestly, Miss Aila!"

Aila's head went down. "But I don't even know if he loves me, Maisie."

Maisie snorted then reached across the table and squeezed the back of Aila's hand. "Miss Aila? I know you think I'm just a simple country girl and I don't have much idea about anything..."

Aila shook her head, her eyes half closed. "No, no, no, Maisie."

"Will you let me finish, Miss Aila! I am quite simple really." She smiled. "I mean as a fr'instance I used to tell myself a bedtime story every night." She laughed and covered her face with her hands. "I'd pretend that you were my older sister and that we'd have lots of adventures. And guess what? I may not be your sister, but we certainly have had lots of adventures. Look at what we've done. Look at the places we've been to, the men we've cared for in the hospital, the people we've met like the wonderful Dr Gillies, the Queen, those generals on the court martial panel."

She paused then looked Aila straight in the eye. "But there's one thing I'm not simple about, Miss Aila, and that's men. I know more about them than you do. Much, much more. Why do you think I've never let one get near me?"

She answered her own question. "Because I know what they're like. I knew from when I was just thirteen, when my dad... Well, that's why I came to Stanwood House. And then when I met you and you were so kind to me. And I felt safe for the first time in a year. And I promised myself I would never leave you." She tossed her head, making Aila smile for the first time. "And I won't unless you throw me out. I mean I'd even have gone to Scotland with you."

That made them both laugh. Aila tilted her head in turn. "Oh, Maisie. What am I to do with you? You're not my maid. I mean you have been, but you've been so much more. You're my closest friend, my confidante, my nurse, my life saver. And why have you never said anything to me before about your father? Does anyone else know?"

Maisie shrugged. "Mr Livens knows. I didn't want to tell you because I didn't want you to feel sorry for me or feel obliged to help me." She frowned severely. "Now, Miss Aila we're getting off the subject." The lobster bisque arrived. "The point is, Miss Aila, that you've met the man you love."

Aila went to speak, but Maisie just waved her spoon at her. "No, Miss Aila. When you first met him, I knew you were attracted to him. And he's handsome. And he's a real man. And he's gentle, not a big show off. And he's special."

She sipped at her soup again. "You told me and Lady Amelia again and again that you wanted to marry for love. Well for goodness' sake just get on and do it. You've seen Will Hammond at his best and you've seen him at his worst. Was the worst so terrible?"

She took a spoonful. And another. Aila did the same. Neither spoke. Aila broke off another piece of bread and dipped it in the steaming soup. "His worst was nothing,

Maisie. Not after all he'd been through. There was anger, but it wasn't directed at anyone else, just at himself. Just at the state he was in. There was despair too. He was planning to kill himself, Maisie, remember?"

Maisie sat still, silent, watching.

"I think, Maisie. I think..." She paused. "No, you're right. I am scared. I'm scared of what he might think when he knows that I saw him at his worst. And I shall have to tell him the truth about everything: about being barren, about being illegitimate, about being Nurse McBride, about lying to him. Everything is a lot, Maisie. And anyway, why on earth would he want me if I'm illegitimate; if I can't have his children? Why would any man want me?"

Maisie finished her soup in silence. Thoughts ticked round inside her head beneath its frame of golden hair. And that afternoon as her mistress slept in her favourite armchair in their suite, she did something for the first time. She wrote a letter.

My Lord,
Please forgive me for writing to you...

CHAPTER SEVENTY

WEDNESDAY 24TH JULY 1918
Stanwood House, Stanwood

The last time he'd been here... When was it that he'd found Miss Aila on the ground with her broken hip? October 1913 it was, not even a full five years ago. More than a lifetime. Funny he couldn't remember the exact date. His mum would know it, of course. She was a walking encyclopaedia when it came to family happenings.

He urged his horse round the Big House towards the stable yard with little more than pressure from one knee, hoping against hope that he wouldn't bump into Miss Aila. But the yard was quiet, the horses nodding at him over the half doors in their stalls. He swung himself down, letting the old mare walk across to the trough to drink, and looked for Juno. There he was, watching him, then throwing his head back in a quick whinny of recognition. He laughed and strolled across to look at his stitching, although all that remained now was just a long white, hair free line down the nose.

"Not a bad bit of stitching, young fella. Not bad at all although I says it myself."

A discrete cough behind him heralded the arrival of the butler. He turned and touched his finger to his hat waiting, as ever, to see the reaction to his terrible scar, but old Livens could never be faulted for courtesy.

"Good morning, Colour Sergeant. You're spot on time, of course."

Will smiled. "Morning, Mr Livens. I'm just plain Mr Hammond these days much though half the village seems intent to remind me of my army days."

"So they should, Mr Hammond. So they should. You're a credit to the village."

Will smiled once more, feeling the flesh tighten again over his wound. "His Lordship here today, Mr Livens? Or Miss Aila?"

Livens shook his head. "His Lordship is in the library, but Miss Aila is in the south of France with Maisie Brown. She has been endeavouring to see if the warmth down there will ease the pain in her damaged hip."

Will nodded, half ashamed at feeling relief that she would not see him. Then Mr Livens was speaking again.

"When his Lordship heard you were coming, he asked if you would call on him after you had seen to the horses."

Will looked down at his riding boots and jodhpurs and pointed to his waistcoat and collarless shirt. "I'm not dressed for meeting his Lordship, Mr Livens."

The old butler shook his head. "His Lordship also asked if you could see what the matter might be with his mare, Scarlet, as he believes she is going lame."

Will checked the nameplates on the stable doors.

He was still examining the Scarlet's foreleg and talking to the horse when he heard a step behind him. He placed her hoof on the ground, straightened, and turned round, favouring his scar–free right cheek. Lord Augustus was leaning on a stick some five feet away, watching him. Will touched his forelock and waited for the other man to speak first.

"Have you found what the matter is with Scarlet?"

"Yes, my Lord. It's her cannon bone."

He stooped once again and ran his hand down the horse's foreleg, lifting it and resting it on his knee. "The puffiness here." He stroked the leg just above the pastern and pointed to the slight swelling. "It happens to horses who try too hard sometimes. It's no more than a tiny fracture on the surface of the bone."

He placed the leg carefully back on the ground and the mare nuzzled against his shoulder. Will scratched her jaw, watching the aristocrat, waiting for a response.

"Will she have to be put down?"

Will growled internally. Why was this always the first question? "No, my Lord."

"Well, if I can't ride her, what's the point in keeping her?"

Will kept his temper. "If I treat her now, my Lord, you should be able to ride her later in the season. Certainly in time for the Boxing Day Meet."

Maybe he wasn't reading his face well. This was, after all, the longest conversation he'd ever had with him. But all he could see was centuries of privilege behind the grey eyes. Lord Augustus seemed to be studying him with equal interest.

"My daughter has always spoken very highly of you, Mr Hammond. Or should I call you Colour Sergeant?"

Was that a sneer? "I prefer to be simple Mr Hammond thank you, my Lord. I was invalided out of the army earlier this year."

"But the war hasn't ended, Mr Hammond. You seem to be perfectly fit now. Is it not it your duty to go back out there and fight for your king and country?"

Will felt the muscles in his stomach stiffen. He took two deep breaths, noticing that Mr Livens had arrived with a glass of some kind of amber coloured wine for his Lordship. The butler looked towards Will, clearly anxious as to how he might respond.

"My Lord, if you don't want to keep Scarlet it would be my pleasure to look after her. I've bought some paddocks over Finedon way, and she can live out her days with a bit of dignity. But as I say, she'll be ready to ride again come Christmas."

Lord Augustus seated himself on the mounting step. He sipped at his sherry. "You didn't answer my question, Mr Hammond."

"Which one, my Lord."

"You are not a fool, Mr Hammond. You know which one."

Will stopped stroking the mare, pulled himself up to his full six feet and rubbed at the terrible scarring on his cheek.

"Funny thing, war, my Lord. It teaches you a lot of things."

He crossed the stable yard. "Would you like to know what some of them are, my Lord?"

A silent nod. Will sucked in his breath and released it, blowing out his cheeks. "Well, apart from the obvious ones like how to get good at killing men you've never met, it teaches you to care for your fellows. In my case it taught me to be a leader. It taught us all patience. Very important thing, patience, when probably eight out of ten of all the orders given to you are at best ill-informed and at worst downright, murderously stupid."

He stepped back. "And it teaches you to read other people, especially officers. It took me a few minutes, my Lord, but I think I can read you now. And do you know what I can read?"

Lord Augustus sipped again at his sherry and shook his head, still silent.

"I can read someone who couldn't care less if I went back to war or stayed at home and became a vicar. You've heard of me – not much chance you wouldn't have round here. And you've just come to see what kind of man I am."

He walked back to where the mare was chewing at her bit. Will scratched her jaw again and spoke in a gentle voice.

"You want me to take Scarlet off your hands, my Lord, do you? Because I'll not stand by and see her sent to the knacker's yard when she has plenty of life in her." He studied the aristocrat, still trying to see beneath the skin. "And why, my Lord?"

He laughed – a short bitter laugh. "Because I've seen death come before his time so many times. I told a nurse in the hospital where they rebuilt my face, that when you're in the trenches you make death your friend. Well part of me, my Lord, certainly this part..." He tapped the side of his face. "... is still back there in the trenches alongside my friend death.

And I can tell you exactly what death looks like too, my Lord. He's a soldier's hand sticking up out of the mud in No

Man's Land at Ypres. He's a row of horses rotting by a road at Passchendaele. He's the body of Rifleman Terry Rogers swinging on the barbed wire a hundred yards in front of us for three days at Flers–Courcelette because the artillery barrage was too great for us to go out and bury him. He's the stink of something my Commanding Officer called putrefaction.

I see death every night when I dream, my Lord. I used to call those dreams nightmares, but they're not. They're real. They're memories. My memories. And, my Lord, I will not let death come to Stanwood before his time. It is not time for Scarlet's death. You call it how you want it, my Lord, but Scarlet lives."

Lord Augustus passed the empty glass back to Livens. "So, everything they say about you is true, Mr Hammond. Very well. Scarlet lives, of course. And you will care for her as I understand you care for every other animal and human in the village. You may be interested to know that Maisie Brown wrote a letter to me about you last week. It was most... aah... illuminating. You have many friends, Mr Hammond. I would like to be counted among them. Good day to you."

CHAPTER SEVENTY-ONE

FRIDAY 20TH SEPTEMBER 1918
Stanwood Forge, Northamptonshire

Sergeant Major Trubshaw joined Will by the forge and worked the bellows for him until the coals were a fierce white once more. Will hammered and shaped and hammered some more then dipped the shoe into the water bucket. He held out the steaming metal to be examined. Trubshaw nodded. "You've got the knack of it now, Will."

Will nodded. "How long's your leave this time, Ernie?"

Trubshaw scratched his jaw. "I'll be going back tomorrow. Looks like the war ain't got much more time to run." With a tilt of his jaw, he indicated the horse standing behind him. "And you reckon this'll help old Scarlet out do you?"

"The crack in her cannon bone's mended fine and a thicker shoe like this should help. She's got life in her still. It wouldn't be right to send her off, now, would it?"

Trubshaw shook his head and smiled. "You don't change, do you? Except now you're running old man Chant's practice you're beginning to sound proper posh."

"Not to worry, Ernie. If you keep dropping round, I'll soon be speaking like a country bumpkin again."

Trubshaw laughed and walked away, touching his forelock towards two figures waiting in the shadows behind the door. Will threw off his sweat soaked shirt, splashed cool water on his hard body, clicked his tongue at the mare, and tapped her foreleg. She raised it obediently and he hammered the nails into the hoof in his neat way, singing to himself as he did so to keep the horse relaxed.

He didn't hear the sound of a quickly suppressed struggle behind him, but in the shadows, there was only one figure now – a figure who had been pushed towards him. His mind drifted and he started another song.

Speed, bonnie boat, like a bird on the wing,
Onward! the sailors cry;
Carry the lad...

He heard what sounded like a stifled sob and the sound of feet stumbling away from the forge, but by the time he had tapped in the last nail and turned there was no one in sight. He sniffed the air. There was a hint of perfume hanging there, a scent he felt he should recognise. The wind blew the half door shut and all that remained now was the scent of horse. He replaced his hammers in their rack and as the horse fretted at the banging of the wind, turned to it with a smile.

"There's a song written about a Scarlet." He stroked her mane. "Only it's about a town not an old mare."

The door banged again and he sang – this time the song that was ever in his heart. The horse listened, tossed its head and blew on his shoulder.

In Scarlet town where I was born
There was a fair maid dwelling
And every youth cried well away
For her name was Barbara Allen.

But there was no one there to sing the descant.

* * *

"Well, what are you going to do, Miss Aila? Run away to the South of France?" She glared at the sobbing woman in front of her. "I knew I should have stayed at the forge. I might have guessed you'd lose your nerve. Really, Miss Aila."

Aila raised her hands towards her maid. "Don't, Maisie. Please don't. It's just that he was singing the Skye Boat Song. He wasn't thinking about me. He was thinking about Nurse McBride. I have made such a mess of everything."

Maisie took her mistress' hands. "But Miss Aila, Nurse McBride was you. You were Nurse McBride."

She watched Aila's tear-stained face for a moment, then pulled her into her arms, rocking her gently. "Dear Miss Aila. Dear Miss Aila."

CHAPTER SEVENTY-TWO

MONDAY 21ST OCTOBER 1918
Glebe Farm, The Stanwood Estate

The farmhouse looked desolate. No smoke rising from the kitchen chimney, the rear porch door hanging open, a single horse in the stable yard turning its head to watch him. Will sat on Lord Augustus' old mare remembering the last time he had been there: that stupid huntsman threatening him, the miserly Alf Naylor dismissing him, a penny from his wages unpaid.

A stable door banged open and a florid faced, self-satisfied, middle aged man walked out leading a shire horse. So, this is why he'd been summoned to come here. Old Dickon needed caring for. Clearly his Lordship had not forgotten Will's lecture. The man walked forward as Will dismounted, holding out his hand.

"Mr Hammond? I'm Edward George, Lord Augustus' new estate manager. Thank you for coming. You'll have heard that Alfred Naylor has passed, and his wife has left the farm to live with her daughter in Wellingborough. Well, we managed to sell the young horse, but no one seems to want this old chap so, his Lordship thought…"

His voice trailed off as Will shook his hand, nodded, and walked past him to talk to Dickon. The old shire horse tossed its head at him. He smiled. "Well, old fella, it's good to see you again. Good to see you." He patted the massive head as the horse bent its neck. He rested his forehead against its cheek.

"You've met Dickon before, then?"

"Dickon and me we go back a long way, Mr George. I was the ploughman here before the war. Best friend a ploughman could have, Dickon was."

"And look at you now, Mr Hammond: one of the most respected vets in the county. Big step up, eh? Extraordinary what a war can do."

Will turned his direct gaze on the man whose eyes were drawn to his shattered cheek. The eyes flicked back up. Will nodded, his own eyes hard, unyielding. "Extraordinary."

The estate manager stammered. "I er. I er. His Lordship asked that you care for Dickon and if you would go and see him when convenient."

"Thank you, Mr George. I've got his Lordship's hunter, Scarlet, here. I promised him I'd have her ready for the Boxing Day Hunt meet and she felt just fine riding over here, so I can bring her over tomorrow."

He turned away, taking Dickon's bridle and swung himself up onto Scarlet's back. He looked back at the estate manager, silent, eyes still hard and watchful as he walked the horses out of the farmyard and down to the lane where he paused, thinking yet again of what he would do if he were ever to meet Miss Aila. Dickon moved his hoofs restlessly on the newly metalled road.

CHAPTER SEVENTY-THREE

TUESDAY 22ND OCTOBER
Stanwood House

"Feel it, Jimmy, see?"

The seventeen-year-old, long since promoted from stable boy to groom, felt the horse's cannon bone, emulating Will's gentle touch.

"It's smooth as it ever was, Mr Hammond."

Will nodded, running his hand up and down Scarlet's leg, feeling for any heat. "I galloped her for a bit and jumped one small hedge." He sat back on his haunches. "Give her some exercise, Jimmy, and a few small jumps and make sure she has that bran mash. Ah, here's Mr Livens. I'll speak to his Lordship about her now."

He clapped the lad on the shoulder not noticing the awestruck gaze, completely missing the hero worship. "Morning, Mr Livens. Does his Lordship wish to see me?"

The old butler had noticed though. He smiled and held out his hand. "Good morning, Mr Hammond. It's a pleasure to see you again. His Lordship is in the library. If you would be so kind as to follow me, please?"

* * *

"Livens, could you bring a cup for Mr Hammond. I'm sure he could do with some tea."

Will walked across the room to the fireplace by which the aristocrat was seated, sipping at a cup, twirling his pince–nez in his hand, his newspaper over his knees, watching him. From the drawing room next door, behind the double doors, Will could hear a piano being played although he didn't recognise the melody.

"So, Scarlet is as good as new then?"

"Yes, my Lord."

Lord Augustus nodded, uninterested. Will watched and waited.

"Tell me, Mr Hammond, what did you think of the state of Glebe Farm?"

"I would have thought your new estate manager would have reported on that, my Lord."

Lord Augustus indicated sheets of typed paper on the table beside him. "He has, but unless I am much mistaken, you had ploughed all the fields on that farm. What is the soil like?"

He picked up the report and turned over a page. Will nearly smiled. Where was this going? He stared at the fire thinking back five years to the October of 1913. "The lower fields are good for wheat, my Lord. The ones by Prior's wood are good for nothing much more than hay and grazing. They might be better with new drainage put in – Alf Naylor was not known for spending money. The upper fields drain well, maybe too well, but barley would be good there."

He paused. The pianist was practising scales. He wondered who was playing. He froze. Aila! He glanced back at Lord Augustus catching his eye just before he looked back down at the papers.

"Er, I believe, Mr Hammond, that my estate manager... yes here it is – disagrees with you. I quote: *'The lower meadows are suitable for grazing only, and the upper fields would carry wheat.'* What do you say to that?"

Will smiled. "He's your estate manager, my Lord. I'm just a ploughman who, as he pointed out to me, by the good fortune of a war is now a vet."

Lord Augustus laughed at that. Will watched him. There was little doubt that this amusement was genuine.

"What Glebe Farm needs more than anything else, Mr Hammond, is someone to farm it. A married man, of course."

He half smiled at this thought and Will was sure he could pick up an undertone of friendly mockery. He cocked an ear towards the double wooden doors that divided the library from the drawing room hearing voices talking and then a new song on the piano – Greensleeves. He half listened to the melody and studied Lord Augustus once more. Of course, if it were Aila in there he would have to leave before she came in to see her father. The door to the corridor opened behind him and he span round, but it was only Mr Livens bringing in a cup for him. Will ignored the proffered cup of tea and walked towards the double doors. The voices were speaking once more. And then a new tune, and this time a voice, singing.

Speed bonnie boat
Like a bird on the wing
Forward the sailors cry
Carry the lad that's born to be king...

That voice, that gentle Highland voice. Nurse McBride? It was Nurse McBride's voice. How could she be here? Two quick steps and he wrenched the doors open, strode through and stopped dead. Aila was looking up at him from the piano in shock. Her grandmother was seated to one side her gaze switching between them, a slight smile on her lips. He tried to pull himself together. "What? Your voice. What?"

She stared back at him, colour draining from her face then bowed her head. "I'm sorry, Will."

It was a whisper. She looked up, colour coming back into her cheeks and spoke. And it was Nurse McBride's voice. "I was Nurse McBride, Will. Do you not see?"

Her grandmother pulled herself to her feet, grabbed her stick and walked briskly towards the library door. She paused beside Will. "Now, young man, this was the best ruse we could come up with to put you two together in the same room." She tapped him on the wrist and pointed with her stick. "I instructed Livens to lock the door to the hall from the other side. And if you try and leave by the library, you'll have to throw my son and me out of the way let alone poor old Livens. So, for goodness' sake the pair of you, work it out! I, for one, have had more than enough of this never-ending melodrama!"

Will stared at her, shook his head to clear it, and stared back at Aila. The double doors closed. Aila came to her feet. She was too pale, too thin, ill almost. He wanted to do nothing more than take her in his arms and hold her – just hold her. He stood still as she walked round from behind the piano and stood before him. Oh, but she was beautiful.

He could feel the pounding of his heart as his eyes swept over her lovely, kind, gentle face.

"Will? Please forgive me."

He shook his head again, eyebrows raised, forehead furrowed. "Forgive you for what? What have you ever done except show me kindness? Why would I need to forgive you? And what is this about you and Nurse McBride?"

"Would you sit with me, please, Will? I have made such a mess of everything, and I must explain."

His shattered face forgotten he allowed himself to be led to the chaise longue on which he had lain her all those years ago when he had carried her broken body back from Prior's wood. She lifted her hand to his face, her cool fingers touching the awful scarring. He turned away from her. How could she bear to touch him? She spoke again. "Harold was so clever with your wounds, Will. He was very proud of his work."

"Harold? Harold Gillies? You know him? What...?"

"I'm sorry, Will, I'm really sorry, but as I just said, Nurse McBride was me in disguise. I've seen your face at almost every stage of Harold's operations. Turn round, Will. Turn round and look at me. Please."

Will dragged himself round and as he turned, he lifted his hand automatically to cover his cheek. She shook her head at him and pulled his hand away from his face. "No, Will. No. Wait. Look."

She jumped to her feet and ran across the room, reaching behind an armchair and coming back with a parcel wrapped in brown paper. She tore the wrapping off and showed it to him. He gasped and sat back hard against the chair, the breath hissing from between his lips. It was the pastel of his face drawn by that man Tonks when he had first been admitted to the hospital. Aila was speaking again, her words tumbling over each other.

"My cousin Amelia – Sister Amelia to you – she asked me to go and work with her in The Queen's hospital, Will, after I had recovered from pneumonia. You wouldn't have known about that, of course, but I nearly died. Maisie nursed me back to life and then I was told you were dead. And I was in despair. So, I finished my training and ended up as the staff nurse in charge of all the admissions in Sidcup, but I arrived there after you had been admitted so I had no idea you were there until the day the Queen presented you with your Victoria Cross." She smiled. "Maisie was the nurse who stood beside you at the presentation."

He didn't realise his jaw could drop any lower. Aila continued. "I went to see Harold after that and told him how you had saved my life and that I wanted to save yours in return." Without her realising it she had clutched his hands. "But Will I knew how proud you were and how you wouldn't want me to see you at your worst, so I invented Nurse McBride. Please forgive me, Will."

Still speechless, he stared at her. "But, but... Why did you run away from the forge?"

"You knew I was there?"

He shook his head slowly still staring at her, still taking in her beauty. "Miss Aila, I..."

She grabbed his hands once more, gripping them, speaking fiercely. "I am not Miss anything, Will. I am just plain, simple Aila."

He looked down at her long, elegant fingers, pale against the brown of his work hardened, weathered hands. "I don't think there's anything plain or simple about you... Aila. I've just realised that I smelt your perfume – at the forge. I didn't make the connection at the time. But why...?"

"Will, I had let you down. I should have written to you, told you I was waiting for you. But I found out something shocking about me, something that filled me with so much shame that I just did as my father demanded of me which I now, so, so regret. And I should have told you that I was a nurse at The Queen's hospital. I shouldn't have lied to you and pretended to be Nurse McBride. I should have told you the truth about everything. And when I saw you at the forge and you started singing the Skye Boat Song... It was Nurse McBride you were thinking of, not me. So, I ran."

Her clockwork ran down. She took a deep, deep breath. "And there is one other thing. You saved my life, Will, all those years ago, but there was one thing you couldn't save. Dudley must have kicked me when I had fallen." She put her hands to her stomach. "He did it to make sure I would never have a baby. And he succeeded, Will." Her head went down again as she whispered the words. "He succeeded. I am barren." She looked up searching his clear blue eyes. "So, all those ridiculous dreams I had been harbouring about you. About running away with you, marrying you..." Her eyes dropped. "Why would anyone, least of all you, want to marry such a person?"

Will tilted his head back, raising his hands to grip the back of his head. "But..." He stood and walked to the French windows, staring unseeingly at the terrace outside. "After you left the forge... The wind was blowing, making the door bang and old Scarlet got spooked so I sang her the song I sing every day to myself." He turned towards her. "Would you like to hear it?"

She nodded and he started to sing, quite unselfconsciously.

In Scarlet town where I was born
There was a fair maid dwelling
And every youth cried well away
Aila joined in, singing the descant.
For her name was Barbara Allen.

Will turned back to the French windows and looked downward at the key in the lock. He spoke over his shoulder. "If I'd known you were going to see me today, I'd have worn the tin plate over my cheek."

Aila shook her head. "Captain Wood's tin cheek. You still don't understand, Will, do you?"

He shrugged. "Not surprising really. All I know is what I've just learned today and I admit to being utterly confused."

"Will, for goodness' sake! Who was it that said '*a scar on the face means nothing? It's what's inside that counts and this is a good horse, gentle, kind and willing. If a man had a scar like that, would you send him to a knackers' yard? Well, would you?*'"

Will half smiled. "I know the answer to that. Mr Chant told me. It was a lad called Will Hammond."

"So you do understand?"

"No, Aila. I do not. I have no idea why someone so beautiful, so clever, so perfect as you, would want a wrecked, monster faced, one–time ploughman with no chance of being anything more than a second-rate veterinary surgeon with a forge in a little village in Northamptonshire."

Aila stamped her foot in frustration. "You idiot. What do I have to say or do to break through your stupid pride? Listen to me, Will. Listen!"

She stabbed her finger into his chest, all but yelling up into his face. "I love you. I've loved you since the first moment I met you. I love you because you understand me, because you cared for me. Because you won't care when I tell you who my mother is - and, and..." "She stammered in excitement waving her arms in the air. "And because you care for horses; because they love you; and because you are the most special person I have ever, ever met."

Will looked down at the furious woman beneath him. The skin beneath his eyes crinkled. His lips turned up. "So would you still run away with me, Aila?"

She breathed out then and smiled, clicking her fingers, whispering the words back up at him. "In the space of a single heartbeat, Will Hammond. A single heart beat."

He smiled back down at her. "You know something?"

She reached up and touched his face. "What?"

"They forgot the key to the French window."

He turned the key, grabbed her hand and they ran out, across the terrace, into the rose garden and across the frosty lawns, where he swung her up in his arms, spinning her round and round in the cold clear morning and they were laughing at each other, laughing at the world, laughing at their love.

CHAPTER SEVENTY-FOUR

SUNDAY 1ST DECEMBER 1918

My daughter, my Aila.

It is the first day of the last month of this year. The awful war finally is over and today is the day I promised myself I would start this letter.

You may ask why on earth I would write to you now after so many years of silence? Well, the truth is that last week I came across a copy of The Times newspaper dating from April of this year in which I saw a brief mention of the court martial of an army officer. His name was all too well known to me and brought back once again the terrible fears for your safety that I have carried with me for the last nineteen years.

But it also stirred in me the first, faint hope that your life might now be safe and that the greatest wish of my life could be realised: that I would see you again, that I would learn about your life, that I would see if you had grown into the woman I have always imagined.

But will I ever dare post this letter to you?

By the time I have finished this missive I will know what I have to do, but for the moment, I beg for your patience as I tell you the story of my life: the story of Alice Haverstock.

The letter grew in length...

* * *

WEDNESDAY 1ST JANUARY 1919
Post Office, Ashley Down Road, Bristol

The queue for the counter was much longer than she had expected and after a couple of minutes Alice Haverstock, known locally for the last twenty years as Miss Alice Smith, glanced at the clock on the wall, concerned that she would be late back for her afternoon classes. Thank goodness, though, the postmaster noticed her presence.

"If you could just wait one moment, ladies and gentlemen, Miss Smith here has only letters for me to stamp and if I know anything about her, she'll be wanting to rush back to the orphanage to help all those poor children."

Alice felt herself begin to colour up. She stepped forward with a nervous smile to the other people in the queue, relieved to see the nods of appreciation directed at her. "I'm so sorry to be a nuisance to you all, but Mr Townsend is correct. Afternoon classes start in ten minutes and I really do hate to keep the children waiting."

The postmaster accepted the first letter, placed it on the scales, fussing self–importantly with the weights. "Three and a half ounces, Miss Smith. Goodness, that must be a long, long letter."

Alice smiled back politely. "It is indeed, Mr Townsend. It's taken me a month to write. How much is it?" She reached for her purse inside her handbag watching as the postmaster ran his finger down the price list.

"That'll be a penny ha'penny, Miss Smith, if you please."

She passed two other, smaller letters across the counter, selected the coins from her purse and watched as the postmaster placed the stamps carefully in the top right-hand corner of the letters and date stamped them. "And they should get there when, Mr Townsend?"

The postmaster picked up the letters and read aloud. "Miss Aila Smythe, Lord Augustus Smythe and The Dowager Countess of Chichester: all the same address – Stanwood House, Stanwood, Northamptonshire. They should be there by mid-morning tomorrow at the latest, Miss Smith."

She bit her lip, started to ask for them back, saw almost in slow motion their trajectory as they were tossed into the huge mailbag hanging on a hook on the back wall and realised it was too late. The die was cast. Her daughter would, by tomorrow lunchtime, know the whole truth about her.

THE END

Printed and bound in the UK by CMP Books, Dorset

DIAMOND CRIME

Passionate about the crime/mystery/thriller books it publishes

Follow

Facebook:
@diamondcrimepublishing

Instagram
@diamond_crime_publishing

X
@diamond_crime

Web
diamondcrime.uk

All Diamond Crime eBooks
now available from

 Books   amazon kindle